MAIMSTREAM

BC FURTNEY

A Comet Press Book

First Comet Press Trade Paperback Edition
October 2013

Maimstream copyright © 2013
by BC Furtney
All Rights Reserved.

Cover Illustration by Amy Wilkins

This book is a work of fiction. People, places, events, and situations are the product of the author's imagination. Any resemblance to actual persons, living or dead, is purely coincidental.

No part of this book may be reproduced or transmitted in any form or by any electronic or mechanical means, including photocopying, recording or by any information storage and retrieval system, without the written permission of the publisher, except in the case of brief quotations embodied in critical articles and reviews.

ISBN 13: 978-1-936964-55-0

Visit Comet Press on the web at: www.cometpress.us

ABOUT THE AUTHOR

BC Furtney was born outside of Pittsburgh in 1972, spending a fair part of childhood reading books, watching television and playing outside, back when kids still did that. Following a year of film school and another year working post-production in a refrigerated room with twenty tons of highly flammable nitrate film stock that could've reduced the building to a crater, he absconded to the sunnier clime of southern California, haunting L.A.'s beaches and byways for the next thirteen years. Crew work, acclaimed short films and a brief segue onto the rock club stages ensued, before he abandoned his adopted hometown to start production on his first commercial feature. *Do Not Disturb* saw wide release in the summer of 2013, by which time fiction writing had flourished and turned our (anti)hero to the page more-or-less full-time. Along with a monthly column, regular guest articles, and an ever-swelling series of ghostwritten hardcore erotica books, he's happy to be afforded the opportunity to deliver his own brand of pulp horror, by way of Comet Press. He lives with his wife in a southern outlaw compound, off the grid and far from the bright lights. *Maimstream* is his second novel.

For Steve Patronas, who'd first ask if this book was making any money, then dig it regardless.

1

Consciousness faded in. Breathing. *In . . . out.* It was dark, warm, moist. Like the womb. Maybe it *was* the womb. She'd get to start over, do better next time. She was enveloped in a muted quiet, like when you held a pillow tight over your ears. Or your head underwater. She tried to move, but her limbs didn't obey. An uncomfortable pressure gripped her abdomen. She opened her eyes, but the world stayed black. *Death,* she thought. *Or birth.* The line between end and beginning wasn't just thin, it was blown all to hell. Was it nothing more than a seamless transition? Break the finish tape and roll back to one—ready, set, go again? She'd do a lot of things differently, provided she was lucky enough to get another go. She wriggled, swiveled her wrists and ankles, flexed her fingers and toes, opened her mouth wide. The air felt strange. *Thicker* somehow. Her lips were numb, a burnt metallic taste in her mouth. She'd tasted it before, but couldn't quite place where or when. Her mind was cloudy, her own name escaped her, her throat felt slick, like the sensation of chugging a drink, only she could breathe. *In . . . out.* She swept her tongue around, jabbing sludgy gums, finding no teeth. Forming again, everything from scratch, clean and new. Her heart surged and felt strong. Forged of iron. *Thump, THUMP . . . Thump, THUMP . . .* She could only hear the steady hiss that kept whatever chaos was outside her carrier's belly at bay. And she felt safe. For the first time in a lifetime—in forever—she felt safe. Some things, though, never changed and she wanted out. With all the strength she could muster, she thrust an arm out and felt a tear, followed by a flush of warm liquid that made her skin tingle. She arched her back and uncoiled, her body lifting from its fetal position. Felt like floating. Was she traversing the birth canal? She twisted around and around until she was even more disoriented, scissoring her legs, moving faster. Rising. Her closed eyelids sensed warmth. She opened them to see a blurry white blob growing steadily brighter. She went for it, kicking harder and faster.

Her clawing fingers broke the water's surface, sunshine hot on her pruned blue hand. A group of dabbling ducks scattered, fearing a predator. Their instincts were correct. Her head emerged, mouth agape, eyes wide. She looked around, seeing her surroundings for the first time all over again—the lake, the dock, the rowboat, the sprawling grounds, the house that seemed impossibly far atop the hill. All familiar, but she recalled nothing of why she was there or what had transpired. A pair of blood-stained pillows bobbed on the surface behind her. The light stung her eyes, so she slipped back underwater where she could see. Where she could *breathe*. She sank to the bottom, passing a ghostly blood-stained blanket that hung frozen, inviting her back into its tight embrace. Her toes dug into the lake bed, a murky cloud blooming around her knees. She blinked, eyes focusing. Dozens of fish surrounded her, staring. They seemed to wonder if she planned to stay. If she was one of them. She had no idea *what* she was. She looked up. The white sun shimmered light years away behind the silent wall of water, not a raging fireball from where she stood, just an impotent and shapeless nothing presiding over a dirty little world full of noise and filth and pointlessness. She rolled her head on her shoulders, felt weightless and unreal, took a step and started walking. The fish parted to let her pass. They knew they were losing her. They also knew she'd return.

She stubbed her toes on a barbell that hid in the murk, kept walking and reached two mossy dock posts. She touched one, looked up and lifted off, effortlessly gliding back to the surface. Her hands grasped the platform's edge and she hauled herself up, every muscle in her body pulling tight. She was nude, her flesh a lifeless shade of white, fingers, toes, ears, nipples, labia, all blue.

She slumped on her hands and knees, shivering uncontrollably, vision slipping in and out of focus on the dock's wood grain. Mucous oozed from her nose and mouth. Her front teeth were gone, bloody gums and a shredded tongue the souvenirs of a slug that blasted through the back of her head, just a few hours earlier. A half-inch of difference would've destroyed her brain stem and cut the lights for good, but she remembered none of it. She only wanted to get up the hill and into the house to clean up. To get on with it. To keep moving, even if she didn't know why. She stood on unsteady legs, staggering up the hill like a mangled marionette with a snipped string. She fell again and again, crawling until she could stand, always pressing forward. The house seemed to recede the more she plodded toward it, making her wonder if it was there at all. When she reached the back patio, it felt like hours had passed. Cobblestones burned her feet as she moved to a window. Her reflection shocked her and she froze, not recognizing herself. She stared for a moment, tried to jog her memory, drew a blank. She tried the back doorknob. Locked. Without hesitation, she punched out a pane of glass, reached in, flipped the deadbolt. The door swung open. She paused, listening. Silence. She entered and scanned the room, padding across the kitchen tile. Deja vu. She knew she'd been there, *just been there*, but the details were lost. Her feet sank into plush carpeting as she moved down a narrow hallway lined with framed photos of people she didn't know, to the bathroom. She flipped the light switch and squinted in the bright fluorescence, her pupils pinning to dots.

    She stared at the mirror, cocking her head. She couldn't remember what she looked like before, but was pretty sure it wasn't what was she was looking at now. She eyed her grisly grill, stuck out her tongue and saw it split down the middle, forked like a snake's. When she flicked it, both sides wagged in unison. The shower loomed behind her in the mirror and she turned, pulling the curtain. A man in an expensive suit stood in the tub, palms raised like he was about to do a magic trick, pants around his ankles, feet lost in fetid red slime. Her heart jolted in her chest. They'd met before, but she couldn't remember that either. He was the one who'd finally given her the last push and unleashed the beast that had grown inside her. An enormous, discolored cock writhed between his legs. It reared back and aimed at her, its meatus curling into a sleazy smile. Then it spoke.

"Hallo, Scarla . . ."

The room spun and she staggered. The floor dropped like an elevator car.

Blackout.

* * *

She woke some time later on the bathroom floor, a pool of dark blood ringing her head like a halo. Again, she didn't know where she was. She recalled nothing of the man in the expensive suit, nor his menacing cock. She pried her matted hair off the tiles, dragged herself into the shower and twisted the faucet after thinking about it for a moment, not reacting to the scalding water that blasted her. Steam fogged the room. She watched her blood spiral down the drain, digging through coagulated blood to find the bullet hole in the base of her skull. Its circumference surprised her. *There's a hole in your head.* She fingered it, felt bone, dropped her hand. Her chest was lobster-red, but she didn't care. She stood, cut the water and grabbed a towel, wrapped it around her head and went to find something soft to rest on for what wouldn't be long enough, all things considered. Threading back down the narrow hallway, she spotted a queen size bed in a small room and ducked in. The sheets were made with military precision, not a crease in sight, and no blanket. She flashed back to the one floating in the lake—the one that held her like the womb not long ago. She let the question hang and stretched out. *Weeeeeee.* Her ears rang louder until she wiggled a finger in them. *Weeeeeeee.* No good. She cracked her neck. *Pop! WEEEEEEEEEEE!* The noise was unbearable. She rose up on her knees, ass in the air, and felt a familiar tingle. She realized she was wet, and not from the shower.

As she felt between her legs, it hit her with force and insistence. Before she knew what was happening, she came.

*   *   *

His hands grasped her hips as he slid into her from behind. He'd wanted her for what felt like a lifetime, but it wasn't how he imagined it. Not even close. The gun sat on the pillow beside her head, easier for her to grab than him, but he knew she wouldn't. It wasn't in the plan and she wasn't even looking at it, her eyes shut tight, mouth agape, fists clenching the sheets, totally submissive. It was their moment and it would be their last. He leaned down to kiss his way up her back to her shoulder, up her neck to her ear, turning her head so he could taste her lips. She wasn't really with him and he knew it, but it was as close as he'd ever get, so he projected her old self into the shell he'd been offered and it was good enough, if only for the moment. Her body was soft, warm. He didn't know about the stiffening or the sudden cold, and how would he? He hadn't done what she had, hadn't spent every last drop of himself in a fixed game, for a hollow cause. Even at that moment, he was getting the sanitized, safety-netted version of the hell she'd lived every night for too long, and he knew it. But it was ending. Finally ending for them both. He leaned back to study her profile, slowing his thrusts. He could see her eyes rolling rapidly behind closed lids, as if in a fever dream. He noted her tensed neck muscles, the twitching in the corner of her mouth. He didn't want to see any more, so turned her away and eased her head back to the pillow. The soft slap of flesh filled the room, hypnotic in rhythm. Her shoulders tightened and flexed. He knew what was happening and didn't want it to. Wishful thinking. Stupid, too. In the end, she'd do her job and he'd do his. It was who they were and people didn't change. Inside, anyway. He almost laughed at the thought, erupting inside her for what felt like an eternity, her muscles seizing and releasing him, holding him in her clutches until he was completely drained. But it wasn't over by a long shot. The cold snapped him to attention, shocking his nerves. He tried to pull out, but couldn't. Her back hunched in lupine posture, her spine's vertebrae so pronounced it seemed they might burst from her skin and shred him like shrapnel. He watched the veins flush blue down the length of her body. Momentarily transfixed, he went for the gun late. A near-fatal mistake. As his fingers closed around the handle, she lashed out with her teeth, slashing his wrist. Blood spritzed her face, the pillows, the wall. Her mouth had elongated into a snout that seemed to sneer with too many teeth. He yanked his arm back, clipping her face with the gun butt. Her head dropped. He put the barrel to the base of her skull and pulled the trigger.

POP!

The wall went red. She crashed facedown on the pillows. Rest in peace, if there's peace to be found, sweet lady.

Her orgasm gave way to nausea and she vomited on the clean pillows. They'd been found in a closet and swapped with the pair she was shot on, the pair floating in the lake, but she wouldn't know that. She flipped the soiled pillow over onto its partner and pushed them away. One puke sandwich on cotton. Staring at the wall, she saw a faint smear where blood splatter had been cleaned and knew it was hers. She pulled the sheets back, eyed the bare mattress. No blood. She stood, upending the bed. Vindication. A huge brown stain smiled back at her. In its outline, she could make out the shape of her own head and shoulders. She'd bled a lot. That much blood loss would kill a person. Maybe, she thought, it killed her too.

Still nude, she stepped outside and surveyed the lake. The two pillows floated silently, yards apart. She heard a caw, looked up, saw a crow perched on a tree branch. It cocked its head, eyeing her curiously. *Don't you want to fly away with me? You can do it, you know.* But she didn't. She didn't know what she could do or what she was, how she'd gotten there or where she'd been, what was happening or what to do next. She was running on pure instinct, fight or flight, and for it she felt thankful. It cut baggage, eliminated bullshit, kept things clear. As clear as they could be for her, anyway. A straight crooked line. She headed back to the lake, footsteps slow and deliberate.

* * *

He cradled her limp body in his arms and plodded to the lake. She was still warm in the blanket he'd rolled her in, her dead weight made heavier by the 35lb barbell plate on her stomach. She had to sink and stay down. He tried not to think about it, his eyes fixed on the small rowboat tied to the dock. He took some solace in knowing it was where she wanted to be, but mostly he just felt numb. He laid her on the boards, caught his breath and eyed the boat, bobbing silently. He climbed in and almost capsized, grabbing the post to steady himself. The blanket suddenly thrashed and he jumped, almost tipping again. He stared hard. She was still. Must've been a peripheral trick. It was mercy, not murder. A monster, not her. Sink the remains and be done with it. Get in the car, go back to the city. If there's a city to go back to ...

* * *

A city to go back to. She looked up, eyed the horizon. What would be lost if it was burned to the ground? If all that remained was rubble? If they were all dead, whoever they were. The thought slipped away before an answer came. She stood on the dock, staring at the boat, knowing he'd rowed her out and dropped her in. The mystery man whose name she couldn't remember, whose face was different every time her mind drew him. He was a complete stranger, though she clearly recalled the feeling of him inside her, still tasted him in her mouth. Underneath the gunpowder. Would they ever meet again? And if so, what would be more appropriate, *fuck you* or *thank you*? Something in the water caught her eye. The fish had gathered near the surface, still staring. She went to raid the house for clothes. And she was hungry, but what she craved wouldn't be found in the fridge. It was time to go.

2

The roadside was craggy, the lake house far behind and out of sight. The late afternoon sun hung low in the sky, bright and scorching, and there were no trees for shade. She walked slowly, eyes on the ground, coordination still dull. She wore rubber flip-flops a size too small with white plastic daisies on the y-straps. The petals poked her feet with every step, pissing her off. Cinched beige shorts, a yellow tee displaying a gap-toothed cartoon kid under the words SUBURBAN MOM, and a blue baseball cap with a jumping fish above the title BASSMASTER! filled out her ensemble. She grimaced and spit blood, looking even shittier than she felt. She hadn't thought of what she'd do when she got to wherever she was going. With no money, no ID, no memory of where she lived or even who she was, it could get dicey.

She was watching the plastic daisies prick her feet when the sound of a distant engine grabbed her attention. She turned and saw a bright red tractor barreling her way from about a mile out. There was a signal for bumming rides, but she couldn't remember what it was. She knew it was easy, but just couldn't think to stick a thumb out. Of course, any woman showing leg on the side of the road would catch eyes whether a ride was needed or not, so she did just that, watching the bobtail approach at well over the posted 55 mph speed limit. It roared past her before slowing, its right turn signal blinking, brake lights burning a deep red and screaming a high-pitched wail as it pulled over a few yards ahead. It sat waiting, growling diesel simmering on the roadside. It sounded mad. She hobbled along the passenger side as fast as she could, her left leg dragging. When she reached the window, the unseen driver made no effort to engage. She stared at a Peterbilt logo beside the door, but it didn't open. She tried to call out, but had no voice. A hand appeared, two meathook fingers motioning her up. She tried climbing with her left leg but it didn't react, so she locked her knee and used the right, boosting herself to the window with lips pursed, figuring if she didn't reveal her mangled grill, she'd stand a better chance of a ride. A man sat at the wheel, silhouetted by the blazing sun behind him. All she could see was the shape of his cowboy hat and the smoke curling from the clove cigarette in an overflowing dashboard ashtray. A green plastic crucifix with a bearded man nailed to it hung from the rearview mirror.

"Sup, lady?" came a guttural voice.

She nodded, said nothing.

"Goin' somewhere?"

Yeah. Somewhere. She didn't *know* where she was going. The city with all the people. Which one, she couldn't say. She nodded to the road and the guy sneered.

"I like a girl knows what she wants."

Pause. He ogled her. She saw the watery whites of his eyes.

"You talk?"

She shrugged. He snickered.

"I like that, too. I like that *a lot*. Go 'head, get in."

She opened the door and slid onto a slashed and gouged leather seat, feeling a strange pang of deja vu as she did. The driver looked her over, took a deep breath, eyed the rearview and pulled back onto the road. Even with the windows down, the cab smelled bad. She breathed through her mouth, watching the countryside roll by. The guy watched her tits more than the road, repeatedly licking his stained teeth. She wouldn't look at him, keeping just enough peripheral track to see that he wasn't making any moves.

He grunted, jabbing a pudgy finger at her. *"Suburban mom?"*

She ignored him. He went blank, eerily silent, jaw muscles clenching and unclenching. She had to look. He was forty-something and unshaven, not obese but sporting the bloated gut and double chin reserved for those with bad genes and a taste for beer and fast food. She followed his gaze down her chest, saw pert nipples pushing through her tee's thin cotton. She looked up and saw the tractor's nose drifting over the yellow line. The road was empty, but that didn't make it better. She tensed as they crossed completely into the oncoming lane. The driver didn't seem to know or care.

"How old?" he asked, in a weird monotone.

She cocked her head at the question. Was he asking how old she was? She looked at her hands. *Twenties? Thirties?* She couldn't say. The roadside sloped into a debris-strewn median on their left. If they were going to barrel into it, she wanted to see it coming.

"Hey!" he barked.

She jumped.

"How old's your kid?"

Kid? What kid? She drew a blank. *Bloody forceps clattering on a cold, hard floor.* The vividness of the imagery startled her. Was it a memory? Was there a baby? *Blood and steel. Something squirming against the wall. Kill it. Make sure it's dead.* She drew her legs together without realizing it.

"Hey!" he snapped again.

She watched his mouth.

"*Ich werde ficken es aus Ihnen heraus.*"

The words didn't match his lips, nor was the voice his. It was lower, harsher, *scarier*. She didn't speak German, so she didn't know how to answer and didn't want to, sitting with a mouthful of blood and nowhere to spit it.

"You alright?"

She heard him right that time, but his tone was disingenuous. He didn't give a shit how she was. She nodded and leaned out the window to spit, watching her blood streak the cab's side. The air felt good on her face and she stayed in the wind, breathing deep. When she sat back, the driver had unzipped and was stroking his cock, steering with one hand. She watched. He sneered. She turned away, felt blood puddling under her split tongue again. He grabbed her left wrist and yanked it into his lap. She tried to pull away, but his grip was steel.

"Jack me a while," he hissed, not letting go.

She wrapped her fingers around his shaft.

"There ya go."

He put both hands on the wheel and took a deep breath, steering them back into the right lane. It took her a minute to get the rhythm going and when she did, she stroked him slowly, all the while staring out the window. He grunted and groaned, hit his cigarette and offered it to her. She took a drag, leaving bloody lip prints on the filter. *Looks like . . . the stuff you put on your lips when you want to look good,* she thought. *But you're not wearing that.* She put it back in the ashtray without a word, kept fluffing him. A big silver belt buckle jingled on his thigh, engraved with *In God's Good Service.*

"Rest stop's up ahead, let's finish there," he grumbled, reaching for the cigarette again. "Gotta piss anyway."

He huffed it down, flicked the butt out the window. She eyed his red lips and jacked him faster, hoping he'd finish before pulling over. He pushed her away, cleared his throat, licked his lips. "Hold your horses, we got time."

Her stomach growled as she realized again how hungry she was. The bobtail's brakes screamed to a halt in front of a sun-baked pavilion. Except for a vintage red Pontiac GTO parked a few spots over, the rest stop was deserted. A disheveled young guy and a pretty sullen blonde were seated at one of the island's two picnic tables, nursing sodas and looking conspiratorial. The driver eyed the blonde as he cut the engine, his fly still open, hard cock nipping the wheel.

"Some o' these lil' lot lizards, *hoo-wee*," he offered.

She couldn't tell if he was talking to her or to himself, but realized for the first time how repulsive he was. It wasn't so much his physical presence, off-putting as it was, as it was the seething bad intentions that radiated from his eyes, his pores, his *being.*

He was rotten to the core, pure pain on wheels, spreading his sickness as far and wide as possible, for as long as he could. She also knew she wasn't his usual fodder. *How* she knew, she wasn't sure. But she could feel him growing weaker by the minute, and though she'd dreaded getting off the road with him, she was starting to feel strangely in control.

"You into chicks?" he asked, licking his teeth again.

She studied the blonde, flattering yellow sundress hugging her pale body. She seemed fragile, but the longer you looked, the more striking she became. Something was simmering just beneath the surface. Something no one needed to antagonize. Maybe it was because all four of them were so bad, they all sensed it in each other at first sight. She shook her head, though the girl did tickle something inside her. The driver sneered, squeezing her thigh with a calloused hand.

"You *sure*? Cos I can prob'ly get her for a twenty spot right now."

Before she could answer, the blonde got up and hurried to the GTO. Her companion sat watching them a while longer, then followed. The driver called to him.

"Nice ride, buddy! '69?"

The guy stopped, his blonde staring straight ahead in the passenger seat.

"'67," he replied, flatly.

The driver smirked. "Oh. I was thinkin' '69."

The guy climbed behind the wheel, gunned the engine, peeled out.

"Oh, well. Looks like it's just us, *suburban mom*."

He squeezed his cock with one hand, her tits with the other.

"*Nice titties,*" he mumbled, pulling up her shirt.

He licked his fingers, squeezed a nipple. She sat still, blank and detached, staring at the soda can left on the picnic table by the couple. Her non-reaction bothered him and he scowled, pulling off her hat and grabbing the back of her head.

"*Suck it,*" he spat, through clenched teeth.

She tensed.

He grimaced, pulling his hand back. *"What the hell?"*

His palm was red with blood. She fingered her wet hair, storm clouds brewing behind the driver's eyes.

"You're *fuckin' bleedin'*, you bitch!"

She laughed out of reflex, revealing her missing teeth. He reached down in a rage, drew a hunting knife from under his seat, swung it hard. She caught his wrist with both hands, stopping the blade inches from her face. He leaned into it, but it was a show. She saw the fear in his eyes. Regardless, he had a hundred pounds on her, so she couldn't afford any tests of strength. She had to move fast. As the point drew closer to her eye, she rammed the back of his elbow with her palm, snapping it the wrong way. The radius and ulna bones snapped and tore through his forearm, spritzing the windshield with blood. He screamed, dropping the knife in her lap. Before she could grab it, he drilled her with his good fist. Her head snapped back, lights popping behind her eyelids. Somehow, she instinctively knew to press the pace and fight harder. She swung the knife and he ducked, banging his head on the steering wheel. He grabbed her arm, blocking another swing. They wrestled around the cab, bouncing off the seats, the doors, the dashboard. Blood splattered everything. His cowboy hat fell off, revealing a red combover and freckled skull. She tangled him up, clinging to consciousness, feeling it slip. *The crowd roared, the flashbulbs popped.* The driver reared back and head-butted her in the face.

Blackout.

* * *

She woke in a bad spot. Facedown on a mattress in the sleeper cabin behind the front seats, wrists cable-tied to a vertical metal bar on the wall. The cinch was so tight it cut off her circulation and she couldn't feel her hands. She blinked to focus, saw photos covering the wall in front of her. Each showed a nude woman, bound and terrified, in different stages of torture. Twisted, crying, begging faces, most under thirty and slim, all captured for posterity in their final agonizing moments as they realized hell had come for them first. And she was set to join them. The sound of the knife handle grinding a chunk of crystal meth alerted her. She eyed the drawn blue curtain to her left, watched the driver's hulking silhouette snort lines like a vacuum. He threw his head back, howled, coughed, spit. The pain of his snapped arm had dulled. She knew he'd turn his attention to her soon. She looked around. Above her was a painting of the same bearded man hanging from the rearview, staring at the planet with arms outstretched and wan smile. She didn't know his name, but recognized his image as the deity that supposedly presides over all things, and she held him in as much regard as she did before, which was to say none. Behind her were stacks of porn magazines and empty cigarette packs. There was nothing to grab but the bar she was cinched to, and the way she was tied, she couldn't even get a grip on that. But the driver had conveniently neglected to bind her ankles. A stupid mistake, considering who he was dealing with, but he didn't know. Neither did she.

She quietly rolled onto her back and kicked off her sandals, drawing her knees up and waiting. She watched his shape as he began speaking in a calm voice, a *different* voice, so different that he sounded like another person.

"Father God in heaven above, I do lift up each lost soul on the face of this earth for your judgement. Grant me thine strength to do your work as only you would have it. In your name, my God. Amen."

He turned and pulled the curtain back fast, eyes wild.

Bam!

Her heels nailed him square in the mouth. Teeth ricocheted around the cab and his head bounced off the windshield, leaving a spiderweb crack. He fell forward and her long legs coiled around his neck, wrapping him in a head scissor choke. She arched her back, squeezing with all her strength. His mouth gaped, blood and spit rolling up her thigh as his face went from red to purple to blue, eyes rolling back as she choked him out. She was on auto-pilot, wondering why the move felt so natural, when she noticed her forearms. The cable tie had dug into her wrists and split the skin, streaking her arms with blood. The driver stopped squirming and she opened her legs, letting him slide down between the seats to sleep it off. She tugged at the bar, testing its strength, wrists stinging like crazy. It was anchored to the wall with four bolts and didn't give. She studied them, trying to twist one until her bloody fingers slipped off. She wiped her hand on the wall, tried again. The bolt turned. It'd take a while, but she'd get them out, even if it meant grinding the flesh off her fingertips. She closed the curtain with her toes to block out the fat bastard while she worked. It was too dark to see the bolts, but she knew where they were. She was tied to them after all. And she had all the time in the world, whatever was left of it.

* * *

An hour later, she climbed out the passenger door, hands raw and bloodied. She'd stripped her fingers to the bone, as suspected. Not ideal wrenches, but they got the job done. She hopped down, bare feet hitting the concrete with a smack.

POP!

* * *

The flashbulbs pissed her off bad enough in the ring, but the cocksuckers were getting into the dressing rooms, lingering like flies on the wall until they saw an opening and then—POP!— swooping in to snap their shots. She understood the importance of interest, coverage, notoriety. She knew it'd have to happen for her journey—for the sport—to mean anything at all. Still, it pissed her off and she felt like decking the squirrelly shutterbug as a warm-up. Maybe that was a good thing. Mindset's half the battle, her trainers always said. Refuse to lose and if you've got the tools, you won't. She felt a hand on her shoulder, the familiar trapezius squeeze that sent a tingle up behind her ear.

"Let's win this," the voice said, calm and steady.

Someone lifted her red hood as the corner team moved for the door. She was Little Red Riding Hood and the Big Bad Wolf rolled into one. She lowered her head, intentionally shouldering the cameraman on her way out. He glared and scoffed, then meekly eyed his shoes when he caught her cornerman's gaze on the way past. He was a bad man, in the ring and out, and though he'd evolved into a soft-spoken, grey-stubbled trainer, it still felt like being in the room with a lion. You didn't want to make eye contact. She was the same way and it came as no surprise. He'd transferred all his bad intentions into her, and she was trouble to begin with. Everyone in attendance felt like the crowning of a new world champion was a mere formality, a matter of when—not if—the belt would be strapped around her lean waist. Pop, pop, POP!

"Leadfoot" Kelli McGray hit the mat like 122 pounds of hamburger. The ceiling lights were blinding. She'd never seen them from her back before, and couldn't distinguish them from the dozens of imaginary ones that spun clockwise around the arena, picking up speed, faster and faster, until a crowd of concerned faces blocked them out.

"Ladies and gentlemen, the winner by way of knockout, at forty-three seconds of round two, and the NEW Lightweight Champion of the Worrrrrld!"

She was halfway back to the dressing room soon after the official ring announcement was over, gratefully fielding back slaps, high fives, and handshakes on the way, but her corner stayed in the ring to soak it up a bit longer. It was theirs too, after all. One more hunk of gold to add to the collection, one more figurative head to mount on the wall down at the gym. The training ground of champions. It had a ring to it. She disappeared off the entrance ramp, thousands of fans whistling and cheering her out of sight.

The Champ.

* * *

The women's restroom door blew open, hitting the wall with a loud steel-on-concrete crack. She moved to a dirty sink, eyeing the knobs for a moment before twisting the H faucet, not knowing what it meant. Nothing happened. She turned the one with a C and it exploded in rusty, stuttering spurts. She held her hands under the spray, splashed water on her face, studied herself in the old mirror. Champion of something. *Of what?* The sport with the ropes, the gloves. Screaming drunks, the haves and have-nots, backroom deals and legitimate beatdowns, bright lights and pain whichever way it went. *What the hell was it called? No time to figure it out. Move. Find something—anything—to jog the memory.* It was worth a shot. And a shot was all she ever needed.

Deep in thought, she didn't hear him coming. The driver blitzed her from behind, slamming her head into the mirror. It shattered and he spun her around, hurling her into the cinder block wall. She crumbled.

"*God's vengeance on the Whore of Babylon!*" he bellowed, eyes glazed, ropes of bloody spit swinging from his chin.

She tried to scramble up, but he punt-kicked her head and pounced on her, slamming her skull into the concrete floor. Dozens, then hundreds, then thousands of voices crowded her brain, all speaking in tongues, louder and louder, until the noise melted into one constant hum, then buzz, then roar, like standing under a waterfall. *Pop, pop, POP!*

Blackout.

* * *

She heard before she saw. Heard his excited breathing and low rumbling growl that sounded strangely like the bobtail parked outside, his blood-clogged snorts seeming to mimic its diesel engine. She smelled his acrid stink, so pungent it seemed to coat her nostrils and throat. But she couldn't see anything and maybe it was for the best, as he stood looming over her sprawled body. She heard *In God's Good Service* jingle and clang like a ring bell as his jeans hit the floor around his ankles. He stepped out of them, leaving his boots on. He tore off her *Suburban Mom* tee with one yank, slid off her shorts, forced her legs open. She winced at the blunt force pain as he rammed himself inside her, opened her mouth wide. He frowned, studying her split tongue.

"The devil bears a forked tongue," he growled, pressing his mouth to her ear and chanting in rhythm with his violent thrusts. "*Drive* the devil from this wench, Lord! *Drive* the devil! *Cleanse* this soiled whore and *drive* the evil from this wretched, diseased body! Created in your image and *defiled* by *sin!* By the *sword* of Adalgar! *Sword* of Benedict! *Sword* of Cajetan! *Sword* of Dominic! *Sword* of Ermine!—"

On he went, rattling off the names of saints he'd either used too many times before or had memorized for the occasion. She tuned him out, hearing nothing but a steady, soothing hum. What the driver was doing to her—or what still lay in store—no longer mattered. He scowled at her blank stare and pulled out, backhanding her in the mouth before flipping her over and slamming her facedown. Her eyesight returned and she focused on a small brown spider crawling along the baseboard in front of her. She swore it met her gaze with an eight-eyed sidelong glance. Her mouth was open, her tongue on the concrete. It tasted of mud, mold, and piss. She heard the driver hock spit into his hand, heard him slapping his wet shaft, felt him force his erection up her ass. He eased in at first, then drove in hard and deep, his hips slapping her cheeks in obscene applause as he took her. She gasped, held her breath. He pushed her face harder into the concrete with his good hand, but she didn't care. Something was happening, seizing her, taking control from the inside out. Something she didn't understand. Something she was powerless to stop. He grunted and growled, pounding without mercy, still bellowing the names of the imaginary friends in whose service he was working.

"—*Sword* of Leopold! *Sword* of Marcellian! *Sword* of Nicodemus! *Sword* of Oswald!—" He closed his eyes, crushing her hip with one strong hand, his other arm dangling at his side. Blood dotted his furry thighs from the damage he was doing to her, but she didn't fight back. She watched the brown spider clomp under the door and out into the sun without looking back. It had seen enough. The thought flashed through her mind that maybe nothing else would happen. That maybe she was meant to wake at the bottom of a lake with a bullet hole in her head, only to die facedown on a dirty bathroom floor under a murdering rapist zealot. Her body ran ice cold. *This is it,* she thought. *This time it's for real.* She didn't know how right she was.

"—*Sword* of Titus! *Sword* of Ulric! *Sword* of Vincent!—"

The driver's body spasmed and he threw his head back, bouncing a loud howl around the concrete echo chamber as he came inside her. She let him have the moment. She could feel the muscles in her arms and legs popping, contorting, morphing into something . . . *else*. Exactly what, she wasn't sure, but it felt *magnificent*. The driver forgot all about his broken arm, eyes rolled back as he rode out his orgasm, oblivious to her ice cold body. When he finished, he slumped over her, sweat and drool splashing her back. His heart was pounding so hard they both could hear it. He noted her cold flesh, figured she was dead.

"Now *that's* what we call an *exorcism,* bitch."

His cock was soft inside her as her hands pressed the floor, fingers spread wide, body coiling like a spring under his weight. He felt her tensing and slammed her face back to the floor with his good arm.

"Be still*, pig!* The *Lord God's* gonna be your judge!"

She grimaced, felt her cheek throbbing on the slimy concrete, let him run his routine. The same one he'd run on the others as they pleaded, cried, and begged for their lives. He probably waited for it, expected it, *thrived* on it. She'd offer none of it. And because she wouldn't, she knew he'd keep her alive that much longer, if only to break her so she'd give him what he wanted. What he *needed*. But she wouldn't. On the contrary, she had something *else* to give him. It was the last thing in the world he expected. He bit her shoulder hard, leaving teeth marks and bubbled blood.

She didn't make a sound, staring into the bright light outside the door just a few feet away. Her pupils exploded, spreading like an oil spill to black-out her eyes. She blinked and they opened wider, stretching insect-like around the sides of her head. She could see both the driver's shoulders in her right and left periphery without turning her head, her vision almost fully panoramic. He watched, befuddled, as the blue spiderweb veins crept over her nude body. Her spine stretched a foot longer and her skin flushed the same sickly aqua color as the walls around them. The driver tried to pull out, but couldn't. Her cold stung his shaft, shriveling him instantly, but he remained stuck. He whimpered, eyes bugging as her anus squeezed him like a vise until he couldn't breathe. Her forearms elongated, sprouting short hard-tissue spikes from wrist to elbow. The driver's boots scraped the floor for traction, trying in vain to get away. He heard a snap and fell back, eyes on the ceiling. The frigid cold gave way to burning heat and a strange sensation between his legs. He lifted his head and saw a fountain of blood gushing from his crotch. He screamed, but it was too late. She sprang up on all fours, almost hitting the ceiling, arms and legs long as stilts. Her head spun 360 degrees on her shoulders and she looked down, big black eyes locking on her prey as she opened her mouth wide, revealing rows of sharp vertical teeth that chomped side-to-side instead of up-and-down. The driver stared in awe and horror, frozen, speechless, *resigned*. She climbed onto him and, in a startling instant, almost too fast for the eye to follow, lunged at his face. He flinched and a chunk of his cheek was gone, blood cascading down his shirt. She chewed fast and swallowed, lunged again. His other cheek vanished, leaving glistening red sinew and bared, chattering teeth. He fell flat, arms outstretched and palms up, as if being crucified.

"Holy Mary, mother of God! Pray for—"

She grabbed him around the neck, lifting his head. The fingers on both her hands had webbed into pincer-like claws that cut into his flesh as she held him.

"—us sinners! Now and at the hour of our death, amen!"

They were fitting last words. He closed his eyes as she plunged again, taking a chunk out of his skull above the left temple. A waterfall of blood spurted from the hole, dousing him red. She chewed voraciously, then bit into his forehead to expose his throbbing, damaged brain. His body convulsed, eyes rolled back, teeth clenched so tight he inadvertently severed the tip of his own tongue. He was still alive, but not for long. Black blood flushed the corners of the room, rolling out the door to turn bright red in the sunshine. Her claws sank deeper into his neck, clipping his jugular, blasting the toilet stall with thick splatter. As his heart weakened, his blood pumped slower and slower. Soon, it babbled from the gaping holes as serenely as a country stream. He blinked, still aware of what was happening. She anchored his torso with her forearm spikes, chewing out his eyeballs and nipping off his nose, forcing his jaw open until it broke and devouring what was left of his bloated tongue like an oyster, gnawing on his head as casually as if it were a cabbage. His fists were balled tight, waiting for the end. She was ravenous, with the luxury of savoring her first meal, so she did just that. He was big. It would take a while. The world would have to fall apart without her. She'd pick its bones when she was ready. She bit into the driver's brain, found the taste pleasing, swallowed and took a bigger bite.

3

Bloody footprints led into the men's restroom, where she stood naked with her head hung in the sink, skinned fingers massaging cold water through her hair. A red swirl spiraled down the drain, fading to pink and finally clear. She'd rinsed herself clean of dirt, sweat, blood, and her body had transformed back to what it was supposed to be, though she wasn't sure she knew exactly what that was. *The chick with the bullet hole in her head.* Every muscle ached like she'd had the workout of her life or had been bludgeoned from head-to-toe, and neither estimate was far from the truth. She turned off the faucet, eyeing herself in the sliver of mirror that remained after years of untended vandalism. Not bad. If she didn't know better, she'd swear she didn't just kill and eat a man in the women's room, not ten feet away. Her thoughts felt clearer too, though she wasn't sure how or why. Ideas just seemed to click a little faster and stick a little longer. She figured it was a good sign and decided not to dwell on it. As she shook her hair out, she licked her gums and hit something hard. Thinking it was a piece of the driver's skull, she leaned close to the mirror and opened her mouth. Small white nubs of teeth were growing in. Forming again, everything from scratch, clean and new. She stared, surprised and confused, and her mind took the next logical step. *If the teeth are growing back . . .* She fingered the hole in her head. Still there, but *smaller.* Was it closing? She wagged her tongue, saw thin scar tissue joining the two halves. She smiled at the insanity of it all, then couldn't help but laugh, and once she started laughing, she couldn't stop. She laughed so hard her eyes welled up, her sides hurt and she lost her breath, which made it worse still. She was caught in a vicious cycle and looking at herself wasn't helping. She ducked into the toilet stall. Seeing the bowl made her want to pee, so she squatted over the stained plastic seat without touching it, knees together. Recalling what she'd done to the driver next door and the fact that she was taking pains to avoid a plastic seat threw her into fits again, making pee impossible. She almost fell, but caught herself on the wall, and the distraction broke the seal. She giggled hysterically at the sound of her stream hitting the water, struggling to breathe.

BIG GAY JIM GOBBLES COCK.

She eyed the stall walls, reading the crude graffiti that was written and carved all around her, mind racing like a child overcome by the rush of new understanding—which, essentially, she was.

SUCK ON THIS, FAG.

She smirked, rocking back and forth as her pee slowed to a trickle.

YOUR MOTHER EATS ASS, FUCKTARD.

The thought crossed her mind that the epithets could've been more imaginative, but she drew a blank trying to think of one herself.

BRONCOS #1.

Look at that. Someone's a big fan of horses. How she remembered them, she had no clue. She burst into laughter again, inadvertently snorting, which destroyed any chance of composure she might've had. Crouching in the stall, she couldn't hear the distant rumble. When the approaching roar finally crashed her one-woman party, she wasn't even sure what it was. Trucks? Helicopters? Giant insects? She crept out of the stall, padded to the door, looked outside. Two Harley-Davidson choppers carrying lone riders sped off the highway toward the rest stop, followed by a small army of the same. The bikes kept pouring off the exit ramp, dozens of them, louder and louder as they closed in. From a distance, she thought they looked and sounded like ugly steel hornets, momentarily distracting herself by realizing she'd effortlessly recalled the names of quite a few things. Helmeted, bearded, sunglass and bandana-masked, denim and leather-clad, gun and knife-toting, some with old ladies on their backs, it was a big motorcycle club with downtime on its mind. Which meant somebody was going to have to use a bathroom. She turned, eyeing the flies swarming the women's room doorway and the blood rolling out from inside, stretching across the concrete walkway into the dirt. There'd be no hiding that. She eyed the window behind her. Seven feet up and barred. There was no way out. Then the obvious hit her. The *bobtail*. The bikers were a hundred yards out and closing. She'd have to run straight at them to *maybe* make it to the cab first. She was completely nude. She wasn't sure how fast she could move. She had no idea if the keys were in the ignition, in the driver's pocket, or in her stomach. It sounded like a challenge. And for some crazy reason, it excited her. She sprinted as fast as she could, legs pumping hard, bare feet slapping hot concrete. Her muscles worked. The lead biker pointed at her, exchanging looks with the rider alongside him, raising a fist to those behind. The cycles flooded the lot, filling it fast, surrounding the tractor. A three-piece patch on their backs read NORTHERN NAZIS, and was emblazoned with a large grinning skull bearing a gold front tooth and double lightning bolts on its forehead. All the faces she could see were white. She reached the bobtail's door to a chorus of catcalls and whistles.

"Shake it, baby!" someone called, and it could've been any of them.

"This the Strip Stop?!"

She ignored the audience, vaulting into the cab, slamming and locking the door. Plastic Jesus spun on the rearview, turning his back on her.

"You charge by the hour or by the stick?!" another voice called.

She reached for the ignition. No keys. Her heart sank. Game over. She sat gazing through the windshield cracks, contemplating Plan B without much hope, when a giant suddenly appeared in the driver's window. Her heart surged, but she didn't react. He was seven feet plus, with a salt-and-pepper goatee, ponytailed long hair, and a deep-creased face. He removed his shades, revealing a milky-white dead left eye.

"Two questions," he purred, his voice calm and deep.

She held eye contact.

"You need help?"

Pause. She shook her head.

He nodded. "You workin'?"

Pause. She noticed one of the old ladies making for the restroom. The chick was tanned leather, late-twenties in a forty-year-old body, bottled blonde with big fake tits to trick Father Time, painted-on jeans and five-inch boot heels to keep it strutty, looking like she could wear 'em out in bed or knock 'em out in a bar and not give a damn which. She definitely wouldn't like the facilities.

"Hey." The giant snapped his fingers. "You hear me?"

She snapped to attention, nodding.

He cocked his head. "Yeah, you're workin' or yeah, you hear me?"

She wondered what he meant by *working,* didn't know how to answer. The bobtail was swarmed on all sides by conspiratorial bikers lighting cigarettes, cracking beers, stretching legs, ogling the naked chick in the truck. The giant waited for an answer, his good eye roaming down her body. He licked his lips. *Maybe he's asking if you're a driver.* She nodded, not sure it was the best answer. He smiled, revealing a gold front tooth.

"*Fuck!*"

The old lady stood frozen outside the women's room door, her face a mask of horror. "*C'mere!*" she yelled, waving to anyone paying attention.

Two bikers ambled her way. Another popped up in the passenger window, ignoring the driver's nude body, but staring intently at her face. He was a twenty-something version of the giant, with eyes and teeth accounted for. Could've been related.

She held his gaze, while the giant turned his attention to the growing restroom commotion.

"*You're Scarla Fragran, right?*" the kid whispered.

The name set off bells in her head. Was he right? She flashed back to the talking cock in the lake house shower.

"*Hallo, Scarla . . .*"

It wasn't coincidence. She wanted to ask questions, but hadn't even tried to speak, wasn't sure she could.

"*What're you doing here?*" he asked, perplexed.

"*Shit, goddamn!*" shrieked one of the curious bikers, stumbling out of the women's room and puking on the walkway.

The other turned and raised his arms, calling to the giant. "*Tully!* Don't let her go!"

Without a word, giant Tully unlocked and opened the bobtail's door, pulling Scarla from behind the wheel and tossing her over his shoulder with ease, moving to the scene of the crime. The rest of the club followed his lead, storming the restrooms en masse. Tully strode to the blood, noting the queasy looks on the faces of his three people. He turned to the biker who alerted him, dropping Scarla into his waiting arms and stepping to the women's room door. The entire club looked on. He grimaced, swatting at flies and shielding his nose from the stench of death, overpowering in the late day heat. The room was painted red, everything in sight dripping with glistening blood and guts. The driver—or what remained of him—was spread across the floor, skeletal arms and legs with the meat picked clean, hands and booted feet intact, pried-open ribcage jutting up from an intact spinal cord, vital organs and head gone, jawbone in the toilet, bloody clothes strewn around it all.

"Fuckin' hell," Tully muttered, swatting a fly off his nose and turning away.

Others started moving in, but he waved them off.

"Back, get back. Don't go in there unless you wanna lose that shitty lunch. Nothin' to see but fuckin' flies anyway."

He pointed at Scarla, still in the arms of the other biker. "Drop her."

The guy complied and backed off.

Tully got down in her face. "Now it's *one* question. What the hell happened here?"

She held his gaze, didn't answer. His eyes blazed, hands clenching into gigantic steel-ringed fists. She didn't blink.

He lowered his voice. "I'm not gonna ask you again."

The kid stepped up, loud and eager. "She's *Scarla Fragran*, dad. The old fighter, the women's champ. Remember?"

She eyed the kid, almost as tall as his old man, but not so iron-forged. She wanted to thank him, but being called the "old" fighter somehow rankled her. *Scarla Fragran, champion fighter.* The vivid images were real memories after all. She wouldn't doubt them again. All eyes were on her. Tully boiled, exhaling through his nose, as close to a dragon as you'd find on two legs—though she could put that to the test if she wanted to. He stared a hole through her.

"Scarla Fragran. I've heard of you," he finally growled, nodding to the bloody walkway. "Did you do this?"

Pause. It was quiet enough to hear a pin drop. She rolled her eyes, looked away. He grabbed her by the neck, yanking her off her feet with one hand, slamming her against the brick wall.

"Darlin', so help me, you got about five seconds to tell me if you had anything to do with that mess in there, or I'm gonna tie your wrists to those bikes—"

He jammed a thumb over his left shoulder.

"—your ankles to those over there—"

He pointed to the road, speaking low and deliberate.

"—and away we go. *Vroom, vroom.*"

She grunted, her face turning purple, unable to speak if she wanted to.

"Just make her your old lady, Tull! They never seem to last the night!" one guy cackled.

No one laughed. Without a word, Tully extended his free hand and the closest man slapped a sawed-off shotgun into his palm. He pressed the barrel to Scarla's cheek.

"Maybe I'll just paint this wall with your fuckin' brains and be done with it."

Wouldn't be the first time, she thought, cracking an smile. Seemed she was bad at keeping a straight face in times of duress. Something to keep in mind. Tully's face went cold. Before she knew that she'd tripped his notorious hair-trigger temper, he reared back and swung the shotgun at her head like a baseball bat.

Blackout.

* * *

She woke in a different place, but the air smelled the same, sky looked the same, dirt was the same. Her ears rang and her head felt glazed in a warm lather that she knew was her own blood. So much for rinsing off. She was on her back in a wooded clearing, surrounded by two dozen leering bikers. The old ladies were gone and it was just the boys. The *bad boys,* the ones who liked to take what they could get, fringe benefits especially. Some of them had rolled in with companions on their backs, but those were just the girls auditioning for old lady status, hoping to hook a member—so to speak—and become official, while still in good graces. They were nothing but a good time until something better, or just something *different,* came along. Scarla was different. Just *how* different, they had no idea. But according to Tully, her ass didn't matter.

"Lose the bitch," he said. "Have fun and don't hold us up. Be quick about it."

It was a half-hour stretch break, smoke break, piss break, any kind of break they wanted to make, so the worst of the bunch scraped her up and carried her unconscious body a few yards out behind the pavilion to blow off some steam. The girls understood what the deal was and turned the other cheek, for fear of losing their spot—or worse. Past prospects who were vocal against such activities had a tendency to disappear, so everyone knew to behave. Scarla lifted her head to see the guys unzipping their jeans and leathers, getting ready for whatever mistake they were set on making. There was no point in fighting. She didn't want to anyway. She still wasn't whole, and knew this gang of fools was a means to that end. Cocks started wagging, some already hard. She felt the tingle deep inside and propped herself up on her elbows, spreading her legs.

"She *wants* it, brother!" growled one bearded ogre.

A different one stepped up and dropped to his knees, licking his palm, fluffing his dick, sliding into her. He pushed in deep, grinning up at the others.

"She's wet as fuck!"

Howls of excitement and shouts of encouragement rang out.

"You like Nazi dick, honey?"

Laughs.

"Take it!"

Surround-sound ad libs came from all directions.

"Gonna get yards of it, baby!"

Claps and whistles.

The biker on top of her looked up again, not breaking his rhythm. "Somebody gimme some blow," he spat, hiking her legs over his shoulders.

A leather-gloved hand reached in, holding a sepia-tinted vial under his nose, but he shook his head and slapped Scarla's chest.

"Put it here," he huffed, to a chorus of laughter.

The hand tapped out a small pile of coke between her tits, as more guys broke out their stashes, getting ready to up the ante. The biker worked her over, bending her in half at the waist and thrusting hard with long, deep strokes. He kept it up, inching forward on his hands and knees, until her toes touched the dirt over her head.

"It's like fuckin' a soft pretzel!" someone cracked.

The biker paused, burying his face in her cleavage and hoovering the white stuff up his nose with one big snort.

"*Whooo!*" he shouted, pinching his nostrils, eyes watering.

"That's some strong shit, motherfucker!"

His voice sounded like Kermit the Frog, drawing big laughs.

"Bust that nut before you lose your bone, Slim!" called a

burly guy who loomed over them, bouncing his dick up and down with no hands.

"Wait your turn," Slim scowled. "And you cum on my back, I'll slit your fuckin' throat."

Chortles from the peanut gallery. Slim pushed down on the backs of Scarla's knees, kept pumping. She watched his face, all slack mouth, hooded eyes, throbbing forehead, bulging veins. He was lost in the feeling and it turned her on. She needed it worse than he did, albeit for entirely different reasons. And, as they'd soon find out, with very different results. She waited for him to thrust in deep, then seized his shaft with her Kegel muscles and didn't let go. His eyes widened.

She smiled.

He smiled back.

"You like that?" he whispered.

She nodded, eyes gleaming.

"You're a live one, ain'tcha?"

The others grew restless standing around jerking off, until one of them spoke up.

"Holdin' up the line, bro. If you ain't cummin', jump off, goddammit. You can nut on sloppy seconds."

She let Slim go and he held her gaze. "See ya soon," he offered, standing up, stepping back.

"Don't make goo-goo eyes!" the burly guy snarled. "This ain't no fuckin' lovefest!"

Hands reached in like a swarm of flesh-crazed zombies, pulling her hair, smacking her face, her tits, her ass. A ringed fist slugged her stomach, knocking the wind out of her. A booted foot stomped her hip, but barely registered. They hoisted her off the ground, flipped her over in the air like a gymnastics routine, body-slammed her facedown in the dirt. She felt one of them enter her from behind, pulling hard on her hair with two hands. A guy knelt in front of her, paint-brushing her face with his dick, then slapping her hard across the mouth. He slapped her again and again, then finally drew back and punched her square in the nose. Blood splattered. She saw stars.

"You like that, *champ?*" he sneered.

The bikers reacted like a fight crowd, screaming for more. The guy behind her let go of her hair and fish-hooked the corners of her mouth, pounding faster until he came.

"*Fuuuuck yeeeaaaah!*"

Her body spasmed as he pulled out and jumped aside to let the next one in.

"That's how you run a train, boy!" someone yelled.

She went numb as the new guy slid in, the tingle in her belly creeping throughout her body. She watched her blood splashing the dirt, shiny ants already scrambling through the slop to attack a fallen bee, writhing in its death throes. She marveled at their efficiency. The bee kicked and bucked in vain, finally succumbing to the myriad of bites, its legs swinging, then twitching, then still. It wasn't all that different from what was happening to her. A hand yanked her head up and a large guy forced himself into her mouth, snaking down her throat until she gagged. He pushed in again, deeper. She struggled for breath, spewing vomit on his balls. The gang cheered. He kept thrusting her face, puke running down his legs. She focused, involuntary tears streaking her cheeks, and finally took him without gagging, her nose bloodying the dark mound at the base of his shaft.

"Take it! *Take it!*" he yelled, palming her head.

His middle finger slid into the bullet hole and he paused, fingering deeper. He pulled out, eyed his red finger, looked around.

"Hey, this bitch has a hole in her head!" he called.

"Does your dick fit?" smirked the guy humping her other end. "If so, *fuck it!*"

The guy grimaced, still humping her mouth. "It's a fuckin' *hole*, man."

Another hand reached in, weeding through her hair to find it. The guy inside her came and pulled out, another taking his place.

"Brock's right, she's got a hole!" called the new fingerer, jiggling her head around.

"Make her talk, Jag!" cracked the guy behind her, miming a hand puppet as he wiggled a finger up her ass. He came, tagged off to another.

The new guy came on his first thrust, then moved to let another in.

"Is it one hole or three? Chop her head off and let's go bowling!" someone screamed.

Laughter. Brock came in her mouth with no warning. She willingly swallowed his spurts, cold permeating her muscles from head-to-toe. He eyed Jag, still fingering her skull.

"Did I hit you with that?" he chuckled.

"Fuck you," Jag replied, pulling his finger out.

He stood up and came in her hair. Brock fell back, laughing. Jag squeezed the last drops from his dick, raised his fists in victory. The gang applauded.

"I ain't touchin' the dirty bitch," he grumbled, zipping up.

Others agreed, following suit.

"AIDS on a stick!" someone yelled.

The guy fucking her scowled and got up, his erection wilted. "Man, you motherfuckers killed my hard-on!"

An empty beer can bounced off his head. He raised a middle finger to the crowd, pulling up his pants.

"Hundred bucks to whoever skull fucks her right now!" Jag bellowed. "Hurry up, we ain't got all day!"

A shaggy scumbag pushed his way to the front, wild-eyed, dick in hand. *"Show me the fuckin' hole!"*

Laughter.

Jag shook his head, peeling a hundred off a wad. "I shoulda known it'd be you, Skunk." He pointed at the back of her head. "Down by the hairline there, it's wide open."

Skunk slapped himself across both furry cheeks. "Wide open's how I like 'em!"

He entertained the boys with a long war cry, yanking Scarla up to face the audience, clutching her head in his big hands. A chant broke out.

"Skull *fuck!* Skull *fuck!* Skull *fuck!*"

He spanked her head with his dick, milking the noise before parting her hair and grimacing at the wound.

Jag cackled. "Careful, it's sharp in there, big man!"

Skunk eyed him, hesitant. "Somebody gimme a beer!" he yelled.

A can sailed through the air like a hand grenade. He caught it, cracked it, chugged it, crushed it in his fist and threw it back, belching deep.

"Alright," he sighed. "I'm goin' in."

More laughter.

He saw her jaw clenched and slapped her cheek. "Open up, let 'em see."

She parted her lips. A coyote skulked along, unnoticed in the distance. Her eyes followed it. It paused, sniffed the air, leveled a piercing gaze on her. *You don't need me. What can I do for you that you can't do for yourself?* Skunk pushed his dick through the back of her head. She felt his rigid shaft slide over her tongue and emerge from her mouth. The crowd howled, in equal awe and disgust. He grinned, holding her head tight, pumping the hole. *In . . . out.* Some guys turned away, having seen enough.

Jag reached over, stuffed the hundred in Skunk's vest. "Goddamn, you win again, motherfucker. Finish it and leave her for the dogs, we gotta roll. I'll be with Tull."

Skunk nodded, taking a fistful of Scarla's hair and slamming his pelvis into the back of her head, for the guys still watching. One of them moved in, stroking himself inches from her face. The thick veins pulsating in his shaft excited her, so she grabbed it for him. He smiled, hooking his fingers behind his head, closing his eyes. "Fuck, let's keep her a while. She can ride with me."

Skunk ignored the comment, pounding his way to climax. His cum shot out her mouth like a squirt gun, splattering his brother's leather chaps, who in turn splattered Scarla's face. The warm spurts turned her on and she kept tugging well after he was done.

Skunk pulled out, her hair still wrapped around his fist. "Look what you made me do to my brother's leathers, he's a mess. Man can't ride with jizz stains, girl."

He pushed her face to the wet chaps. *"Clean him off."*

She stared at the milky-white streaks on black leather, desire swelling so intensely, she shook all over. Skunk forced her lips into the dripping ejaculate and she stuck her tongue out, licking up a thigh-long streak and savoring the taste before swallowing. Suddenly, the switch flipped and her throat went cold, eyes rolling back white, fingers and toes instantly sprouting sharp black claws. None of the dozen or so remaining noticed it. Skunk nodded to the group. Someone handed him a length of O-ring motorcycle chain. Without hesitating, he turned and lashed her across the face.

Thwack!

She crumbled to the dirt, silent and still. He stepped over her, raised the chain high, swung again. The flesh on her back split open, spurting red. He swung harder and harder, thinking she might already be gone and it would be easy. He was wrong. Very wrong. Deep lacerations criss-crossed her back and sides, blood splashing everything within twenty feet. She took the beating without flinching, head down, face hidden. Skunk paused and scanned the dirt, lifting a twenty-pound rock. He stepped on her neck, raising it for the final blow. A hand grabbed his arm and he turned. It was Slim.

"Hold up, Skunk."

Skunk seethed with bloodlust, boot still on Scarla's neck. "The fuck you mean, *hold up*? Tull's orders."

Slim raised his hands, nodding. "I know. *I know*, man."

Skunk stared. So did the few who remained. If Slim was trying to break up the party, he'd be joining her. Club rules. She recognized his voice and listened, far more conscious than they knew.

A smirk crept across Slim's lips. "She felt fuckin' *good*, man. I just wanna hit it one more time."

So much for human compassion.

Skunk shook his head, unmoved. "You can hit it after I'm done."

Slim's face dropped. "But—"

Skunk pushed him away.

The closest biker chuckled, amused. "Looks like *cold* leftovers for you, Slim."

No one noticed her hand between her legs, bloody fingers massaging her swollen clit, and they wouldn't have understood if they had. Skunk raised the rock again, turning back to her. What looked like a dog's maw was the last thing he saw before she removed his foot, leather boot and all. Tasted gamey, but it was all the same when you got right down to it. He never had a chance to scream as she sprang straight up, twisting in the air to lock her teeth around his throat, thrashing her head as she took him down. He was dead before he hit the dirt, a red fountain gushing from the ragged stump on his shoulders. His head rolled to a stop, eyes blinking. He could see his body. In his final seconds of awareness, he watched Scarla mount his carcass on all fours, slicing the length of his torso with her claws and ripping it open like a birthday present. She looked more lupine than human, her flesh still as smooth and supple as a young woman, her body gashed and blood-streaked from the savage beating. He chalked it up as a hallucination, his eyelids fluttering shut. *Slim stabbed me in the back,* he thought. *Fuck Slim.*

The scene erupted in a stampede of leather and denim. Slim ran for his life with the others, whimpering in a mad dash to the pavilion, just a few yards away. *Run. Don't look back. Lure it to the club and they'll shoot it to shit . . . shoot it . . . shoot it . . . shoot!* He got a few feet from the walkway, before being run down and slaughtered like the fresh prey he was. Before he knew it, he was facedown in the dirt, his left arm gone. His brain said *kick,* but she'd taken his legs, too. He still felt like he had moving appendages and might get away, despite the flood of gore that pumped from stumps where they used to be. Everything around him went red and he knew the blood was his. He heard slashing, ripping, chewing, then commotion, screaming, finally shooting. *Finally.* Her claws hooked his mouth, ripping his head off above the jaw. The last thing he saw was the pavilion wall spinning wildly at him. His severed head slammed against it, splatting to the ground, a fly already stuck to the eyeball.

"*Kill it! Kill it!*" someone screeched.

Gunfire erupted. The dirt around her seemed to explode all at once, dust filling the air. Sharp stings speckled her arms and legs. She knew they were bullet hits. Bikers surrounded her on all sides, guns aimed. She lifted Slim's eviscerated carcass, using it as a shield. His remaining arm flailed like a rag doll's, bullets shredding his torso as she charged straight through the gang, sending bodies scattering. A flurry of rounds drilled her back and leg, but she made it around the pavilion and lurched into the women's room, slamming the door.

Silence.

The bikers stood stunned, wild-eyed and out of breath, sweaty brows and shaky trigger fingers. All eyes instinctively looked to Tully, who maintained his reptilian cool as he reloaded. After what seemed an eternity, he calmly turned to Jag, who stood close with scared eyes.

"Don't care how we do it, we ain't leavin' without that bitch's head on my handlebars."

He fired a shot into the women's room door, looked around at all the faces.

"Blow that house down."

Every hand on deck raised what they had. Handguns, shotguns, semi-automatic machine guns, all leveled on the small brick restroom. Everything fell so still and quiet, the scene felt like a photograph as the seconds ticked by. Scarla slumped beside the toilet, tired and hurting, wolf-like eyes blazing white, drool oozing from her razor-toothed mouth, body hunched in a sinewy arch. She let the frenzied flies swarm her, using a claw to dig bullets out of her side. The lead slugs bounced on the concrete, one after another, rolling away like pinballs. She heard the sharp crack of weapons unloading, saw the wooden door turn to Swiss cheese, bowed her head and waited. Laser beams of light sliced through the room, dust jumping off the cinder block walls as they absorbed the barrage outside. She contemplated going outside, just to see if she'd die, but decided they didn't deserve her. The window exploded overhead, glass shards blowing around the room, some of it falling into the gashes on her back. Two huge shotgun blasts rang out, splitting the wall from floor to ceiling. The symphony of firepower faded as some paused to reload, before coming back even stronger. Half the door crumbled in. Ceiling plaster fell on her head. The porcelain sink exploded, water spewing from its orphaned pipes, flushing Slim's wrecked torso and the tractor driver's bones against the wall. A section of bricks caved in. Sunlight and bullets blasted the metal stall serving as her cover. She sank lower, her mind racing for a plan and coming up with nothing. The bikers closed in, crowding the openings, peering inside.

"Is that her?" she heard one of them ask, referring to the picked-clean bones near Slim.

Tully's deep voice replied. "Naw, that sack o' shit was already there. So, our little piggy must be—"

Boom!

A chunk of the toilet stall blew out above her. She stayed low.

"Come and get it, wolf girl!" he taunted. "Whatsa matter, ain't hungry no more?"

Pause.

"Your head's gonna look real nice leadin' this club down the highway, bitch. Ain't leavin' til we get it. You took two of mine, I'm takin' *you*, bottom line."

Boom!

Buckshot blasted the stall wall apart and shattered the toilet bowl. She felt a burn and looked down, saw her hip shredded, her leg spurting blood. Her fangs and claws receded, eyes returning to bleary normal, adrenaline giving way to crippling pain. She saw bodies crowding the perimeter, all wide eyes and trigger fingers. She stared down more barrels than she could count.

Tully smiled, signaling them to hold their fire. *"There* you are, piggy. Wanna get up and take it like a woman? Or you like it on all fours?"

He dropped his gun, swung his legs over the wall, stepped inside. All eyes followed him.

His kid spoke up, alarmed. "Dad. *What the fuck, dad?*"

"He knows what he's doin'," croaked Jag, a smoking Glock in each fist.

Tully kept his good eye on Scarla. "How long you had it?" he asked.

She slid back against the wall, plumbing flooding the floor under her, cool on her mauled leg. Tully rolled his head on his shoulders, cracked his neck. She shifted uncomfortably, wondering if her old self would've seen any options she was missing. He hooked his thumbs on his belt, tapping a boot in the muck, his eye dissecting her mauled body.

"I can see outta both eyes when I'm overcome, y'know," he purred, before raising his outside voice. "Move it out! Everybody on your bikes!"

He eyed Jag, who nodded grimly before seconding the order. "You heard him, clear out! Half-speed on the highway!"

A doe-eyed chick, with big tits stretching the limits of a baby tee, hesitated. "Should we bury Slim?" she squeaked.

Jag glared. "You wanna bury Slim, go in there and get him. Then stay here and bury him, but I'd hitch a ride with the next club that rolls through, if I was you."

She hung her head.

He nodded to the lot. "Get your ass on that bike."

She obeyed. Jag raised a Glock and made eye contact with Tully, concerned but resigned, before setting it on the wall and walking away.

"Start 'em up!" he shouted. "Let's roll!"

He kickstarted his hog, the doe-eyed girl on back. They both watched the restroom.

"He'll catch up," Jag mumbled. "He always does."

Engines roared to life. Tully Jr. shook his head in disgust, revving his bike hard and peeling out. His father was an animal he just didn't understand. The club rolled after him, somber and confused, slowly streaming back to the highway without its leader.

4

Inside the women's room, Scarla and Tully stared at each other, neither blinking. The bulge in his jeans turned her on and the pain wracking her body faded. She felt her cells springing to life. His gaze fell between her legs and she knew he felt the same. She opened them wider, letting him get a better view, watching him unbuckle and unzip. Her eyes floated down his chest and kept floating. He was riding commando and already hard, with a cock the size of her forearm. She met his gaze again. He smiled. She pulled away from the wall and crawled across the blood-smeared, glass-strewn concrete to him. He stood waiting, feet planted wide. She bowed her head, tongued the tip of his boot, licked up his leather-chapped leg to take one of his pendulous balls in her mouth. He watched, breathing harder.

"You ever been with another one?" he asked.

Another *what,* she wondered. Had she? She couldn't say for sure, so she stayed quiet and closed her lips around his other nut, sucking softly. He laid a ringed hand on her head, wrapping her hair around his erection and gyrating his hips.

"Yeah, baby," he groaned, letting her lick the length of his cock and roll her tongue around the head.

He was too big to suck, so she stroked him with both hands, studying the black swastika tattoo emblazoned across his stomach. She couldn't recall exactly what it signified, so she took it as another club logo. She leaned back to accommodate his growing size, cupping his balls and tonguing his shaft.

"Spit on it," he commanded.

She obliged.

"Now lick it off," he added.

She did. Her leg was still bleeding freely, blasted almost to the bone, but all she could feel was the tingle. The *urge*. She looked up at him, gripping his cock like a club, and smiled. He softly thumbed spit from the corner of her mouth, then grabbed her wrists.

"Let's fuck."

She didn't know what that meant, but it sounded good. She nodded. He lifted her off the floor and she wrapped her arms around his neck, legs around his waist, wanted to kiss his mouth, but somehow knew it wasn't that kind of encounter. With two big strides, he slammed her against the wall, reaching down with one hand to guide himself in. She gasped as he filled her, using his shoulders as leverage to ride him, long and slow. *Up . . . down . . . up . . . down.* A shudder tore through her body and she came without warning, digging her fingers into his leather, gumming his ringed earlobe with bloody lips. Her body seized on his cock, squeezing and releasing, over and over, taking him to the edge of orgasm.

"Stop," he ordered.

She kept grinding her hips.

"I said *stop!*"

He drove his forearm under her chin, pinning her head to the cinder blocks. She held eye contact, electric aftershocks rippling through her body. He struggled to stay focused, but it was too late. His shaft ran cold inside her, eyes rolling over white, face stretching into a coned point at the nose, mouth gaping wide to the farthest corners of his jaw, rows and rows of jagged teeth sprouting behind a front line of silvery razor-tips. Despite the transformation, she wasn't afraid. Hanging in his arms, impaled on his monstrous icicle of a cock, she only felt more frenzied. *Stronger.* She was right where she wanted to be. He opened his mouth wide and she counted hundreds of teeth that could to rip her to shreds. He lunged at her, but didn't make it. In the blink of an eye, her arms and legs morphed into squid tentacles and coiled him, encircling his neck and waist, holding him frozen. He chomped air wildly, trying to get a piece of her, but could only move where she'd allow him. Inch-long hooks sprang from her tentacles, digging into his flesh. They weren't lethal, just deep enough to sting and keep him from escaping or fighting too hard. He winced and cocked his head, surprise clear in his bright white stare. Insatiable hunger swelled inside her. So did his erection, still primed and ready to burst. She liked the feel of it, splitting her attention between bleeding him out and getting him off. Her muscles went gelatinous, her bones bowing like rubber, as she sank more hooks into his sides, back, abdomen, shoulders, neck. His legs gave out and they both crashed to the concrete. She landed on top and rode him, pumping with short fast strokes as he lay helpless in her grasp, giant mouth agape in a mute pain/pleasure combination until he came, spurting a torrent of what felt like ice water inside her. She tensed, eyes shut tight, climaxing again herself, despite the shock of his frigid semen. She threw her head back, blue veins bulging in her neck, and bared sharp, black, shiny teeth that weren't in her mouth a moment ago. They were hard and murderous, yet she didn't use them on him. She felt his muscles relax as his orgasm wound down, and she rode hers out until she was spent.

She slumped on Tully's chest, their hearts pounding like jackhammers. The reprieve didn't last. The fight-or-flight instinct kicked back in and her eyes popped open, fists clenched. Fists. Her tentacles were once again arms and legs. She eyed them, disoriented.

"Was it good for you?" he asked.

She looked up, startled. He lay flat on his back, grinning ear-to-ear, back to normal, whatever that was. Just a gigantic, rough, ugly biker with a big dick. She sat up, felt his cock softening inside her and climbed off, watching the glazed slab flop onto his stomach. He tucked his hands behind his head, ignoring the plumbing still flushing across the floor under them, strangely relaxed in his afterglow.

"You don't talk much," he said.

She didn't bother trying to answer, reaching up to feel the back of her head. The bullet hole was even smaller. She smiled when her finger wouldn't fit. He saw her expression and sat up, staring intently.

"Y'know, it's been a while since I fucked something I didn't kill."

Pause. She steeled herself to fight.

He chuckled, tracing a finger down her arm. "It's kinda nice."

She touched her gums, felt teeth. *Her* teeth, inexplicably grown back. He watched her feel around in her mouth.

"It's okay, you'll be fine. Get used to it, happens every time."

She smiled, showing off her new pearly whites.

He started stroking his cock. "Wanna go again?"

She had other things on her mind. "Do you know me?" she asked, her voice rusty and cracking. The sound of it was strange and familiar at once, but she was glad to have it and knew she'd get used to it. He glanced at her nude body, cock hardening in his hand.

"I know you better *now,* but yeah, I remember you. Watched you fight a few years back. You were a bad girl." He grinned, swinging his dick in circles. *"Are."*

She clenched her fists, studied her scarred knuckles. "I was bad?" she asked, not understanding.

He dropped his dick, its big head splatting on the wet concrete, and leaned closer.

"Listen. I can use a girl like you. Old lady who can fight *and* fuck's hard to come by, y'know?" He gently raised her chin until they locked eyes. "We'd make one helluva pair."

She watched him. He was probably right. And she'd have a small army at her disposal, for whatever was out there. Of course, she'd have to kill a couple dozen of them for raping and trying to kill her, but there'd still be quite a few left—who'd probably not appreciate the downsizing and carry some serious grudges. It was a hornet's nest, not worth it. And her gut feeling told her she'd operate better alone. She decided to heed the instinct. It was all she had. Tully was staring, lovestruck. She cleared her throat and eyed his cock, propped on the floor like a third leg, heavy balls waiting just behind. She suddenly felt like she hadn't been fucked in forever and found herself salivating at the prospect of having him again. *Strange,* she thought, unable to quell the urge if she'd tried. She surrendered to the idea, rolling over on her hands and knees, ass in the air. She glanced over her shoulder, not needing to offer any more of an invite. He rose up, planted his feet wide, entered her from behind and pounded hard, punishing her for wanting more, putting all his weight into piledriver thrusts. She moaned, savoring every second, her hair plastered on the wet floor. She knew she had to stay aware, be ready for him to turn. She had to be ready for her own turn, too. The danger of it all was so arousing, she orgasmed on the spot, warm juices gushing around his shaft with each booming thrust. He came inside her again, bellowing at the top of his lungs. A cold so intense shot through her bones that she thought her knees might shatter on the floor. Before the change even registered in her mind, her shoulders rolled back and she reached for him, hooking his ribs with sharp pincers that were soft hands seconds before. Her feet slammed into the small of his back to hold him inside her, hooks for toes gouging the nerves in his tailbone, elongated tongue sweeping back and forth to strangle anything in its reach. He looked down, saw blood streaking his sides, didn't care. A smirk flashed across his lips before they sprang into a pointed snout with jagged teeth, bared and ready to snap. A shadow darkened his face, staying as a coat of fine black fur. He lunged, clamping the back of her neck with a bite strong enough to draw blood, but not to kill. He didn't want her dead. He wanted to keep her. Whether she shared the feeling remained to be seen.

Locked in a stalemate, neither of them moved. His teeth on her neck, her hooks in his flesh. He was unable to withdraw, but still rock hard. She didn't mind. The transformations made her feel strong and she had the idea that she'd grow even stronger after each turn. Besides, she was still horny and judging by Tully's raging erection, so was he. His drool gushed around her throat, hitting the floor with a weighty *plunk . . . plunk . . . plunk*. He humped her to the rhythm, his body twitching as her hooks pricked nerves with every thrust. He didn't care. He'd finally found another one, and it was even hotter than he imagined. She'd keep up with him, not submit and die like the others. They'd been nothing but chum to quell the Hunger, and he almost always lost hours after the fact masturbating over their bones, his libido a runaway train with no conductor. He'd just begun coming to terms with the fact that he'd never truly be satisfied, when out of nowhere, like a gift from the heavens, there she was.

Scarla.

He liked the way it rolled off the tongue, imagined calling it out for years to come, but somehow knew they weren't meant to last, neither together nor individually. It didn't matter. Nothing mattered in the moment. The moment was all they had, so it would suffice. Her muscles squeezed his shaft, driving him to the brink before stopping. They both froze on the edge, knowing they'd explode with the slightest move. She felt no urge to kill or eat, she just wanted to fuck, over and over, all night long if she could—and she had the idea that she could. The two of them teetered on the precipice as long as they could bear it, then she backed into him with a quick bump and he erupted, his pleasured wail carrying clear to the empty highway.

* * *

Scarla sat with her back against the cinder blocks, knees drawn to her chest, watching through the crumbled wall as the afternoon sun waned and shadows crept across the ground. Tully was propped up on his elbows in front of her, leather-clad legs splayed wide, flaccid cock draped over his left hip, waiting to see if she wanted more. She didn't, but she also wondered if her mind would change in the next breath. She knew he wasn't an immediate threat, but still made sure not to turn her back, just in case. Neither of them were the most trustworthy to be left alone with, after all. She kept a poker face as she thought about his earlier offer, again weighing the pros and cons. The gang would be good insurance, but she might end up killing every last one of them to avoid being killed herself, which would leave only Tully. Two were stronger than one—not to mention the fact that the two of *them* might've equaled six—but how many more like them would they find? Six vs. six-thousand was a losing bet any way you looked at it. The sex was good—epic, actually—but she had the feeling it was just a means to an end. Fucking Slim's rigor mortised torso might rock her boat just as hard. She eyed it. A slab of nothing, still in its club cut, arms pale and rigid, bullet hits from neck to crotch, resembling nothing more than discarded mannequin parts. She studied Tully, who couldn't have been less bothered by his brother's dismembered corpse over his shoulder. The idea of mounting Slim aroused no sensations, so with curiosity squelched, her gaze floated back to Tully's big dick. She studied it, feeling for the bullet hole in her head, finding only a small divot. She smiled. Forming again, everything from scratch, clean and new. Tully saw her watching him, began stroking himself.

"Wanna go again?" he smirked.

She thought about it. *Yeah.*

He wagged his winger. "C'mere."

The tingle seized her inside and she got wet. She pulled herself up the wall, hands over her head, curves on display. He studied her body, stroking faster. She stepped toward him and he quickly sat up, turned on, on guard. She sauntered past, bending over the collapsed part of the wall and wagging her ass, until he leapt up and stalked after her. She braced herself on the jagged cinder blocks and smiled, noting the Glock resting within her reach as he grabbed her hips. She watched another coyote lope by in the distance. It was scavenging. Tully slid in again, one hand on her ass, one on her shoulder. She gasped as his length filled her.

"*Oh yeah,*" she cooed, "*fuck me.*"

Sexy voice, she thought, listening to her smoky delivery. He grinned, took a deep breath, began thrusting. She noticed another coyote a few yards out, then another. They stood frozen. Watching. Listening.

"Fuck me *hard*," she ordered, and he delivered.

They went at each other with frenzied abandon, bodies stretching and contorting into strange hybrids, identifiable only for an instant before morphing into something else. They slashed and stabbed with teeth and claws, drawing blood without dealing death blows. In some strange way, she knew it was all part of the ceremony, the unholy union of whatever the hell they were, and she kept her senses as her body whipped and spun and betrayed her expectations, all the while feeling better and better. Feeling *electric*. She wanted it, *needed it,* with a desire more intense and overwhelming than any addiction she could imagine, and she knew she'd be chasing that sensation to the end of the earth. Or the end of her life. Somehow, she had the idea that the former was coming a lot quicker than any of them realized. Without warning, she grabbed the Glock and turned, blasting a baseball-sized hole in his face. He fell, his body twitching in a puddle of muck. The image was vivid, felt real, but was fleeting. His hips were still clapping her thighs as he fucked her. On that note, she came.

* * *

They sat side-by-side on the wall, Tully's boots on the ground, Scarla's bare feet dangling, watching the last rim of sunlight sink below the horizon. The sky was starless, the highway still empty. The birds had gone, leaving the night for the crickets to score. They buzzed loud, rising and falling in pitch, thousands of different insects chiming in and cutting out from all sides, making her wonder if they were trying to communicate something to her specifically. The idea made her laugh. She slid her tongue over her teeth, still glad to have them back. The Glock was on her left, loaded and ready. Tully was on her right, watching. She didn't care. He wanted to fuck til sunrise, but she was done with him and wasn't going to do that. He also wanted to ride off with her on his back, but she wasn't going to do that either. As for how he'd handle the rejection, she didn't care. As far as she was concerned, they both got what they needed and their time was over, no reason to make it anything other than what it was. Besides, part of what made him attractive was how nasty he was. She didn't sign up for a big bad puppy dog, not in this life nor, she somehow knew, the previous one. She wondered about the bobtail keys. They had to be in the driver's clothes. It was either that or take Tully's bike and leave him behind, which she didn't want to do, mainly because she was naked and his hog wouldn't provide any protection other than speed and maneuverability if she ran into trouble. Someone—or some*thing*—could pick-off a rider like a bee picking pollen, whereas the armored bobtail would mow down most anything in its path. Plus, the Northern Nazis were probably all Tully had. Granted, he'd kicked her ass and ordered her gang rape and murder. The big bastard was hardly deserving of mercy. She pondered it. If not for the club, she might still be trying to figure out what she was—and what she was capable of. She felt strangely indebted to them, and a bit sick to her stomach because of it. Then a lot sick to her stomach. She bowed her head, vomiting in the dirt. He touched her back, concerned.

"You alright, Scarla?"

She didn't like hearing him say her name. He had no right. Her stomach turned again and she hopped off the wall, crouching in the dirt, puking bile. Tully stood and zipped up, carefully pulling her hair back as she retched. She wiped her mouth with the back of her hand, then stood and hopped the wall into the dark restroom. He heard her moving around and lifted the gun, tucking it down the front of his pants. She found the light switch and the room sprang to yellowish-green life, similar to her puke. She scanned the bloody clothes scattered around the floor and snatched the driver's pants. They jingled. *Keys.* Tully watched grimly from outside, knowing she was leaving him.

"What're you doin', baby?" he asked, in monotone.

She yanked the keys from a pocket, tossed the pants aside, faced him.

"It's been fun, but I have to go."

She grabbed her shorts, wrung them out. He played nice guy, watching her pull them over her hips and cinch them.

"Well, I was thinkin' you could ride with me."

She smiled, shook her head. "Sorry. Go find your gang, they're probably worried."

His face darkened. "They know how to roll, they don't need me. Let's take off, just us. We'll go where we want, do what we want."

She spotted her torn *Suburban Mom* tee, then eyed the Northern Nazis leather on Slim's torso, with its constellation of bullet holes. Slim was a wiry fucker and the cut was about her size. She leveled a cool gaze on Tully.

"Your kid's out there. He needs you."

He smiled and leaned over the wall, gold tooth gleaming in the ceiling light.

"I was upstate for eight years, junior'll be fine. We're tough stock. You're with *me* now, bottom line."

She stripped Slim's corpse. Tully nodded approval. "There you go, put it on. Spot open, spot filled. You're a Nazi now."

She slipped it on, zipped it as high as her cleavage would allow. He smiled and extended his hand, in mock chivalry. *"M'lady!"*

She ignored him and hopped back out, headed for the bobtail. He let her go and didn't turn to watch, listening to her footsteps fade before calling out, with controlled intent.

"Get on the bike, Scarla. I'm gonna say it one time. You get behind that wheel, I'll kill you before you step on the gas."

Her footsteps stopped. He didn't budge. "I'm old enough to be your daddy, so I'll give you some advice. Sooner or later, life shows a fork in the road. In that moment, you wanna choose wisely. Very wisely."

Silence.

Tully nodded, satisfied.

The bobtail roared to life.

He drew the Glock and turned, hesitating, letting her decide. Scarla watched him through the cracked glass, releasing the clutch too fast. The tractor jackrabbited, jumping the parking block. She braked, threw it in reverse. He fired, blowing out the windshield. She shook glass from her hair, flipping him off. He rushed the cab in four long strides, back in her window like they'd met, this time with a gun to her head. She hit the brake.

"What'd I say, girl?"

He felt the cold steel on his throat before he knew what it was. She had the hunting knife.

"I wasn't listening, why don't you repeat it?"

Pause. He grimaced. "Choose your path wisely, that's all."

She arched her brow, pressed the blade deeper. "Thanks for the advice."

He eased back. "You're not takin' that cut with you," he said, referring to Slim's vest.

She shrugged. "I take *your* cut, or you take *mine*. Leave the gun."

Pause. He tossed the Glock on the passenger seat, and in a flash, chopped her elbow and twisted her wrist. She dropped the knife, hit the gas, and the bobtail shot back. Tully tried to keep his grip on her, but his sweaty palms slipped off. The tractor hit the curb, lurching to a stop. He charged. Scarla went for the gun, but not fast enough. He elbowed her in the face, dragged her through the window by her hair, threw her to the pavement. She tucked and rolled, looked up to see his boot heel.

Bam!

Blackout.

* * *

When she came to, the stars that were suspiciously absent from the sky were swirling in her eyes. Tully had her off the ground by her neck, his raging face inches from hers.

"*I'll break your fuckin' neck right now, bitch!*"

And to think, she was just going to walk away when he wanted a last dance. Hanging in his iron grip, she started to laugh. He fumed, grabbing the back of her head with his other hand to execute a fast, clean break. Out of nowhere, she blasted his torso with a flurry of rapid fire knees that knocked the wind out of him, then staggered him with a hard shot behind the ear. He dropped her, backpedaling. She landed on her feet in a side stance she didn't remember, but that served her well in the past. Without thinking, she spun on the ball of her left foot and nailed his chin with her right. She had to spread her legs wide to reach his face, but was no stranger to larger opponents and caught him on the button. It was a pinpoint-perfect spinning hook kick, a taekwondo move, one of her old signature knockouts. He staggered, but didn't fall. She set herself, threw it again. Telegraphed as it was, he still didn't see it coming.

Bam!

She popped his jaw just right and down he went, skull bouncing on the concrete, out cold. She stayed poised for a fight, fists clenched, setting and re-setting her stance, before finally realizing he wasn't getting up. *Ok, then.* He'd have a bitch of a headache when he woke. Probably a nice concussion, too. It was a minuscule price to pay, all things considered, and she hoped he'd count it as the price of admission and leave it at that. She'd leave him where he fell, to his own devices, to find his club or to seek hollow revenge. Worst case scenario, it'd be both. She'd cross that bridge when and if she came to it. The bobtail sat purring, the trusty steel steed, waiting to get on with it. She climbed into the cab, taking more care with the clutch as she rolled out. Whatever awaited her, she was as ready as she'd ever be. The plastic Jesus spun to face her again. *Thanks for nothing, Mr. Savior.* She snatched him from the rearview, dropped him out the window, hit the gas.

5

"What's *causin'* all this?! Women's college hoops *bloodbath!* Rutger's and UConn throw down in a *vicious* war to settle the score that ends in a *melee,* leaving fourteen hospitalized and one *dead!* This ain't your momma's basketball! Plus, we've got *all* the sordid details on the *death* of quarterback Michael Vick! The shocking murder caught on video, *as it unfolds!* Send the kids to bed cos we're showing *all we can* and it ain't much, baby, but it's *nasty! Catastrophe* or *karma? You* decide! All this and *more,* if you can stomach it, on tonight's edition of *Suchoza's Scoreboard!* Blitzing your behind in just a *few* minutes, baby!"

Channel 4 sportscaster Josh Suchoza—or Such, as his friends and colleagues referred to him—swiveled away from the broadcast desk, gliding a few feet to a group of newsroom workers crowded around an open laptop screen. Still fit after forty, he acted younger than he was, with the air of a former athlete and intense blue eyes calling attention away from a deep-lined face and receding buzzcut.

"*Watch* this, you guys," he said, excitedly slapping a young intern on the back and hitting the space bar.

Barry was all of twenty-one, freckled and gawky. He chuckled nervously, adjusting his glasses, licking paper-thin lips. Beside him stood another intern, Karly. Short, bespectacled, and busty, she was even more hesitant to watch the footage than Barry was. The others braced themselves, having already seen it. News producer Nancy Brenheiser grimaced, watching the kids' faces instead of the onscreen action. She was a tall brunette and the walking definition of the term *cougar,* never crossing a room at the station without having her ass scoped by every guy within eyeshot. Those positioned behind her were even brazenly staring as she spoke.

"*Ugh*. I just had my chicken salad, I can't watch this shit again," she groaned.

Such didn't care, salivating at the prospect of initiating the newbies. Chickening-out at the last minute, Karly quietly excused herself.

"I have to use the restroom, I'll watch it later."

Brenheiser offered a smile. Such ignored her.

"Five minute warning," called a bearded guy in a headset, on his feet in the control room, a wall of timezone clocks looming behind him. It was floor director, Dale Forrest.

"*Shhh!*" Such waved him off, eyes darting from the screen to Barry. "Give us a minute, it's cued to the good part!"

In the video, notorious NFL quarterback Michael Vick was handcuffed to a bed's ornate oak headboard with his knees drawn to his chest, naked and mauled, shaking and crying uncontrollably. His left eye and ear were missing, his left bicep shredded to the bone. The sheets and wall were covered in blood. The camera angle was static, from a vantage point across the room. Something streaked back and forth in a dark blur, circling the king-sized bed in a lurching gallop, randomly rearing-up to make Vick flinch, never stopping long enough to allow a good look.

Such cackled, clapping his hands. "The most fucked-up sex tape of *all time!*"

Others scoffed, nodded.

"Couldn't happen to a nicer guy," chimed a burly grip.

Barry watched their reactions with a forced smile. Such grabbed his shoulders, not letting him off the hook.

"Watch, watch, *watch!* It's about to get good!"

The kid gulped, obeying orders, feeling queasy. "How'd you get this?" he asked, prompting a mischievous grin from Such.

"Tricks of the trade, young man, tricks of the trade." He leaned closer to the screen than all of them, eyes wide, fists pumping. "Here we go, *here we go!*"

Brenheiser exchanged looks with the cameraman beside her, both of them concerned by Suchoza's snowballing enthusiasm. The cameraman stole a glance at her tits when he thought it was safe, but she never missed a thing.

Onscreen, a shadow lunged onto the bed and began thrashing. Vick screamed, kicking his legs in a panic. Blood blasted the ceiling like it was shot from a cannon, drizzling back down like rain. The shadow slipped back to the floor, racing in circles, faster and faster. Vick's wild eyes followed it, his midsection gored wide open. Barry watched, slack-jawed, as the quarterback's large intestine unspooled from his side like glistening rope. He begged for his life between high-pitched sobs.

"*Oh, God!!! Oh, Jesus, no!!! No, please God!!!*"

Such snickered, reciting the rest by heart. "'*I'm sorry! I'm so sorry, God in Heaven!* Listen to this fuckin' shithead. He's been apologizing for being a *scumbag* for years, it's never gonna *stick*."

A piece of Vick's innards fell from the ceiling, landing on his face.

"Not even to the *ceiling!*"

The crew laughed. The shadow leapt onto the bed again, its back to the camera. It was dog-like, with muscular shoulders and a thick neck. It was also feminine, with smooth skin and hourglass curves. It lowered its head and tore into Vick's throat, turning his shrill wail into a drowning gurgle. His body went rigid, stiff as a board from head-to-toe.

"Look, he's planking," laughed the grip, popping a pretzel from a nearby bowl. "Nike could release this and call it an exercise video, make a killing."

The comment drew guffaws from everyone but Such, who never reacted to someone else's jokes.

Brenheiser rolled her eyes. "Don't give the assholes any ideas, for fuck's sake, they'll get in bed with their mothers for a buck."

The dog-woman grabbed Vick's ankles, slamming his body into the wall above the bed. He hit hard, sending framed photos and awards flying. A cheesy Subway/BET Sportsman of the Year plaque hit the bed, face-up and in-focus.

"*Eat fresh,* baby!" Such chortled.

Vick landed in a heap, his wrists badly broken in the handcuffs. The thing burrowed into the hole in his side with a chomping maw, emerging with a bloody mouthful. It chewed, swallowed, and hurled his body into the wall again. He came down with a spray of blood and cracked ribs. It threw him again, breaking his ankles. His body seemed to deflate like a blow-up doll, crumbling and gasping for breath, collarbone, ribs, pelvis, kneecaps, all shattered.

Brenheiser stepped away. "O-*kay,* then. I'm glad it was him too, guys, but I don't need to keep seeing it, okay?"

Everyone ignored her, eagerly awaiting the finale. A Just-For-Menned tall guy and buxom bottled blonde strolled in, both poker-faced in pancake makeup, both more interested in cue cards than real conversation. They cast curious glances at the computer screen, taking their places at the desk to the sounds of Vick's pathetic death rattle.

"Is that the Vick thing?" the female anchor asked, wrinkling her nose.

Everyone scrambled to get in position for the 11 o'clock broadcast. Such jumped up, punching a shell-shocked Barry in the arm.

"*Showtime, baby!* Cue it up to right before she turns on him, when his eyes get big and he goes *duh-duh-duh!* and pisses himself, that's our in," he deadpanned, straightening his tie.

"It's a family show," mumbled the male anchor, flipping through his desktop notes.

Barry nodded, cycling the footage back, focusing on the video timecode instead of the hyperspeed maiming. When he started his internship, he figured the worst he'd witness was a nasty game injury once in a while. In that regard, his present task was far beyond the pale, but he agreed with the crew's prevailing sarcasm. It *couldn't* have happened to a nicer guy. He'd hated Vick since the dogfighting disgrace and subsequent prison sentence that put an asterisk on his career years ago. Barry might've been naive to a lot of things, but he knew people didn't change, not really. Advertisers, sponsors, even the league, may have forgiven those heinous crimes in the name of shameless capitalism, but they were corporate shills, their soullessness and selective memory to be expected. Real people didn't forget. Real people *never* forgot. Barry cracked a smile, slowing the footage as he closed in on the requested moment, :05, :04, :03, :02, *bingo*. One wide-eyed asshole in clear focus, *duh-duh-duh!* He was glad Vick was dead. So were a lot of others.

Forrest raised three fingers, counting them down. "In three, two, one," he pointed to the floor and the station recording boomed through the newsroom.

Your undisputed news leader, 14 years and counting! Welcome to KBLM, news at eleven! The anchors suddenly sprang to life, charming the cameras with warm smiles.

"Good evening and welcome to KBLM news at eleven, I'm Thad Jaworsky."

The blonde continued, in a well-practiced sing-song. "And I'm Marcie Unrue. A three-alarm fire tore through *another* block of Southside row housing this afternoon, marking the *fourth* such incident this week. Channel 4 has unfortunately learned there *are* civilian casualties, more *specific* details on that information still to come. *Three* city firefighters were hospitalized before the blaze was brought under control, shortly before seven o'clock this evening. Their injuries bring the city's *current* number of wounded servicemen to *eighteen*. The *mayor*, this morning, announced a new deal for *federal funding* to rebuild areas damaged in the recent rash of fires, and interim police chief Tommy Delmones has vowed to immediately increase street patrol by *fifty* percent, in the eastside and downtown districts hit hardest."

* * *

Karly sat in the women's room stall, struggling to moderate her breathing. *In . . . out.* She'd felt herself slipping all day, fighting the strange sensation that had been growing inside her, stronger with each passing week. She'd tried to ignore it, tried to work through it, to no avail. She sometimes curbed it by taking a break to practice her breathing exercises, by going to her car to listen to one of her audio book CDs, or by popping one of her roommate's recreational pain pills, which seemed to help. Sometimes, if it hit her late at night, she'd masturbate to take her mind off it, floating back to sleep on the wave of the unusually intense orgasms she could suddenly achieve. They were better than any guy she'd ever been with, and her mind was delving into some strange kinky territories to keep up. She'd been interning at the station for three months and had no health insurance, but was about to be hired on full-time, so was avoiding a doctor visit for as long as possible, in the hope that benefits would kick-in or whatever the problem was would pass. But it wasn't passing. It was getting worse. She didn't know what it was, didn't even know how to describe it, but something was wrong with her. Her heart pounded like a runaway train in her chest, controlled breathing not doing the trick. She wasn't there to pee, still in her black stretch dress pants, but the urge to do something else suddenly overcame her. Her hand slid between her legs and she tingled all over, opening them wider. It was usually over quick. She'd just rub the sweet spot until she had one, then casually rejoin the newsroom. Same as she'd been doing, whenever she couldn't bear it, for a few weeks. Something felt different, though. It wouldn't suffice. She dropped her pants and strawberry undies, touched her clit and realized she was soaking wet. She could feel the blood surging through her brain, grew dizzy from the rush. The stall spun as she rubbed faster and faster, arching up on her toes, leg muscles flexing hard, taking short sharp gasps of breath as she neared climax. She arched her back, dilated pupils staring a hole through the ceiling, a warm sensation filling her whole body until . . .

Release.

Unable to control herself, she squirted the stall door, the floor, her pants. She'd never done it before and was embarrassed, her cheeks flushing the same shade as her panties, but she couldn't take her hand away. She kept rubbing, kept gushing, mouth open wide in mute ecstasy. Whatever it was, it was a spectacular problem to have. If only she could harness it, not let it run roughshod over everything else in her day, her work, her life, she wouldn't *want* to be fixed. She wouldn't want another boyfriend either. *Hell,* they never lived up to their promise anyway. No, solo would do just fine. Maybe she'd make a friend that would evolve naturally, but even that wouldn't be on the agenda for a while. Alas, it wasn't so easy. She was fucked-up and she knew it. Her hands were shaking. She unspooled a length of toilet paper, wiped her fingers, dabbed between her legs, and the urge walloped her again. The tissue slipped away, floating under the stall door and across the floor, carried by the powerful central air blowing through the room. She closed her eyes, massaging her temples. When she opened them, she saw her legs covered in goosebumps. She tried her breathing exercise again. *In . . . out. Fuck it,* it wasn't working. She was still dripping wet, steadily secreting into the toilet bowl. *Plop . . . plop . . . plop.* She wondered exactly how long she'd been away from the newsroom, but didn't care. She wanted more, had no choice but to continue. It didn't matter if it imperiled her job, her health, her life. She needed *more*. More than fingers would provide. She eyed the mounted toilet paper holder, yanked out its chrome roller. It was eight inches long and cool to the touch. She sucked one end to warm it up, then lowered it between her legs and carefully inserted it. It felt amazing. *In . . . out.* She worked the smooth cylinder, pumping faster, slower, faster, slower, rolling it in a wide circle and bobbing it up, down, up, down. She came again, gushing a torrent that soaked the toilet seat. It took some of the edge off, making her think it might be time to get back to work. She replaced the roller and pulled up her damp pants, checking to see if it was noticeable. Reaching for the stall latch, she heard the bathroom door open, decided to wait.

  Beth Larrissey was an amiable news researcher, a pixie-like blonde who stood five feet and weighed ninety pounds, if that. She wore her hair in pigtails that made her seem child-like, despite the fact that she'd recently turned thirty. Water cooler rumors pegged Beth as gay, but no one knew for sure. Karly'd never been with a woman, never even flirted, but was fantasizing more and more. Watching Beth kill time at the sink so she'd be alone to pee, Karly felt the tingle rising again. Hypothetically speaking, if she ever chose to jump the fence, Beth would be her type. But hypothetical fantasies didn't come true, unless pursued. Karly unlatched the stall door and strode to the sink, smiling at Beth's mirror reflection.

"Hi."

"Hi," the pixie replied, turning to enter a stall.

Don't let her go.

"*Beth,* right?" Karly blurted, unsure of a follow-up.

Beth stopped, flashing wide eyes and an innocent smile. "Yeah?"

Karly fidgeted, feeling her damp pants and wringing her hands, trying not to draw attention. She drew attention and Beth glanced down.

"I, um . . ."

Pause. The pixie stared, her smile flickering. Seconds felt like hours.

". . . I'm sorry. I lost my train of thought." Karly laughed, out of reflex. "I'm Karly."

Beth nodded, somewhat confused. "I remember, we've talked before. It gets busy, I know. I started with an internship too, don't sweat it." Pause. "Do you need something for the newsroom, or . . . ?" she asked, letting it hang.

Do you need something? Or? Karly just stared. Beth stopped smiling.

"Well, if you remember, lemme know. I'm just down the hall, extension 313," she offered, moving into the closest stall.

"Ok. I'll let you know."

Beth closed and latched the door. Karly reached out and touched the red metal, leaving moist fingerprints. She listened as the pixie raised her knee-length skirt.

Silence.

Beth sat on the bowl, staring at Karly's feet. She liked her shoes, but was more concerned with why she was still standing there.

"Are you okay?" she called, unable to pee until the room was clear.

Karly didn't answer right away. When she did, it was with a dazed drawl, like she'd just woken up. *"Huhhh? Yeaaah. I'm . . . I'm okay. Sorry."*

Beth watched Karly's feet step away, then stop again. The intern was starting to irritate her.

"Hey Karly, if you don't mind, it's hard to go and I need to get back to my desk. I'm pulling an all-nighter and I'm swamped."

"Do you wanna go out sometime?"

Beth grimaced, dumbstruck. *"Excuse me?"*

"Do you wanna—um . . . Do you wanna hang out sometime?"

Beth laughed, studying the thick black straps and white buckles on Karly's block heel shoes, wondering how in the world she worked in them. She'd never addressed the rumors that swirled about her since her first week at the station, when she was shooting guys down left and right. *Must be a dyke,* they reasoned, because it couldn't possibly mean they weren't smooth, smart, or even *nice* enough to interest her. Truth was, they were half right. She was emotionally invested in women, which made the sex easy and fun, when she had enough free time to find it. That didn't mean she didn't like some dick every now and then. The boys just had to use a little more TLC to catch her, but they never could quite figure that out. Karly was cute. Young, soft, supple, and clearly new to it. The strangeness finally making sense, Beth was flattered.

"Are you asking me out on a *date,* Karly?" Silence. She watched the intern roll her block heeled foot and it turned her on. She bit her lip, smiling, and started to pee. "This week's busy, but I'm off Sunday. That work for you?"

"Mm-hmm," Karly replied, under her breath.

Beth finished, dabbed, stood, lowered her skirt, flushed. She paused, hand on the latch. The intern's shoes were still right in front of the door. Reflexively, she got spooked and wondered if it was some kind of set up. Growing up in a small town, she'd seen her share of bigotry and unprovoked violence. The big bad city, sky-high crime rate and all, was utopia compared to the backwater swamp she came from. She'd endured more than her share of teenage harassment, and it was most unbearable after making out with her best friend. The girl just couldn't live with herself after the fact, so she told the whole town that queer Beth had tried to force herself on her. Of course, to really sell the story, she'd had to sever their friendship and help make Beth's life a living hell, whenever and however she could. Had to make sure everyone knew Beth was the freak, not her. She liked boys. She liked dick. To compensate for her suppressed urges, she quickly became popular with the guys who liked it fast and easy. And some of the teachers, too. Beth stood on the sidelines, not a friend in the world, watching her first crush blossom into the school skank and degrade herself in every possible way, all in the name of being accepted as *one of them*. Beth made up her mind to get out, to never be one of *them*. To get out and never look back, which is what she did. Her friend, however, took a very different route to a similar destination. After multiple abortions and miscarriages, she finally had a baby. She married and moved into a double-wide, becoming a young battered housewife who knew to keep her mouth shut, even looking the other way when her toddler began taking the brunt of the abuse, until finally reaching her breaking point and snapping. Forced bondage and electrocution not being her idea of a healthy sex life, she started thinking of how she could get away with killing the evil sonofabitch she'd married. When she found the photos of their daughter on his computer, she stopped giving a shit, waited for him to pass out drunk, and blasted his dick with his own 12-gauge shotgun. Afterward, she lit a cigarette and took her little girl outside to read a story and wait for the police to arrive. By that time, the hubby had bled to death. The cops were his childhood friends and treated her none too kindly, but she didn't care. She didn't feel a thing. The kid went to foster care, she went to prison, the end. That is, until last month, when the new parolee looked Beth up and got in touch. She was living in a downtown weekly, fully out as a lesbian and happy for the first time, or so she said. Nothing helped a girl find herself like soul-shattering life mistakes and six years in the state penitentiary. She'd thought of Beth often, she said. Wondered what became of her, wanted to reconnect. Beth was sad to hear all the details, but wasn't interested. *Had your chance. On and up. No what-ifs. No looking back. Want to undo your past mistakes? Find your daughter, not your old bestie.*

Was the intern just testing her to see if she was queer, before blowing her brains out in the bathroom stall upon affirmation? The things that ran through her head, well into adulthood, well past the point of accepting herself for who she was. *Don't be silly, she's just like you were once. Meet her for a drink, she could use a friend. Lose the PTSD already, get back to work.* Beth chuckled, feeling ridiculous, unlatching the door. She opened it and stood face-to-face with Karly, seeing a shocking change from moments earlier. The girl didn't look so good. Pale and sweaty, with hooded eyes and unsteady feet, she seemed about to keel over.

"Are you alright?" Beth asked, bracing to catch her if she fell.

Karly offered a half-smile, watching Beth's lips.

"C'mon, sit down." Beth took her hand, led her to a bench near the sink, felt her forehead. "You're cold. Are you on something?"

Karly shook her head. Beth didn't buy it.

"Pills? Cold medicine? Anything. You could be having a reaction."

Karly shook her head again, her eyes floating down Beth's chest.

"Alright, wait here and don't get up. I'm getting you some water and calling a cab to take you to the hospital. You need to see a doctor." Beth turned to exit, but Karly grabbed her arm with surprising strength. Beth winced, tried to pull away. "*Ow,* you're hurting me," she remarked, prying the intern's fingers loose and backing toward the door.

Karly sprang off the bench, rushing Beth and slamming her against the wall, pinning her wrists on either side of her head. Beth's heart raced. She wasn't much of a fighter. And she was right, it *was* an attack. In the workplace, on the job. Her shitty luck.

"*I'm sorry!*" she blurted.

Sorry for what, she wasn't sure. It just slipped out. Karly stared with intent, mouth slack, lips moist. Beth's eyes darted around in a panic, but Karly's were dilated to complete black. She pressed her bosom to Beth's heaving chest, their mouths inches apart.

"I just wanted to help, I won't say anything, I *swear,*" Beth pleaded.

Karly thought her breath smelled like coffee and chewing gum, noticed her bottom lip quivering. It made her smile.

"I don't mean to scare you," she whispered.

Beth frowned, not sure how to take that. Before she could say anything, Karly kissed her. Hard. Beth's eyes widened, her body tensing. She felt the intern pressing closer, felt their tongues touch. Karly released Beth's arms, caressed her hips, began sucking her tongue. Beth stood frozen, felt sick. Force was force, and it wasn't her scene. She mustered all the strength in her tiny frame and pushed Karly away.

"*Stop!*" she yelled, loud enough to be heard in the hall.

She ran to the door, keeping her eyes on the intern. Karly gave up, resigned. Beth wiped her mouth and straightened her skirt, exiting in her best power walk.

"*Shit,*" Karly muttered out loud, at a loss to explain her own actions.

She slunk back to the bench and started to cry. Without even realizing it, she slid her hand between her legs. It felt good. Her eyes focused on the dripping water faucet. She sat staring, whispering a song under her breath.

"*The itsy-bitsy spider went up the water spout. Down came the rain and washed the spider out . . .*"

6

The bobtail tore through the countryside, Scarla hunched over its steering wheel like a speeding demon, eyes unblinking, foot to the floor. She hit a grade on the highway and floated gears without even thinking, blasting onward. She'd been driving for close to an hour, with no sign of civilization. Inky black clouds had overtaken the moon, blanketing the rural ride in impenetrable night. She watched the yellow line and the horizon, knowing something would appear sooner or later. She couldn't drive forever, but didn't plan on stopping until there was something—or some*one*—to see. Alive or dead, standing tall or reduced to rubble, she didn't give a shit. There was some kind of world out there and she'd find it, if it was the last thing she did. And the thought crossed her mind that it might be. The bobtail climbed up, up, up, finally reaching the crest of the hill when, as if by invocation, there it was. Scarla's eyes widened. She blinked to see if she was hallucinating. Still there. City lights glowed in the far distance, shimmering bright under the impossibly black sky. She was lost in the sight, when a figure suddenly appeared in the bobtail's headlights, facing her down. The man in the suit stood in the road, his slithering cock doing its serpentine dance between his legs. He made no attempt to move, but her reflexes did, and she jerked the wheel to the right.

Smash!

The bobtail veered into a tree at top speed. It was a giant oak and didn't fall, but the tractor hit with such force that its headlights were face-to-face, shining directly into each other. Scarla's arm and leg muscles kept her from being thrown through the missing windshield on impact, but her head snapped back with enough force to inflict one hell of a concussion. She lay sprawled across the passenger seat, dazed but conscious. She touched her fingertips to her thumbs, forward and backward. Coordination intact, she tested her memory by silently mouthing the alphabet song. *A, B, C, D, E, F, G* . . . She got that far, before forgetting what came next. She started over. *A, B, C, D, E, F, G* . . . *H, I, J, K, LMNOP* . . . She snowballed the last five, in cadence with the childhood tune she was singing, and it was good enough for her. She dragged herself up the dashboard, ashes from the ashtray coating her hair and face, and peered out into the dark. No sign of the German creep. She tried to listen, but only heard the ringing in her ears. *WEEEEE!* With both the doors popped open, she slid out of the cab, stepping on a fallen branch and stumbling, catching herself on a front tire that stunk of burned rubber. She limped away from the bobtail, onto the road. Rocked by lightning bolts of pain every couple steps, she held her head and looked around for the suited man. He was nowhere to be seen, if he was ever there at all. Their history was still foggy, but she knew he'd also popped-up in the lake house shower. She felt inexplicably let-down, a part of her *wanting* him to be real. She wasn't sure she needed to rediscover that part of herself. She scanned the shadows, turned back to the ride. It was totaled, more accordion than tractor. She eyed the city lights. A mile or more away. A bitch of a walk in bare feet. Then she remembered.

Daisies.

She ran back to the bobtail, climbed into the cab and felt around the sleeper, tossing porn mags until she found one sandal, then another. She slipped them on and gingerly climbed out, so as not to give herself an aneurysm jumping down. Maybe it was a blessing in disguise. The bobtail would be seen and heard from a distance, but one woman on foot, in the dark, still held the element of surprise. Whether it would even matter, she hadn't a clue. She started walking, those plastic daisies jabbing her feet with every step.

7

"Where the fuck is Karly?"

Brenheiser stared at the intern's empty desk as the broadcast went to commercial. People criss-crossed around her, getting ready for the segue to sports.

"Cued up here, Such!" Barry called, snapping his fingers with nervous energy, like he did every time his handiwork was about to go live.

Such smirked and nodded, taking his seat to the left of the anchors. He swilled the last of his coffee, raised the styrofoam cup in the air. Barry ran in with a waste basket. Such waved him back. The intern stopped on a dime, held the basket out. Such sank a free throw, did a fist pump, eyed Jaworsky's hair.

"You dye your hair again, or is that a weave?"

The anchor scoffed. "It's all mine." Then, eyeing the sportscaster's thinning dome. "I see you forgot your dulling spray tonight, *Josh*."

Such's eyes bugged in mock indignation, drawing snickers from around the room. Jaworsky turned his back, too good for their antics, and started whispering to Unrue. Such put a fist to his mouth, poking the opposite cheek with his tongue to mime a blowjob. Laughs. Unrue looked around, missing the joke. Jaworsky touched her knee, urging her not to pay attention, continued whispering.

"One minute warning," called Forrest.

Such fiddled with his tie. "Am I straight?" he asked, to no one in particular.

Jaworsky raised a brow, unable to resist. "From what we hear, *no*."

Unrue smiled, shaking her head. Such took offense.

"*Ha, ha!* Hey Marce, soon as you stop doing your overtime under the desk, you'll be doing the weather in Barstow, mark my words. Now, *that's* funny."

Unrue's face dropped.

"Thirty seconds," called Forrest.

Jaworsky spun around, livid. "Maybe *you'd* fit the Barstow team, Josh. You don't seem able to do much around here, and your ratings are in the *toilet*. I'll put a word in."

Such didn't miss a beat. "Well, after fifteen minutes of your pilled-up monotone, anyone who's not invalid switches to Channel 2. *That's* the problem, cock jockey."

Jaworsky was hot to retort, but Forrest chimed in. "We're back in three, two, one," he pointed at Such, who wooed Camera 2 with a snarky grin.

"*Wake up, people!* And *welcome* to another *action-packed* edition of your *favorite* segment, Suchoza's Scoreboard! Tonight, we've got it *all* for ya! A *nail-biter,* a *head-scratcher,* and a *stomach-turner!*"

Having reached the breaking point with her intern's sporadic disappearing acts, Brenheiser quietly made for the door. She knew the guys were watching her ass, so she threw some extra bomp in her she-bomp, as always, before slipping out into the hall to find Karly and fire her on the spot. She waved down a rookie station reporter.

"You seen my intern?"

He stared, quizzically. "Which one?"

"Karly," she replied, holding her hand flat, about five feet off the floor.

"Little girl, big tits?"

Brenheiser rolled her eyes. "Yeah, *that* one."

The reporter shrugged. "Nope."

Brenheiser stomped away, her heels echoing down the hall like thunder. She paused in the research office doorway, saw Beth Larrissey sitting in the glow of her computer screen.

"You seen my intern?"

Beth jumped, looking up like she'd been shot. She was sure the girl had gone back to her boss with colorful lies and accusations, as revenge for rebuking her advances. Pause. She pondered her answer to the point of seeming suspicious. Whose word carried more weight, the solid researcher or the sinking intern? The answer was easy, so Beth nixed the self-doubt and sat up straight, looking Brenheiser in the eye.

"I saw her sitting in the women's room a while ago. She seemed upset."

Brenheiser's nostrils flared and she stomped away, thunderclapping toward the restrooms. Beth listened to the footsteps fade, then got back to work. Served the little bitch right.

* * *

Brenheiser barged into the restroom, ready to rumble. As soon as she passed through the door, she walked right out of her high heel pump, her nylon-stockinged foot landing in something sticky. She frowned, tried to step back, but the stocking was stuck. She looked down, saw a gooey membrane coating the floor.

"*What the fuck?*" she spat.

She pulled free, ripping the heel off her nylon in the process. Her other foot was also stuck and she stumbled, rolling her ankle. She caught herself on the wall and winced, unable to pry her hands free.

"*Fuckin' hell!*"

She pulled back as hard as she could, losing her balance. A loud ripping sound reminded her of a scheduled waxing appointment, right before her head slammed into the wall behind her. She sat in a daze, feet and ass glued to the floor, head and shoulders glued to the wall. Stunned by the fall, she looked up and saw a peculiar image. Two glistening red handprints on the wall in front of her. She looked down, saw her palms stripped to the bone. It took a moment for her to process it, but she didn't scream. She only ever raised her voice when she was fighting or fucking, never in fear. Fear wasn't in Nancy Brenheiser's operating manual, but the room's decor finally caught her eye. The color drained from her face before she even saw what was coming.

The restroom was completely covered in silky white webbing, draped in dense sheets over the sink, the mirror, the stalls, funneling into a two-by-two black hole in the far corner. As Brenheiser struggled to get up, she made the web vibrate, sending shock waves rippling through the murky tunnel. Something stirred, just out of view. She thrashed, ripping out a chunk of her own hair to free her head, accidentally sticking her other hand to the floor.

"*Motherfuck!*"

She froze in horror, watching a face emerge from the hole. It was Karly, eyes blazing white, sharpened teeth oozing venom. The intern advanced steadily, spider-like, hand-over-hand. She was nude, her wet flesh a sickly shade of grey. Another pair of arms appeared right behind hers, crawling in rhythm. Then another, making a total of six arms. *It's not real,* Brenheiser told herself, certain she was seeing double, then triple. Karly looked like she was on playback, her movements fluctuating between fast-forward and slow-motion with each step. Brenheiser feigned rage, freely pissing herself.

"*You're fired!*" she yelled, struck by the absurdity.

It was all she knew how to do, really. Even with her life in the balance.

"*Clean out your desk and get the fuck out! Now!*"

Karly's legs were bowed wide and disjointed, as fast and efficient as her arms, making the case that she didn't have six arms at all, but rather eight legs. Brenheiser dropped her other hand, relinquishing both to the adhesive floor. She shook her head, at a loss to comprehend what was happening. Not that it would've made a difference. She knew she was dead, knew it before the thing appeared, sensed it in the air. She developed her killer instinct in the boardrooms, knew a loser when she saw one, and the big L was finally glowing bright on her own forehead. She had no idea what her intern had become, but she knew it trumped her.

Touché, you little bitch.

Karly sank her teeth into Brenheiser's cheek, taking a crunchy bite of the producer's eye socket. Brenheiser grimaced, not making a sound, not even as her eye flopped out on bloody tendons.

"*Choke on it!*" she rasped, hard-assed to the end.

Karly chewed and swallowed, then bit again, crushing the boss' eyeball in her mouth. She *was* sweet and juicy, just as the guys suspected. Karly pressed Brenheiser's head back to the wall, tore open her expensive silk blouse. Her tits were smaller than they appeared, courtesy of a padded bra. She could hardly be faulted. She knew what it took to make it to the top, and offering a little T&A was simply part and parcel of getting where you wanted to go. Karly undid the bra's front hook and let two cream-colored pads fall away, eyeing a pair of solid B's. She liked them just the way they were, but there was also another thought process at work. A *stronger* process. If it were thirty minutes earlier, she'd have kissed those full lips, caressed that soft flesh, gone down on that sweet spot and done things the guys in the newsroom only dreamed of doing. But that was then, this was now. Now, she'd follow only *one* urge, *one* desire, until it was met. It had already won. It would win every time. She bit deep into Brenheiser's left breast. The producer felt eight legs grabbing her all over, felt the searing pain of bite after bite, saw the white tiles splashing red around them. Karly—or *whatever* it was—kept attacking, as relentless as a wild animal. The intern opened her mouth, all bloody teeth and shredded flesh, lowering her head again. She bit until she heard it. Shrill, loud, *afraid*. Outside in the hall, heads began poking out of doorways. Nancy Brenheiser was screaming.

* * *

People filtered out of their offices, confused and alarmed, slowly filling the hallway.

"What's going on?"

"Where is that coming from?"

"Omigod, who's *screaming?*"

"It's coming from the bathroom!"
"Somebody call the police!"
"Check it out!"
"We can't wait for the police, go in there!"
"Who *is* that?"
"Get *in* there! Somebody, *please!*"
"Oh God, make it stop!"
"Where the hell's Leach?"
"I'm calling the police right *now.*"
"I know he's in the building, but—"
"*Jesus Christ,* is there no security?!"
"Somebody call Leach!"
"Watch out! Move, *move!*"
"Everybody move back!"

Two big guys from tech support bulled their way through the gathering crowd, clearing space around the restrooms, moving bodies out of harm's way. Reggie and Mike both stood well over six feet, both big-boned and broad-shouldered. Despite their pressed shirts and ties, they looked like they could handle trouble. With blood-curdling screams still booming from behind the door, many of the women started backing off, along with several of the squeamish men. A bookish guy from web design peeked out of the men's room just a few feet away, face pale and drawn, eyes full of fear. Reggie jabbed a thumb over his shoulder.

"Get outta there, man. *Go.*"

He watched the guy skitter to the far wall and huddle with the others at a safe distance. Mike nodded to Reggie, banging on the door with a slab-of-ham open hand, his wedding ring popping like a gunshot on the varnished aluminum.

"*Hey!*" he shouted.

The screaming abruptly stopped. The entire floor fell silent. The support guys eyed each other. People coming off the stairwells at both ends were hushed by onlookers, but kept advancing with careful footsteps—some out of desire to help, some out of morbid curiosity with cell phones ready. Reggie watched Mike, unable to contain himself, ready to move in.

"*Let's do it,*" he urged, under his breath.

Mike steeled himself and kicked the door as hard as he could. It flew open, hitting the wall hard, sticking in place instead of bouncing back. The guys looked down, their faces twisting. The crowd gasped. Some turned and ran. What was left of Brenheiser sat glued to the floor and wall, her stripped torso mauled and gutted, her head missing. She'd have resembled a rag doll's shell, if not for all the blood. Mike looked around at the webs and the splatter, for a moment thinking—hoping—it was some kind of sick joke. But what they were seeing was all too real. Suddenly light-headed, Mike took a deep breath and projectile vomited, staggering down the hall in a trot that turned into a sprint. He kept going, bowling over a little guy on the way, barreling straight through the stairwell door. Reggie stood still, shell-shocked, staring at the body. He knew from the clothing that it was Brenheiser. He made a point to check her out every day, always thought she was a fine piece of ass. Behind him, the braver staff members jockeyed to get a good look, some snapping pictures, some taking video. They stuck together in a huddle, clinging to the nearest arm, shoulder, back, anything they could hang onto for comfort, reassurance, or just to keep from fainting. And they had no idea, but the worst was still to come.

"Omigod, who *is* that?"

"Get back! Someone's *in* there, goddammit, can we call the *police* now? Did anyone call the *police?!*"

Then, barely coherent, through deep sobs. "*Who is it?*"

Reggie didn't turn to see who he was answering. It didn't matter.

"It's Nancy," he said, flatly.

Stunned gasps rose from the crowd, as if it were somehow more horrific that it was a senior news producer, than say . . . an intern. Beth Larrissey, who'd been watching from her door down the hall, overheard and covered her mouth, eyes welling with tears. She'd thought crazy Karly was probably being ejected from the building and putting up a fight, peaking on whatever drug cocktail she was under the influence of, making a royal scene and further embarrassing herself. She didn't realize something was terribly wrong until seeing the onlookers' reactions. Had she gotten Brenheiser *killed?* No, no, no. *It isn't happening. It didn't happen. It didn't* . . . But she knew inside that it did. She leaned on the door jamb to keep from collapsing, felt her knees going rubbery, remembered the anxiety meds she kept in her purse. She'd just taken one after her calamitous bathroom break, but it hadn't had a chance to kick-in, and she really wanted another. Since she began filling the script, she'd tried to beware of getting hooked, but lately found herself popping a pill whenever *anything* agitated her. And Beth was agitated a lot. It wasn't about to get any better. She started drifting off to her safe place, or *glazing,* as her yoga instructor put it, which was kind of a New-Age mental trick she'd been using to cope with stress, something that would hopefully ween her off the pills. Something dark dropped right in front of her face, thumping the floor at her feet with a heavy smack. The first thing she noticed was her hand, and the door jamb around it, speckled red. The web design guy got her attention next, pointing and screaming from down the hall.

"Oh my—*watch out! Beth, watch out!!!*"

He was pointing up, but she looked down. Nancy Brenheiser's head, all dead eyes and gaping mouth, stared up at her. She watched it, unable to move, or even react.

"Oh, God! What *is* that?!"

"*Get outta there!*"

"Beth! Beth, get back in the office, *now! Beth!!!*"

Reggie's voice sounded like it was coming from the bottom of a well. She saw his alarm, saw the panic of everyone still in the hall, knew something bad was right above her, but just couldn't move a muscle. Maybe it was all too much. Maybe more than her mind could handle. Maybe life-or-death situations just didn't compute. Whatever the reason, Beth Larrissey resigned herself to whatever fate had in store for her on the night shift.

"Run, *fucking run!!!*" called a strange voice that she didn't bother identifying.

Time slowed to a stop. Run for what? *To* what? Her overpriced walk-up single apartment? Her cat that jumped two stories to run away every time she opened the window? Her nonexistent love life? There was no reason to run, but she was the only one who knew it. She was touched that they really seemed to give a shit about her safety in that moment, but it didn't mean they'd call to see how she was doing on her next night off. They'd go their way, she'd go hers, until Monday morning anyway, when it was time to smile and punch the office card again. *And how was your weekend?* She didn't care about that charade. She needed a nice, long vacation. Anywhere would do. She dropped her hands to her sides, stepped out into the hall.

"No, get back! Get back!!!"

Her co-workers were really going apeshit, but they also kept their distance, which probably meant the predicament was worse than she knew. And with the boss's head being tossed around the hall, things were pretty dire. Her perceptions had become muted, buffered, the pill finally taking effect. She heard some kind of snarl, couldn't tell from where, then felt silly. *Duh.* She looked up. It was the strangest, most fascinating and terrifying image she'd ever seen, and it only lasted a second. A grey spider hung from the ceiling on a short length of thick web, ten-foot-long legs drawn close, except for the front two—the two that reached for Beth in the moment before she could collect the breath to scream. Almost anyone could've picked up Beth Larrissey like she weighed nothing, and the thing hoisted her off her feet accordingly, lifting her up, up, up, until she hung face-to-face with it. Beth looked into its glowing white eyes, awestruck, as it stared through its prey, passionless. It was intern Karly, but it wasn't.

"*Beth!!!*"

More shouts from people who didn't matter and couldn't do anything about it if they did. Beth swung her legs like a little girl, losing a shoe in the process. It landed with a clap beside

Brenheiser's head. The web design guy stared at it, unwilling to witness what would happen next. Inexplicably, Beth smiled. She was fulfilling something she always told herself she'd do before she died, and it made her feel good. *I'm going to die with a smile on my face.* She'd never considered it before, but she was ready to go. Life hadn't been fun for longer than she cared to remember. She studied Karly's face. The lights were on, but the girl herself was long gone. Beth kept smiling and closed her eyes, hoping it would be quick. It would be . . . kind of.

8

"What the *hell's* going on out there?" Such whispered, still seated at the news desk.

The anchor team was distractedly reciting the night's final stories, everyone aware of the commotion outside. In the midst of the broadcast, no one was able to investigate, but it was obvious something was going on. Barry floated out of the shadows to Such's end of the desk.

"Something's going on outside. Should I check it out?"

Such shook his head, snickering at a mental image. "*Nah*, Brenhitler's probably just firing the whole fuckin' station. Let her play, we'll have leverage for raises tomorrow."

Barry chuckled, uneasy. "*You'll* have leverage, *I'll* have unemployment. If she's chopping heads, mine'll roll as soon as that door opens."

As if by invocation, the newsroom door flew open, smacking the wall. The sound was buffered by rubber padding, but some intruder had brazenly disregarded the *On Air* red light glowing outside. Barry jumped out of his skin, as did Marcie Unrue, who was in the middle of a sentence. Jaworsky scowled, looking past her to see who'd committed the cardinal sin. The door swung shut, no one in sight. Such grimaced, balling his fists. He might've hated the anchors, despised the union guys, taken advantage of the interns, but he respected the news and wouldn't stand for *anyone* fucking with the broadcast, Nancy Brenheiser included. He eyed Forrest, standing near the clocks, belying no emotion. Their eyes met. Forrest held up two fingers. Such nodded, jaw muscles clenching, ready to unleash hell fury on the sorry sonofabitch who held no regard for newsroom sanctity. Two minutes to smackdown. Barry watched the door close in slow motion and wasn't sure why, but couldn't tear his eyes away. Time seemed frozen. Karly was suddenly in his face, upside down.

"*Whoa!*" screamed a grip from across the room, effectively nuking the show's last minute.

On-camera, Jaworsky kept talking, struggling to stay composed, eyes darting around the room. Such jumped up, irate. A warm spray hit his face and he flinched, one eye burning like hell. Barry's body crumbled like a house of cards, his head plopping down on Such's desk. Unrue tried to run but fell off her chair, too shocked to move. She squeezed Jaworsky's alligator shoe until he kicked her away.

"Cut, *cut!!!* Go to commercial!" yelled Forrest.

For some in the room, it was the first time he'd raised his voice. Such stared at Barry's head, stunned. The crew scattered.

Bang!

Someone tripped over a cable, bringing down a light stand and plunging half the room into darkness. Such looked up, saw the Karly spider spinning slowly from a length of web, eight long grey inhuman legs spread wide. She snagged a fleeing grip, hauling him off his feet like a rag doll.

"*Yeeeaaaarrrgh!!*" screamed the poor flailing bastard, before she nearly decapitated him with a bite that left his head dangling from bloody sinew.

Jaworsky, white as a sheet, sprinted for the makeup room behind the news set. He shoved a guy out of his way and straight into the wall. The guy hit face-first, his nose exploding on impact. He still tried to follow, getting the door slammed in his face as a bonus. He tried the knob with shaking hands, blood streaming down his shirt, but it was already locked.

"*Jaworsky, you miserable Polish prick!*"

He stepped back and flung himself at the door with all his weight, but it wasn't like the movies and he only bounced off. The guy collapsed in a heap, writhing in pain, his shoulder dislocated.

Inside the cluttered room, Jaworsky stumbled past Jackie, the station's longtime redheaded makeup girl and closet drunk. She sat with a cigarette burning in one hand and a plastic cup of burgundy red in the other, rattled by the sudden explosion of chaos.

"What is it?" she spat, losing the cup and keeping the butt, as she leapt to her feet.

Jaworsky shoved a wheeled clothing rack aside, searching for anything that could be used as a weapon.

"Don't open that door," he replied, offering nothing more. He gave her a metal folding chair. "Wedge this under the doorknob, *tight*."

Jackie gulped and took it, cigarette dangling from her lips. "Is everything okay?" she asked, slinking to the door, jamming the chair under the knob.

Jaworsky's shoulders sagged. "*No*, everything's *not* okay. I don't—is there a *knife* or something?"

She grimaced, realized it wasn't the time to ask questions, reached for her bag. He fidgeted, sweat streaking the makeup around his hairline. Screams and crashes on the other side of the door quickly sobered Jackie, who rummaged through her things, heart pounding.

"*Mace!* You have mace?" he asked.

She found what she was looking for, shook her head. "Better."

He waited, sweat glistening under his nose. She brought out a Beretta Bobcat .22 caliber, dropped the bag.

He leapt to her side, wide-eyed. "It's loaded?"

She glared at him, struggling to focus, riding the drunk-sober-drunk rollercoaster. "*Of course* it's loaded, I walk to the subway."

He snatched the gun, aimed it at the door, rolled his head on his shoulders, flexed his fingers.

She stared, finally taking the smoldering cigarette from her mouth. "You know how to use it?"

He scoffed, sweat rolling down his face, soaking his collar. "*Yes,* I know how to use it."

"The safety's on."

Jaworsky eyed the gun, not exactly sure where the safety was. Jackie chugged the rest of her wine, tossing the cup in a trash can, turning back to see him still looking. She reached for the gun, but he wouldn't give it up. She eased her hand over it, speaking softly.

"Calm down, Thad. You're shaking."

He scoffed, a drop of his sweat hitting her hand. "And *you're* drunk," he shot back, trying to pull away.

Pop! Crash!

The gun went off as they jockeyed for control, shattering the makeup mirror, raining glass shards on Jackie's table. She backed off, first surprised, then pissed.

"*Fucking asshole,* you ruined my kit! You know how much that cost?! How 'bout I spackle your fucking face with *broken glass* tomorrow?!"

Jaworsky didn't care, hushing her with a finger to his lips, creeping back to the door to hear what was happening. His face dropped as he listened.

* * *

Crouched behind the news desk, Such could see his surviving colleagues scrambling, fighting, or cowering for their lives, depending on their constitution. The Karly spider hung upside down, spinning around and around, in total domination of the room, her legs seeming to grow longer with every rotation. She snagged the unlucky and killed swiftly, ripping out throats with her teeth, wrapping the limp bodies in web membrane and casting them aside. Four cocooned corpses lay in a heap against the wall, with two more severed heads on the floor beneath her—one of them Marcie Unrue's—and Barry's still staring from the news desk. Such looked around in dismay, spotted a ballpoint pen under the anchors' chairs. It was better than nothing. He thought about his big brother, Johnny, murdered while serving time for possession, done-in by a makeshift shank of wadded toilet paper and dried Elmer's glue. *Where there's a will . . .* He army-crawled to the pen and white-knuckled it, to a soundtrack of frantic grunts and struggling. He peered over the desktop, shank ready. Having cleared the control booth, floor director Forrest was fighting like hell in the spider's clutches, to no avail. Hauled off his feet, he clung to a batch of power cables with all his might, pulling down a wall of monitors as he went up, two long grey legs coiling his torso, claws at their ends digging into his flesh to weaken him.

Ba-boom!

The screens exploded on the floor, some catching fire. The severed cables whipped around like a bundle of snakes, propelled by the force of flamethrower-like sparks, current still raging through them. Such looked on, helpless, as Forrest blocked a lethal bite with his shoe, forcing Karly's razor-filled mouth back with his heel. It was only a momentary reprieve. She lunged again, tearing a chunk from his thigh and severing the femoral artery. Blood sprayed like a fire hose and the director thrashed, determined to go down swinging. Such pounded his fist on the desk, in a strange surge of adrenaline. He'd always been drawn to the macho ethic, spent three months covering bull fighting in Spain for a documentary project that turned out too harsh and unflinching to air, ran with the bulls in Pamplona, dove off the coast of Australia sans shark cage, hiked the Serengeti alone, and twice attempted to climb Kilimanjaro, succumbing to dehydration both times. He knew he was wired differently, but didn't give enough of a damn to care. It was one of the many reasons guys like Thad Jaworsky didn't like him, and that was just fine by Such.

If you can't stand the heat, stay the hell out of my kitchen.

In contrast, he'd always liked Dale Forrest, but never had a real reason for it . . . until now. In some strange way, Such enjoyed watching Forrest fight certain death with every fiber of his being, tooth and nail. It trumped their working relationship, even their friendship. Never give in, never surrender, never say die. Go out in battle, head up, teeth bared, fists balled, all or nothing. Forrest swung haymakers at Karly's face, most of his punches connecting. As his blood rapidly drained, his energy began to fade. He knew he didn't have long, so he grabbed one of the deadly arms and bit it hard. Black blood sprayed his cheeks. Such was giddy at the sight. It didn't matter that his friend was being eaten alive, not when he was dying in valor. Hell, he was trying to eat the spider right back! Such fought the urge to cheer, envious that the director was getting to show his mettle. He found himself bobbing and weaving, like it was front row at the biggest fight of the year. Taking advantage of the chaos, another grip scrambled out the door. Such glared in disdain as the door swung shut, though he could've easily escaped himself.

"Fuckin' pussy," he muttered, drawing curious looks from the people still plastered to the far wall, hiding in the shadows.

Forrest lost consciousness and fell limp in the spider's grip, waking suddenly to kick hard with his good leg, smashing Karly's sharp teeth down her throat.

"*Ha-haaa!*" shrieked Such, jumping to his feet with arms raised, like he'd just seen a slam dunk at the buzzer.

Trying to assist, he grabbed Unrue's chair and hurled it at the spider's head. It hit Forrest instead, opening a deep gash above his eye. Such flinched, frowning.

"*Sorry,* Dale."

The blow sapped what was left of Forrest's fight and he wilted, never saw the claw coming. It slashed deep, nearly decapitating him, leaving his head flopping on his shoulders like a broken doll. Karly spun him in her web, then flung his one hundred-eighty pounds at the wall. He landed with a thud, face down on top of the pile. Game over. Such stood, blank-faced and dejected, like a winning season had just ended in overtime. A fingernails-on-chalkboard hiss got his attention and he turned, locking eyes with the Karly spider. She had all eight legs on the ceiling, poised to strike, and he knew *he* was the next meal. His heart triple-slammed in his chest, like a car doing 80 mph being thrown in reverse. Another surge of adrenaline, fight-or-flight times ten. For Josh Suchoza, there was no choice. He eyed the damaged monitor cables spewing bright orange sparks across the polished concrete floor. It was a long shot, the kind of madness that only worked in the movies, but it was all he had. He palmed Barry's head and hurled it like a basketball, thumping Karly on the chin. She didn't flinch. Knowing the news desk was gimmicked, he snatched up the top board like an oversized shield, kicking the hollow base aside and charging. The spider's legs reached for him like a dragnet, but he spun the desktop like his old street corner sign spinning job and blocked them. A claw slashed his pant leg, opening a deep gash he wouldn't feel until later. He pushed the spider back with the desktop and dove out from behind it, dive-rolling to the bare cables, stopping inches short to avoid electrocution. Wide and watery eyes peered from uncertain hiding places, dreading what they might witness next, but compelled to see if Suchoza could make a difference. Since they'd known him, he talked shit for no good reason other than to hear himself, a tough and blustery bag of wind at best, a delusional and egomaniacal asshole at worst. He'd never outlined a course of action in the event of a giant man-eating spider attacking the news staff, but no matter how impossible the scenario, it was the card dealt. Could Josh Suchoza back up his bullshit? *If anyone could,* the hopeful among them thought. *If anyone could . . .*

Before allowing himself to second-guess, Such grabbed the bundle of cables and sprang up, thrusting the frayed and sparking ends into the Karly spider's underbelly. She froze, her grey skin blazing fluorescent green. What sounded like a tornado siren filled the room, ricocheting off the soundproofing, brutalizing any ears still trapped inside. Heads disappeared behind whatever would shield them. The sound—the most shrill and demonic anyone had ever heard—was Karly's screaming. Such clamped a free hand over one ear, keeping the electricity on the spider with the other. His arm cooked in a shower of hot sparks, the smell of scorched flesh filling the room. The spider skittered away, doing donuts across the ceiling, a black hole charred into her navel. Such chased after her to finish the job, his shirt sleeve incinerated, his arm blackened and bubbling. Seeing the thing on the run prompted the others to grab makeshift weapons and come out of hiding. Suddenly, five livid crew members surrounded the spider. She turned left, a broomstick cracked her face. She turned right, a three-pronged electrical cord plug struck her eye, ripping it from the socket. She fell off the ceiling, landing on her back, surrounded by the maddening crowd. Collective bravery seized them and they attacked, whipping, pounding, stomping, kicking, throwing everything they had into killing it. Such lowered his cables and backed off, letting them take over. Knowing Ali's classic rope-a-dope, he feared the spider wasn't as hurt as it appeared. The monster with the intern's face was down, but not out, and if those suckers found themselves gassed when it rebounded, they'd be shit out of luck. But Josh Suchoza'd be fresh for round two.

Fuck you, go ahead and set it up. I'll finish the bitch off and take the credit.

He defiantly eyed his burned forearm and waited, watching the guys grow more assured with each passing moment. They swung for the fences, every one of them starting to suck air.

"*Get* it, Donnie!"

"*Yeah!*"

"Fuck you! *Fuck you!*"

"Fuck it up! *Kill it!*"

"Let's mount this fucker over the news desk!"

"Chop its legs off! Get the legs!"

They sounded like the weekend warriors they were. The spider balled-up and drew its legs in, lying still in their midst. The guys eased up to catch their breath.

"Watch it, *watch it!* Don't let it up!" shouted Such, on guard.

They didn't heed the advice, staring like he'd just spoken Greek. Brave Donnie's head was the first to fly, whizzing by Such's face and leaving a bloody splat on the Channel 4 logo. The body crumbled like a house of cards, leaving the other four guys stunned and flat-footed. One of them let out a war cry, raising a news camera high with both hands. Before he could use it, a clawed leg swiped his abdomen, eviscerating him where he stood.

The camera hit the floor. Such rolled his eyes.

"Fuckin' forty *thousand* dollar camera," he grumbled.

A flood of gore spilled from the guy's stomach, splattering the others' shoes as he sank to his knees, pathetically trying to hold his innards in. The closest guy slipped in guts as he backpedaled, feet flying out from under him. A long grey leg caught him in mid-air, using his flailing body like a battering ram to drop the other two like bowling pins. The last man standing, Such set himself and lobbed the live cables. *Just like fly fishing.* The guy in the spider's grip caught them, electrocuting himself instantly, but the current didn't pack enough juice to do much more than piss the beast off. Such scowled, unable to drag the cables back from the guy's blackening hands. The spider dropped its fried victim and crawled onto the nearest screaming worker's back, ripping the spine clean out of his body. Such ducked as it spun through the air at him, head still attached.

"Help! Help me!" screeched the last poor fool, helplessly flopping in the spreading red pool, unable to get up. His eyes were terrified, his clawing fingers swiping at Such's legs.

The Karly spider rose up tall, bumping the ceiling with her legs fully extended, spitting out bits of bone and gnashing the new teeth that had suddenly grown in. Such pulled the begging man to his feet. The guy smiled, thinking they had a chance. Such smiled back, shoving him into the waiting spider's clutches. The guy never had time to scream, which was good, because it was the last thing Such wanted to hear. Two claws speared the fool and lifted him high into the air, conscious as he hung impaled, mercifully dead before he hit the floor with a splat.

And they all fall down.

The spider slowly raised its head, Karly's blood-smeared face staring at Such with its empty white eyes. A chill shot up his spine. He tried to gulp, but had no spit and couldn't swallow. He looked around. Nothing left to grab, so he reached in his pocket with a shaky hand, finding the ballpoint pen. Sometimes things happened for a reason.

Stranger things have happened, he thought, ogling the spider intern.

Presumably, she'd be the last thing he'd see. He steeled himself, considering his final words. The thought that no one was left to listen bummed him out a little. Then something caught his eye. Across the room, a red button glowed on Camera 2, mounted alone in the shadows. It had been recording the entire time. Such smirked, projecting his voice to make sure they got every word, whoever *they'd* be. He'd only get one chance.

One shot to go down in history as the baddest motherfucker of all time, he thought.

"You're on camera, you ugly bitch. I can give you an autograph—"

He raised the pen like a sword.

"—or I can shove this up your ass. *You pick.*"

He winked and flashed a cocksure grin, hoping the angle didn't highlight his piss-stained pant leg. The urine stung like hell, reminding him he'd been slashed pretty deep above the knee, though it hardly mattered with the spider lurching at him on those murderous clawed stilts. He knew he was about to suffer much worse than a cut. For maybe the first time in his life, his interior running monologue was silent. There were no more words, no consequences to weigh, no repercussions if he made the wrong call. All that was left was to fight and die, and he knew he had a lot of fight left. He damn sure wouldn't make it easy.

"Come and get it," he sneered, wondering if he'd be able to get the pen into her eye when she came at him, likely his only shot to do some damage before being torn to pieces.

He wasn't going to survive the attack, he was sure of that, but since they were being recorded for posterity, he at least wanted the damn thing to suffer some damage. Or, best-case scenario, they could die together in mortal combat. The thought of it made him hard.

"AAAAAAAAAAARRGGHH!!!"

A crazed wail, followed by a firecracker flurry of shots. *Pop,*

pop, pop, pop, pop! The spider froze in its tracks. Such watched Thad Jaworsky charge from the makeup room, gun raised. He ran full-speed at the spider, emptying the clip and continuing to pull the trigger, oblivious that he'd fired all the rounds. *Click, click, click, click, click!* Karly eyed him, blood streaming from a bullet hole in her cheek—the only one that hit. Jaworsky eyed Such, at a loss.

Such shrugged, indifferent. "Reload?"

Jaworsky's face dropped. The spider lunged. The anchor raised his arms in self-defense and Such watched them both hit the floor, severed at the elbows, one hand still clutching the .22. Jaworsky collapsed in shock, the spider climbing over and around him with speedy precision, cocooning him while he was still alive. Such watched blood flush the web from inside, flooding the whole six-foot-three package deep red.

Douche-sicle, he thought, managing a chuckle.

Jaworsky's face twisted in mute agony, as he slowly drowned in his own blood. Such spotted Jackie cowering in the makeup room doorway, her wine buzz replaced by a terror that would lead her to even harder addictions if she managed to survive. *If . . .* In her, Such saw his way out.

Wrong place, wrong time, doll.

With the spider occupied, he waved to her, mouthing *c'mon!* She hesitated, in a daze, so he waved harder. Damning the consequences, or maybe just unable to weigh them, she blindly ran to him. The move would cost her. She reached Such's side and he swept her off her feet, cradling her in his arms. She eyed the spider, then the door. They could make it. They *would* make it. Her head screamed *go!*, but her body was paralyzed. The spider finished with Jaworsky and lobbed him onto the corpse pile. Not a bad haul for a few minutes of work.

"Hey!"

It turned, salivating at the sight of Such and his curvy friend.

"*Eat this!*"

He tossed Jackie at the spider, catching a glimpse of the mortal terror in her eyes, instantly regretting his words. They were being recorded, after all. Did it constitute murder? He knew the answer, but wasn't about to stick around and contemplate. Not when the distraction was his only chance to get out alive. He bolted for the door, as the spider sunk its teeth into the makeup girl's wine-marinated flesh. Someone in the building had pulled the fire alarm. A shrill whistle and flashing emergency lights greeted Such as he blew out of the news room, past the *On Air* warning light and down the empty hall. He threaded bloody pieces of Beth Larrissey without so much as blinking, thinking he'd never seen the place such a ghost town.

Should've hired a giant spider years ago, he thought, cracking another smile.

He even remembered calling Karly a *killer* intern a few times, briefly dubbing her just that, albeit sarcastically. Killer was too meek and not long for the broadcasting life, in his estimation, hence the nickname. Little did he know. With such random thoughts bombarding his brain, he didn't see the clear puddle of Beth's urine. Before he knew what was happening, he was flipping upside down. He landed on his head with a smack and sat up, disoriented.

Bang!

The spider crashed through the news room door and galloped at him upside down, claws punching through the fiberboard ceiling tiles, bloody shards of flesh hanging from its mouth. Was there no waking from this nightmare? Such slipped and slid to his feet, falling against the nearest doorjamb, waiting to meet death with his head held high. Alas, the reaper wouldn't be pulling his card yet. Just a few feet out and closing, the Karly spider lost traction and fell off the ceiling, a bundle of power cables wrapped around her foot.

ZZZZZAP!

Such watched the thing writhe and convulse in the piss puddle, the electric current of the entire floor flowing into its monstrous body and frying it on the spot. Karly's tongue went black, lashing back and forth like a bullwhip. Her eyeballs exploded, leaving black craters where the gleaming whites used to be. The smell reminded Such of family barbecues when he was a kid, and he suddenly felt hungry. The thought crossed his mind that he should be more troubled than he was, but truth be told, Josh Suchoza felt nothing at all. He looked up and down the hallway, but there wasn't a soul in sight. If he'd had a knife and a fork, he might've taken a bite of the big bitch. He'd never tried spider, but guessed it tasted like chicken. It always did.

9

Scarla was thankful for the paved highway, having discarded the damn daisy sandals almost a mile ago. The balls of her feet were scraped and sore, but nothing she couldn't handle, all things considered. The city loomed beyond the next exit, close enough for her to see into the lower windows of some high-rises. All was quiet. She knew the business district after hours was given over to the dregs, drifters, street urchins, shadowy figures and ne'er-do-wells. Not too long ago, it was her nightly stomping ground, but her mind had so far chosen to block those gory details. No use for them. Maybe down the line. Once upon a time, she was on a mission. But that was before she found out just how high the fence she'd been straddling was, just how hard the wind was blowing, and just how far she could fall. Fall she would, and with no right side to land on, it would only hurt. All the King's horses and all the King's men might've come running, but she wasn't sure she wanted them to. She didn't have a great track record with gangs, and besides, only *she* could put herself back together again. So there she was, walking the road to who-knew-what and reconstructing the pieces, however many were left. The last thing in the world she wanted or needed or cared about anymore was an obligation, a duty, a calling. She'd live in the moment, let someone else sweat the big picture. She'd been reduced to survival at its rawest, and was acutely aware that her mind—and her libido—could force a hard left at any moment.

Stay focused. Control it.

It was a good mantra, and while she didn't know how well it would do in practice, she decided right then and there to give it her all. A vivid image suddenly formed. A middle-aged, mustachioed, buzz-cut, square-jawed guy in a suit, grinning like a Cheshire cat with steely eyes, the same skyline laid-out in a panoramic sprawl behind him.

"Give it the old college try," he said, glancing left with a chuckle.

She heard someone else's laughter, loud and hearty, but a face didn't form. She didn't recall square jaw's name or history with her, but knew it was a memory and it made her uneasy. He seemed like a real asshole. She made a mental note of his face and voice, but he was already cold and dead, by her own hand. Not realizing how used to the dark her eyes had become, Scarla cleared a roadside tree and flinched, her face illuminated like a Christmas tree. The neon sign shined so bright, she had to turn her head and read it sidelong:

ADULT FIXXX
His & Her One-Stop Shop,
Drop & Pop for the New Sex Nation

What the fuck did that mean? She stopped and stared at the garish pink-and-blue electric sign, perched atop a four-story high metal pole, towering over the highway like a cryptic beacon to hell. She studied it for too long, before curiosity got the best of her and she hopped the guardrail, making her way down a rocky slope and up a grassy hill, heading straight for the non-descript, warehouse-type structure that sat beneath the sign. She had no idea what she'd find inside, but the butterflies were gathering in her stomach again, her palms sweating and heartbeat quickening. She reached a chipped yellow guardrail at the top of the hill, stepping over it into a small parking lot with four cars. An immaculate black Mercedes-Benz SL550, a white Ford F150 pickup on monster truck tires, a grimy purple Dodge van with no hubcaps, and a sticker-bedecked red Toyota hatchback that looked like someone had practiced teeing-off into it a few hundred times, watched silently as Scarla passed. Brutal fluorescents blasted her from above, as she stepped up to the front door. A sign on the glass read, *Every Wednesday's Ladies Day! 25% Off All Toys & DVDs!* She peered inside, saw two life-like female mannequins staring back at her, skimpy lingerie barely covering their ample curves. A chill ran up her spine and she instinctively stepped back, noting the security camera that watched from the upper right corner of the building. A tinny voice shot through her brain like an electric shock, nearly staggering her.

The furnishings are very valuable to me and I don't wish to replace a thing. Thank you. Continue when you're ready.

Her stomach suddenly turned and she doubled-over, puking yellow bile, not knowing why. She straightened, wiped her mouth, approached the door again, every cell in her body screaming *turn back!* Not interested in orders, she flung the door open and stepped inside. The place was empty and smelled of rubber, plastic, and decay. Straight ahead, thousands of porn DVDs created sensory overload on shelves angled toward the entrance. She looked around. To her right, a long glass case was filled with bongs and paraphernalia, the wall behind dominated by poppers, whip-its, performance enhancers, and pricy designer vibrators. To her left, three aisles split the showroom into sections of bondage, butt plugs, cock rings, condoms, dildos, lingerie, lubes, and pocket pussies. The sounds of someone being fucked echoed loudly. She couldn't tell exactly where it was coming from, until spotting the yawning black doorway at the far end of the room, velvet ropes leading the way into the dark unknown.

Scarla wandered the aisles aimlessly, listening to the disembodied squeals, biting her lip as the tingle exploded between her legs and swept upward, hardening her nipples and catching in her throat. She grabbed an endcap to steady herself, repeating that questionable mantra, over and over.

Control it . . . control it . . . control it!

All the while, she drifted closer and closer to the velvet ropes, to the black doorway, to the dark unknown. Overhead, in large carnival-esque rainbow letters, was painted:

ARCADE
MUST BE 18 TO ENTER

And taped to the right side door jamb, a misspelled handwritten scrawl:

ABSALUTELY NO WOMEN ALLOWED IN THE BACK ROOM!

A ban? Well, that was all it took. Without hesitating, she stepped to the entrance. The squeals grew louder, becoming screams. She couldn't tell if it was coming from a live person or a TV screen. She glanced left, spotted a pair of fuzzy handcuffs hanging on the wall. Right under them hung a stainless steel police-grade pair. *You never know.* She arched her brow, slid them off their display hook, disappeared into the shadows. She followed a neon pink stripe down the floor of a pitch black hallway, barely able to see the walls and corners. On both sides were small booths, detectable only by the flickering TV screens playing inside each. In the first, a petite blonde was being gangbanged by a group of rough-looking guys. Scarla eyed the action with no emotion, kept moving. In the second, a burly, furry-chested guy hung suspended in a leather-and-chain harness, being face-fucked by a smooth, lean frat boy until he gagged. She noted the twitching work boot of the booth's occupant, coupled with the sound of slapping flesh and pathetic grunting. She slid the handcuffs out of their box, letting it fall with keys still inside, and kept moving. A booth-tanned guy in a baseball cap, Polo shirt, checkered shorts, and flip-flops stared from the doorway of the third booth.

What's up with the fucking flip-flops around here? she wondered, locking eyes with the weirdo.

He quickly looked down at the cell phone in his hand, though there was no incoming call.

He's afraid of you. He's not a threat. He's here for something else.

She got the picture, kept moving. Loud noises came from the last booth on the left, obvious screen action with the volume cranked, but something else was going on, too. She reached a T, where the pink stripe split to the left and right, and hung a left.

"Deeper! *Deeper!*" howled an on-screen participant, indistinguishable as male or female.

The command was met with a muffled cry that rose in pitch and volume, more real than the tinny speaker sound. Scarla wrinkled her nose at a nasty stench and looked down, saw human shit streaking the lower three feet of the black wall, collecting in a steaming mound of chunky slop on the floor. The flies had already found it. The patrons didn't seem to care. She kept moving, if only to get away from the mess, no longer sure why she was there—if she'd had any idea in the first place. The butterflies were gone, the tingle had abated. She was repulsed by her surroundings, not turned on. And she liked the feeling, in some strange way. Maybe her soul wasn't as lost as she thought. She padded slowly and reached the last booth, handcuffs dangling at her side, and glimpsed the screen. Some generic rough gay sex in a shower stall, barely worthy of note. The scene playing out around it was what she needed to be concerned with.

Three men were jammed into the single-seat booth, two of them older, with saggy paunches and greying hair. Ron sat naked on the vinyl seat, gagged by a leather strap that buckled behind his head, legs spread wide, feet propped up on the wood-paneled side walls, the nub of a black rubber plug poking out of his ass. Randy stood over him, clad in a local bowling league tee, with khaki shorts around his ankles and a raging hard-on.

"What'd I tell you about popping a boner, huh?"

He slapped Ron hard in the mouth, causing saliva to ooze from his chin. The third man was younger, in his twenties, tall and wiry, with shaggy hair and a glazed look in his eye. White foam bubbled in the corners of his mouth, as he furiously stroked his erection to the show. Looking closer, Scarla saw a pink-and-blue nametag hanging from a lanyard around the kid's neck.

HELLO, MY NAME IS NICK
ALLOW ME TO SERVICE YOU!

Randy reached back and gave Nick's cock a few tugs, then looked the kid in the eye.

"Give it here. It's time to show this little bitch what happens when you get hard without permission."

Nick reached in his back pocket, producing a smooth, curved, surgical steel rod, ten inches long and almost an inch in diameter.

"Here it is, daddy," he whispered.

Randy took it and sucked the end, then grabbed Ron's cock with an iron grip, killing the burgeoning hard-on.

"Apologize," he ordered, his voice flat and cold.

"*I orry,*" was as close as Ron could get.

Randy slapped him again. "What?"

"*Orry!*"

Scarla felt strange. She wanted to leave, but couldn't tear herself away. She lingered in the dark, just outside the booth, just outside Nick's eyeshot, and kept watching. Randy got down to business, squeezing Ron's dick with one fist, inserting the rod into his urethra with the other. Ron howled behind his gag, then settled into euphoria, wide eyes rolling back, head thumping the wall as he writhed in acquired ecstasy. Randy pushed the penis sounding instrument deeper, driving it all the way up Ron's shaft and looking over his shoulder at Nick, who stood masturbating in a daze.

"Don't you cum til I say so, boy. And you blow it on his chest, you hear me?"

Nick nodded, then shuddered all over, as Randy turned back to his work and Ron gurgled like a baby, sweat beads glistening on his flabby grey belly. Excitement overload, Scarla assumed, until the employee's head jerked like someone had yanked his string.

It was like a skip in playback, wasn't natural. She watched his glassy eyes, saw them roll back white just for an instant, knew he was about to turn.

"There you go, punk," spat Randy, finishing the urethral implant on Ron, slapping it and stepping back to admire his handiwork. "Hold that for me. Maybe I'll let your little dick get hard later, if you're good."

He started stroking himself, beckoned the kid to join in. Nick stepped up, shoulder-to-shoulder with Randy, both of them staring at Ron's plugged piss hole. Nick's dick was considerably longer than Randy's, which bothered the old man, but the kid didn't mind. Randy scowled and glanced up, did a double-take, noticing the white foam that now streaked Nick's jaw.

"What the fuck is that?" he asked.

"What?" answered Nick, keeping his eyes on Ron's pathetic image.

"That shit on your mouth. Looks like someone shot a wad in your face."

Nick shrugged, breathing deep, closing in on climax.

Randy ogled him. "You want me to cum on your face, boy?"

No reply.

Scarla knew things were about to go bad, not that they weren't already. Something moved in her periphery and she turned, looking down the hall. The guy with the cell phone from Booth 3 stood on the pink stripe, staring at her, rubbing his crotch. She met his gaze. He didn't look away. *Looks like we got us a cowboy*, she thought, her stomach turning because the voice in her head belonged to the bobtail trucker. She nodded and he unzipped his shorts, revealing no underwear and a big cock. The tingle hit her like a thrust kick below the belt. He motioned to Booth 3, slinking back to it with his dick in hand to wait for her. She watched him disappear around the corner, suddenly able to see everything around her in hi-def, like a special spotlight was shining for her eyes only. Jizz stains, blood stains, piss and shit stains, splattered everywhere she looked. She preferred the dark.

"Fuck my ass! *Oh yeah,* fuck my asshole!" wailed the bottom on screen, his cheek pressed against the shower wall as the top hammered away without mercy.

The screen suddenly blacked-out in a splash of dark liquid, catching Scarla off guard. She looked up, saw Randy staring right at her. She braced for a fight, but he didn't see her. He didn't see anything. He was in a stupor, with the lights on but nobody home, anesthetized against feeling anything, be it a good orgasm or massive blood loss. While she was distracted, the kid had gotten on his knees to please Randy, but didn't stop at sucking his dick and was in the process of sucking his blood at alarming speed. His legs no longer able to support him, the old perv tipped back, head smacking the booth wall, face white as a sheet. Ron sat up, still gagged and sounded.

"*Aiee! You o-ay?*"

Nick lifted his head from between Randy's legs, revealing three sharp blades set at a Y-shaped angle to each other in his mouth, with a gaping pharynx greedily slurping blood behind them. It was the mouth of a leech. Trapped, Ron kicked wildly, banging his fists on the wall, screaming through his gag. It was all in vain, of course, since the only one who'd remotely lift a finger to help was the same one running amok. Randy crawled out of the booth in slow motion, pasty and weak, blood spurting from a Y-shaped gash in his scrotum, fully half his body's blood gone. Scarla stepped back, watching him drag himself down the pink stripe, leaving a red streak as he went. He never saw her.

In the booth, Nick mounted his prey, latching onto the neck and tapping the jugular. Ron made a sound like air being let out of a balloon.

"*Aaaaaaaaaaah . . .*"

The harder he fought, the faster his fight faded. Scarla slipped away, moving along the wall. No reason to get involved. She passed Randy, who finally noticed her and reached out, weakly grazing her leg. She didn't stop, rounding the corner and making for the exit. The showroom's bright fluorescence gleamed at the end of the hall. She stopped, overcome by déjà vu. Another robotic voice crackled in her head.

Initiate intercourse.

She broke into a cold sweat at the sound of it, not sure why, and couldn't take another step. She turned, saw the guy still clutching his cell phone in the doorway of Booth 3, glanced down and saw his dick hanging out of his shorts, half hard. The tingle hit her again and she shed the creeps, suddenly in the mood.

"Everything okay?" he whispered.

She pushed him back into the booth and followed, dropping her shorts and leaving the Northern Nazis leather on. He looked her over, smirking nervously.

"I like your vest." Then, noticing the cuffs in her hand. "And your, uh . . ."

She eyed his TV screen. Two bearded guys were 69'ing in the grass. She arched her brow.

"What do you want with me?"

He hesitated. "Uh, my hook-up didn't show." He shrugged, wagging his dick. "Gotta get off, right?" He pointed to the cuffs. "Wanna use those on me?"

She paused, shook her head and dropped them, turned around and bent over, feet spread wide, hands on the wall.

"Pretend," she purred.

He gulped, grabbed her hips and entered her from behind, keeping his eyes on the TV. Four strokes later, he was done, pulling out and finishing on her ass. She would've been disappointed, in both him *and* herself, but the switch had been flipped. She stood and turned, felt his semen rolling down the backs of her legs. He saw her white eyes and darted. She let him go and stepped out into the hall, leaving her shorts on the floor. They didn't fit anyway. She eyed the pink stripe, shining so vibrant in her eyes she had to squint. A pair of work boots stepped up to the line. Startled, she looked up to see a sun-weathered hillbilly with a moussed flattop and double chin. He was no taller than her, but everything about him was too wide, wider than any two men.

He looked like he'd just gotten off work from the nighttime road crew, and probably did.

"You the one causin' all the commotion out here?"

She cocked her head, didn't answer, eyes still glowing.

"Nice contacts," he complimented, oblivious to her transformation, his gaze floating lower. "Nice kitty cat, too."

It felt like something was pushing against her skin from the inside, swirling and churning to bust loose. He reached for her with a meat hook hand.

"Mind if I pet your kitty?"

She let him feel her, butterflies raging in her belly, goosebumps prickling down her legs. He moved closer, crossing the pink line.

Control it . . . control it . . . control it . . .

"Ooh, looky here. I stepped outta line. I'm all up in your personal space, huh?"

She snaked an arm around his wide waist, holding him tight. He smiled, slipping a finger up her ass, grimacing and grunting. He looked like a grunter.

"Nice n' tight."

He withdrew his finger, sliding his hand over her wetness, finding her clit. She watched the wall with a thousand-yard-stare, feeling sharp teeth with her tongue.

"How'd a pretty little girl like you get back here? Didn't ya read the sign?"

The black wall in front of her suddenly lit up bright, revealing the ominous words, *Abandon Hope,* scrawled in big blazing letters. She eyed Work Boots to see if he saw what she saw. He didn't. The vision was just for her, apparently. Again, she knew it was a memory from some other life, but the details were as murky as the arcade. Work Boots raised his hand, licked his fingers, put it back between her legs. He leaned close to her ear and she stifled a gag, having smelled corpses less offensive than his breath.

"I got a boy 'bout your age," he whispered, jamming two fingers inside her.

Sick fuck.

Something down the hall caught her eye and she looked over his shoulder. Randy was crawling around the corner, blood still gushing from his crotch. His skin had gone from white to blue.

"Lemme show ya how we do it at home," Work Boots growled, in what she assumed was his best abuser voice.

But Scarla didn't want to fuck and/or run, she just wanted to eat. Tightening her grip around the bastard's bloated waist, she shifted her weight and hip-tossed him onto his back. He landed like a sack of potatoes, with no clue what was happening as her snapping wolf maw locked around his face, squeezing and thrashing so violently that it crushed his eye sockets, cheekbones, jaw, and snapped his thick neck in three places. His boots rattled like bobbles and piss soaked his pants, but he was already dead. She hunkered down, resting her elbows on his chest, savoring sloppy bites of that disgusting double chin. It was fatty and greasy, the cannibal's version of fast food, and the thought crossed her mind that she wasn't so much *cannibal* as she was *carnivore*. She still couldn't grasp what the hell she was, seemed to be different every time, but felt stronger and more present than she'd been since dragging herself out of that damned lake. As she swallowed a mouthful of slimy flesh and sinew, she felt physically *and* mentally ratcheted. If she was lucky, maybe the mysterious snatches of memory would start to make sense. Or maybe they didn't matter. Maybe all that mattered was the *now*. She liked the sound of that, biting deep into Work Boots' throat, gulping a huge blast of arterial blood. She swiped her face with an arm and licked her fingers, savoring the taste, wondering if there'd be a sink to wash up in.

Clang! Clink, clink, clink!

She whipped around to see the steel sounding rod bounce across the floor and spin slowly down the pink stripe toward her, past Randy's motionless carcass, stopping against Work Boots' heel. She stared, looking like herself again, the maw receded. The rod was bloody, shards of soft tissue wrapping it like bacon.

She eyed the work boots. They were just about her size, so she reached down and started unlacing one, when a guttural hiss echoed from the shadows. She stood up fast, peering down the hall, listening to something ominous slosh closer. The six-foot-long flesh-colored worm slithered around the corner, leaving a thick trail of bloody mucous in its wake. Nick's nametag hung from the lanyard around its neck, pulled taut around its girth, without much slack. The three-bladed sucker chomped hungrily as it closed in, gliding halfway up one wall, sliding back down and shooting straight at Scarla. She thought fast and jumped aside, pushing off the wall with her bare foot. The leech slammed into Work Boots' gut, siphoning his blood on impact. She somersaulted over the thing's head, landing with her feet planted on either side of its squirming body, executing an agile backbend to grab the lanyard. Once she had a firm grip, she dropped and rolled over its slimy back, cinching the nylon tighter with each rotation, until its body bulged around the makeshift garrote as she cut off its air and blood flow. The lethal sucker gaped wide and the thing reared up, bucking like a bronco and slamming off the walls. Scarla hung on for the ride, taking a brutal hit on the right and wondering if her shoulder was dislocated, and a vicious head blow on the left that flipped her station to static for a second. She managed to hang on, laying her weight into it, forcing it to the floor, where it whipped and thrashed like a runaway rollercoaster, its sheer force smashing holes in the walls all around them.

Relax ... breathe ... wait it out ... make it carry you ... wear it down ... down ... down ...

Sound fighting advice, wherever it came from. The monstrous thing faded fast, gooey spit blowing from its sucker like a flu sneeze, splattering in what was left of Work Boots' face. She straddled it like a horse, pinning it with her knees and rearing-back on the lanyard with all her strength, every muscle flexing, every vein bulging, until the beast hung limp in her grasp, its slack sucker aimed at the floor. She let go and it face-planted with a splat. She slumped, catching her breath, her body on fire. *Helluva workout,* she thought, surveying the collateral damage all around her. She felt her teeth. Back to normal. She had ridden it out, quite literally. She wasn't hungry, she wasn't horny. But she *was* covered in blood and slime, and it was no way to march into a city, so she pulled herself up and strode back into the showroom, trailing red footprints as she went. She flipped the closed sign and locked the door, eyeing the lingerie and taking note of a plaid schoolgirl skirt that was way too short, but would do the trick better than the rest. But, first things first, she needed running water.

A door marked EMPLOYEES ONLY caught her eye, at the far end of the room. She went to it, glancing into the arcade's gaping black jaws as she passed, making sure no other surprises were creeping her way. All quiet, *all dead*. She threw the door open, braced for a surprise, and sighed with relief. A utility sink sat surrounded by cleaning supplies. Her mind was clear, with no more confusion as to how things worked, and she knew she'd rounded an important corner. She unzipped the Nazi's cut, threw it in the sink, turned on the water, grabbed a fat blue sponge and started scrubbing. When she was done, she hung it on a nearby rack, unscrewed a bottle of Wecks all-purpose antibacterial soap, dumped it over her head and climbed into the deep bin, crouching under the faucet and washing herself clean. It felt like the greatest shower in the world.

Naked and dripping wet, Scarla eyed the mannequins' attire and browsed the lingerie section, lifting a pair of black panties from a bin and pulling them on. She turned, yanked the schoolgirl skirt from its hanger and stepped into it. She warily followed the pink stripe back into the arcade, wrinkling her nose at the rotting stink that already permeated the unventilated space. She stepped over the giant dead leech and knelt to untie the work boots, moving fast. She pulled them on, finding a perfect fit, then fished the guy's keys from his pocket. Old and oily. Had to be the shitty van outside. She guessed the Mercedes belonged to the one

that got away, then eyed dead Randy and bet he drove the F150.
Take that one.

She scrambled over, raided his pockets, and *bingo*. Ford keychain. She grabbed her almost-dry leather from the utility room, zipped it to her cleavage and headed for the door, grabbing another pair of police-grade cuffs as she passed.

You never know.

The keys hit the floor on her way out. Outside, under a peaceful night sky, the women's world lightweight champion of some other reality climbed into the Ford, revved the engine, and laid rubber for the city.

10

Such bounded down the station's east stairwell, clutching cameras one and two from the news floor, a bundle of power cables slung over his shoulder. The building's blaring fire alarm was lighting his skull up with a monster migraine, a condition that contributed in part to his usual bad disposition, making him far more pissed-off than afraid, even with the conceivable threat of more giant mutations around every corner. He jumped the last seven concrete steps to the third floor landing, hitting a huge painted number 3 with his shoulder and needing a breather, bad. He set the heavy cameras down like a pair of dumbbells, shook his arms, found his cellphone and hit call on a contact called *Truck*. It rang. A woman shrieked from somewhere. Sounded like upstairs. Such rested a hand on his knee, trying to catch his breath and keep his heart from exploding. A man's voice answered, all deep bass and concern.

"Say you're okay, bro."

Such spit his words with no breaks. "I'm good my man I'm good what the fuck's goin' on fuck's sake?"

"Some crazy sonofabitch rolled up in the lobby down here and jumped off on security. Marcus n' Mike're *dead,* bro."

Such looked up, reacting to loud crashes from the fourth floor. "Jesus brother shit hit the fan up on eight too." He took a deep breath and settled, speaking more coherently. "Our intern turned into this . . . *thing,* I dunno. I barely got the fuck outta there in one *piece.* Nobody else made it, Whitey."

Silence. Such eyed the phone for a signal.

"Whitey?"

"Your cameras were live. I saw everything. Bro, you—hang on."

Such waited, cringing at the thought of a witness to his actions, listening to chaos-ultra erupt above him. Next thing he knew, the madness was in stereo.

"Whitey. *Whitey?!* You okay?"

He listened to what sounded like a swordfight on the other end of the connection, when suddenly a section of wall exploded in the stairwell above him, raining cinder blocks down the stairs. Such bit the phone and held it in his teeth, grabbing the cameras and racing to ground level. Behind him, half a young executive in a jacket-and-tie flopped down the stairs, his body severed clean at the waist. Such glanced back at the sight and jumped the rail, free-falling the last ten feet to the bottom. *Lotta good it did you, dipshit,* he thought, knowing how much the kid paid for suits to keep up his image. He heard something else coming down the stairs, but didn't dare look back again. He kicked open the exit door and ran outside. The midnight air smelled of fire.

11

Scarla sped down the exit ramp into downtown, almost smashing into the concrete median, leaving smoldering black strips on the asphalt of the sharp curve. She cruised to a stop at the red light, engine purring. She realized the sliding cabin window was open behind her and pulled it closed, noticing the big metal tool box mounted in the bed. She looked around. At first glance, nothing was out of the ordinary, and as opposed to previously, she thought she had a pretty good grasp on what constituted normal. Downtown was quiet. Maybe too quiet. Eyeing the empty streets to her left, she didn't notice the dark drop hit the windshield. Another drop escaped her, then another, until she finally caught the fourth. Her eyes focused on the gathering black spots, watching as they ran red. She knew it was blood, and rolled down the driver's window against her better judgment. Another drop. She leaned out, looked up. A small nude black girl, no more than five, perched atop the traffic signal box, fifteen feet up. She clutched a bloated, writhing rat in her little hands, lowering her head to take greedy bites of its plump belly. Her head darted back and forth as she chewed, bird-like, white eyes piercing the night like LEDs. Scarla stared, letting the light change from red to green to yellow and back to red. The girl devoured the rat, leaving nothing but the head, legs, and tail strung to a ragged, picked-clean spine. She dropped the carcass on the F150's hood and spread enormous bat wings, wider than she was tall, taking flight with effortless and eerie grace.

Scarla watched the girl silently fade away, then lowered her gaze back to the ground and froze, not liking what she saw. Shapes were creeping out of the shadows to slowly advance on the truck, from all sides. They were the dregs, the throwaways, the street urchins, the damned. But the night was theirs. Newly-infused with purpose, passion, and hunger, they'd not go unseen, unsung, or unneeded again. Tonight, they'd take what they wanted. Tonight, they'd feast. A dirty-sleeved arm smashed through the passenger side window, clawing to get ahold of her. She hit the gas, mowing down two lurching guys who didn't even try to get out of the way. The truck jumped the curb at the far end of the intersection, barreling into a tree-lined park surrounded by office buildings, the attacker still stuck to the passenger door with his feet dragging.

    She threaded trees at top speed, jerking the wheel hard to avoid an elm. A sharp pain stung her and she looked down, saw long claws that used to be fingers, gored right through her shoulder muscle and into the driver's seat padding. She had the presence of mind to grab the guy's wrist and hold him still, preventing any further damage to her arm, though it meant pushing the claws deeper through her rotator cuff. She'd torn the same muscle years ago, toward the end of her storied title reign, and remembered the searing pain and lengthy rehab that followed. But, the thought occurred, she hadn't been impaled by monster claws that time. *Shit fuckin' ow!* It was definitely worse.

    She floored the pedal and spun the wheel, shredding the grass with a 400-horsepower donut and side-swiping a tree, ripping her attacker's arm off at the shoulder. It seemed fitting. The mystery man fell off and rolled back into the night, minus the limb that still held her tight, and vice versa. She let it be, deciding it could wait until she navigated her way out of trouble. Besides, it had gone numb and wasn't so bad. She'd already been killed, after all. A *few* times, in her estimation. She'd tally them all up later, choosing to stay in the present as long as she had fight left. If she had nine lives, one of them was bound to be lucky. She wouldn't take any for granted. The streetlights surrounding the park cast hard tree shadows, making it difficult to distinguish between solid objects and tricks of the light. More difficult still, since the shapes were moving, charging the truck, transforming the picturesque lunchtime business park into a deadly shadowland obstacle course. She didn't give a damn who she ran over or through, but most of the trees were big enough to do more damage to the truck than it would do to them. Hit one head-on, it was game over. And she hated to lose, felt it in her bones.

Smash!

Unfortunately, something hitting *her* was just as much of a threat. The bat-like thing smashed into the windshield out of nowhere, its long dark muzzle and horseshoe-shaped snout stuck in the broken glass, toothy mouth chomping futilely, inches from her face. She punched it out of reflex, ripping the impaling claws from the seatback and freeing her right arm, sending a lightning bolt of pain through her chest. The severed arm hung limp against her own, claws still embedded in her shoulder. The thing kept reaching for her, glass cutting deep into its neck, blood splattering the dash and steering wheel, making it tough to grip with her good hand. She slugged it again, breaking its front teeth and slashing her knuckles, but knocking it out of the truck. The jagged windshield slashed its throat, spraying her face with hot blood, and the thing slipped off the hood.

"Fuck!" she growled, spitting a mouthful.

Her head smacked the ceiling as the truck bounced over shadowy figures left and right, plowing and grinding body after body under the treads, not slowing for anyone, not stopping for anything. If they wanted the prize, they'd have to work for it, just like anything else. The park edge was in sight, boulevard traffic lights just beyond blinking yellow. Several vehicles sat abandoned in both lanes, doors open, engines running, a station wagon on fire, a coupe's windows painted with blood all the way around. The truck clipped a low-hanging branch and dried leaves exploded through the shattered windshield, floating around the cab in slow motion.

Like dead fairies, Scarla thought.

She kept the pedal floored, sailing over the curb into the street, swerving past the stopped cars and jumping another curb to get around the log jam, cruising the sidewalk for half a block, before screeching out onto an empty side street. She saw a stray dog slink between two parked cars—or *was* it? Didn't matter. She looked around for anything familiar. Nothing rang a bell. She hit the brakes, grabbed the severed arm's wrist and gritted her teeth, pulling the claws out of her shoulder. The throbbing pain gave way to a searing burn. She threw the limb out the window, stepped on the gas.

Keep moving. Move until you find it. You'll know it when you see it.

She hit the door lock even though the windshield was half gone, looked around. Rows of brick walk-ups on both sides, some lit up, some dark, some in flames. Smoke detectors chimed relentlessly, but there were no sirens, no help on the way. A guy in a button-down shirt and boxer shorts hung from a second story window, bed sheets tied around his neck. Piss and shit streaked his fly-covered legs. She didn't bat an eye as she passed.

12

Such stormed through the parking lot, past a row of sculpted shrubs and a gigantic neon blue 4 that they always joked could be seen from space. Dozens of satellite dishes led to a group of unmarked white trailers at the lot's far end. He looked around without breaking stride, half-expecting something to jump out from behind one of them, bee-lining for the first trailer, leaving one red shoe print as he went, his slashed leg still bleeding freely. Jacked on adrenaline, he didn't feel it. Maybe later.

"*Whitey!*" he shouted, closing in on the trailer, its door badly dented and scraped, with light leaking from what looked like a long swath of claw marks.

A large silhouette appeared in the window, pulling the blind slats down to peek. Such waved one of the forty thousand dollar cameras. The figure ducked out of sight, leaving the blinds swaying. Such grimaced, then heard the hiss over his shoulder. He froze, watching his long shadow on the concrete to see how close the thing was. Nothing there . . . yet. He couldn't bring himself to turn around. The thought occurred that his mind had processed all the horror it could handle for one night. Or for a lifetime. Unsatisfied with that bullshit as a final thought, he decided he'd get at least one good shot in with Camera 1, maybe bash in its goddamn brains and record it for posterity with Camera 2. Was that realistic? *Who fuckin' cares? You didn't get where you got worrying about reality, you dropped out of college freshman year, for fuck's sake, and you're the greatest goddamn sportscaster since Cosell.* In his mind he was, anyway.

New sweat bullets sprang from his buzzed head. *You're gonna die this time, champ. Law of averages. Fuckin' hell, it was a fun ride.* Such whipped around to face whatever it was, not wanting to die and not giving a damn, all at once. As he turned, the trailer door flew open and a once-famous wide receiver rushed him, but he only saw the four-foot-tall horned cockroach running him down fast on the naked, oily arms and legs of a man. He had no time to process the sight before being bowled over from behind and face-planting on the concrete, cameras and cables flying from his hands. He looked up, braced for attack, and instead caught a blast of blue-black blood in the face.

"Glaaagh!"

DeWade "Whitey" Collins was electric in high school, if not downright legendary. He made the cover of Sports Illustrated at seventeen, as the face of the *Future Greats* issue, which should've been called the *Kiss of Death* issue, since the jinx hit hard and not one of the players featured from around the country went on to fulfill their promise. Upon graduation, DeWade sparked a college draft frenzy, accepting a full scholarship to play for the Rattlers, where he logged twenty-seven touchdown catches and 1,996 receiving yards his freshman year, setting four state records along the way. One year later, a badly blown knee would kill his pro aspirations and end his career before it began. There'd be no second act for DeWade, though his image would wow fans via archive footage on countless sports shows for years to come. Nothing could erase the magic he created in such a brief time. That was six years and forty pounds ago. He put his size 12 sneaker on the roach's head to yank out the fire axe he just buried in its brain, letting it fall dead, limbs bent under and out at unnatural angles. As if anything about the thing was *natural*. He eyed Such, bloody axe still in hand.

"You alright, bro?"

Such squinted up at him, wiping blood from his eyes. "Been fuckin' better, man." He extended a hand, letting Whitey pull him to his feet. "Thanks."

"Don't mention it. Saw that damn thing runnin' you down, had to move fast."

"Well, that's what you do." Such pointed at Camera 1, running to get 2 and the cables. "Grab that for me, will ya?"

Whitey complied, keeping an eye on the lot.

"I don't know what the hell's goin' on, but we gotta get inside, bro," he called, snatching the camera and jogging back to the trailer.

Such stayed put. "No, we gotta get the fuck *outta* here, where's your car?"

Whitey paused in the doorway. "In the shop, bro. I'm on the fuckin' bus."

Such frowned. "The *bus*? Why didn't you *say* something, you could ride with *me!*"

Whitey thumped a big fist on his chest. "You're a brother, Such." Then, peering into the shrubbery across the lot. "C'mon inside, bro. Shit's been steady buzzin' out here, won't be long til something else comes."

Such eyed the trailer, didn't budge. "I'm parked in Lot B, ground level. We can make it."

Whitey shook his head, pumping Camera 1 to his words for emphasis. "I already called the cops, bro. Should be here anytime."

Such held fast, cradling Camera 2 like a newborn. "You don't know what I went through to get these outta there, man. I should be *dead* right now. We have golden footage, *crazy* shit. It was bad."

Whitey nodded, then lowered his voice, his tone grim.

"Listen, if you're worried about it, I cut the live feed before the shit really jumped off. Erased the footage from the hard drive, too. Ain't no proof o' anything that happened in that room, bro. You're good."

Such nodded, understanding the favor. "Thanks." Then, after a beat. "I still have the master tapes. We get these cameras to safety, they'll make our *careers.*" Then, sheepishly, ". . . with a little editing."

Whitey laughed out loud. "Your career's already *made,* Such. Mine's *behind* me. How many favors you *want?*"

"Whattaya *mean,* behind you? You're *clutch* out here, man! You're my broadcast VIP every night!"

"Big difference between the broadcast truck and the field, bro. Bum wheel's a career-ender, so that's where my career *ended,* know what I'm sayin'? I'm twenty-five years old, bro. *Done.* This shit here's about paying bills, but I appreciate the support."

Such followed Whitey's eyes to the shrubs, watched them rustling.

"We're wasting time, big man."

"I *know* we're wasting time. And you're all fucked-up. Get your ass in here."

Such stood firm, shook his head. "We'll *die* in that sardine can."

"Die quicker out here, from the looks of it."

A sly smirk crept across Such's lips. "You still run?"

Whitey cocked his head, shrugged. It wasn't like he was lame.

"Ran the forty in four-point-five last week, but I'd never get through a camp."

Such beamed his on-air grin. "You're a bad-ass."

"I *know,*" Whitey nodded, straight-faced.

He watched a long, hairy, triple-jointed leg reach out of the shrubs and step onto the concrete.

"You said Lot B?"

Such nodded. Whitey eyed the glowing B on a distant parking garage, at the far left end of the lot. Another leg stepped out of the shrubs. Then another. It was likely to turn into a dead sprint. He eyed Such, who didn't turn to look. He didn't want to know.

"Can you keep up, bro?"

"*Hell,* no. Don't worry about me, just find the white Escalade. I'll get there."

He handed Camera 2 to Whitey, who swung the axe into the trailer wall and curled both cameras like dumbbells, rock hard biceps bulging.

"Escalade used to be my back-up. I *will* catch a ride with you from now on, motherfucker . . . if we live through this shit." He watched the legs across the lot, nodded to Such. "Go, I'll cover you."

Such slung the cables over his shoulder and jogged off, looking back. "Cover me with *what?*"

As if on cue, a hundred-pound mosquito with a woman's head rose from the shrubs, buzzing wings flapping faster than the eye could see. It flew in a square pattern over the shrubbery, gleaming eyes scanning the area, fixing on Such's streaking body.

"I don't know," Whitey mumbled, under his breath, before shouting at the top of his lungs. *"Run!!!"*

The mosquito woman flew at Such, closing in fast. He bolted, pushing himself harder than he thought possible, but Whitey still caught up with ease.

"Don't look back, bro, trust me!"

Whitey didn't need to say a word. Josh Suchoza's eyes were shut tight.

13

Scarla sped down a two-lane boulevard, eyed the speed limit sign, slowed to the posted 35. There was no one in sight, least of all cops, but she didn't want to chance any stupid mistakes. A man's deep, soothing voice popped into her head.

Play by the rules, until you got a good reason to break 'em. Then once you get dirty, stay *dirty. Ain't no goin' back, girl.*

She didn't know who it was, but knew she could trust him. She felt a void open inside her, a feeling she couldn't control, a bottomless pit of sorrow. She wanted to find the guy, whoever he was, but somehow knew that couldn't happen. His memory would have to suffice. He'd answer so many questions, if not all of them, of that she was sure. She could even see his face. Carved from stone, brown and kind, hard but compassionate, with deep lines of experience and regret, twinkling eyes piercing right through her. A lump crept into her throat, but just like she never allowed him to see her cry, she willed it away. His image was so strong, he may as well have been sitting with her.

Stay strong. You're a warrior, not a little girl. He's just a man, he doesn't want to deal with your shit. Break down on your own, it's not for anyone to see but you.

It was a mantra she'd obviously repeated more than once. She pulled to a stop at the corner, collected herself and looked right. At the end of the block, a pack of coyotes skulked between shadows. She looked left, saw a row of vultures perched on the power line between two second-story apartments, still as statues.

Pop, pop! Pop, pop, pop, pop, pop, pop, pop!

Gunshots echoed in the distance. She didn't bother wondering from where. She stepped on the gas, rolled through the intersection.

Thump!

Something hit the driver's door, hard. She looked out the window, didn't brake. An indistinguishable possum-like thing spun in circles, blood dripping from its fuzzy head, spritzing the concrete with thick spiraling dots.

Thwack!

Another hit, this time on the passenger side. A large, mangy shape popped up and fell out of sight, too fast to get a good look. She floored the gas.

Tha-dump!

The truck jumped, front tires running over something.

Ba-bump!

It jumped again, back tires finishing off whatever it was. Scarla looked in the rearview, saw a bulky thing smashed in the street, long fleshy tail thrashing and whipping from side-to-side. Suddenly, the truck was besieged by flying objects . . . things . . . people . . . Pummeled from all sides, she held the pedal to the floor and tried to outrun them. An emaciated guy with crude web membrane under his arms that formed wings and bones poking against his torso's thin skin crashed through the open windshield, slamming into the passenger headrest. Before he could do anything, Scarla split his head open with a hard elbow, crumbling him against the door. She reached over, opened it, shoved him out. But he didn't hit the ground, just hanging in the air, flapping his wings and bleeding. She kept driving with the door open, racing, swerving, trying to get clear. There could only be so many of the things . . . she hoped. Everywhere she looked, the streets were abandoned, and where they weren't, she wished she hadn't seen. Things had definitely gone poorly in the city. Understatement of the year.

Bang!

At first, she thought someone had fired a shot, then realized a tire had blown. The truck fishtailed, side-swiping a row of parked cars. Alarms wailed, headlights blinked. Something lunged into the cab through the passenger door, teeth locking around Scarla's throat. She kept the pedal to the floor.

Kill me if you're gonna, motherfucker. Good luck in the crash.

In the rearview, she saw her assailant—a stunning blonde bombshell with the jaws of a wolf. Butterflies. The woman's teeth, lips, breath, all turned her on. She could feel soft tongue flicking her skin, saliva dripping down her neck, rolling warm and wet under the leather. She also knew she could take the bitch. Not even recalling all her abilities, she *was* aware that she was a weapon—in any form—and physical confrontation didn't intimidate her. The truck rocketed toward another intersection and Scarla's eyes widened. She blinked to see if the image was real. A wall of bodies blocked the street, from corner to corner. Must've been hundreds of them. Writhing, mutated, hideous and fascinating, all at once. Some on the ground, some in the air, too many to try driving through. It would surely be suicide. *If suicide's even an option,* she thought. Death didn't scare her either, though she'd fight it with everything she had, until the last breath, whenever it came. She felt teeth pierce her skin, but the bite wasn't a finisher. More stilling than killing.

Okay, sweetheart. You want me? Let's find some privacy, see if you can give more than a hickey.

She zoomed toward the wall of flesh, claws, teeth, wings, tentacles, pincers, pussies and cocks—again, getting more of a glimpse than she wanted—and spun the wheel hard left, attempting to escape down another side street. The move backfired. Driving too fast, the truck couldn't handle the sharp turn and rolled, spinning around and around in a shower of sparks, cutting a swath right through the bloodthirsty horde and coming to a rest on its passenger side. The toolbox in the truck's bed fell open, spilling hardware into the cab, a hammer to the temple rattling Scarla's cage. She realized she was lying in a heap with the wolf woman, jaws snapping in her face. She head-butted her in the nose and pinned her to the bloody, glass-strewn concrete with a forearm under the chin. The woman kept biting. Her eyes were a striking blue.

If only you'd calm down, girl.

Unnamable creatures swarmed the truck from all sides, climbing over its upended metal belly, reaching through its shattered windows. A hand grabbed Scarla's ankle, squeezing tight. Claws swiped her back, slashing the Nazi skull in two. A stinger stabbed her thigh, hitting bone. Strange heads lunged in, biting and missing, closer each time. She closed her fingers around a long screwdriver, swinging at anything that moved. She buried steel in a guy's eye, impaled another's cheek, slashed an arm, cut a throat, but kept her lupine girlfriend alive. *Alive,* if that's what it was. They kept attacking, relentless, her efforts making no difference. She knew it was hopeless, that they'd overtake her soon if she didn't find a way out. Everywhere she looked was a threat, a body, a chomping maw, or something she couldn't even identify. She slumped on the wolf woman, careful not to lean too close, hope fading fast. Then she saw it. Directly under blondie's head, where the passenger window used to be, was her only chance. It was a longshot, but she was proof positive that stranger things did happen.

She eyed the tools lying all around them, spotted a crowbar and grabbed it, kicking off a slimy bug man trying to bite her leg. A hand grabbed her hair and she couldn't break free. Blondie lunged for her throat again, mouth open wide. Scarla jabbed her under the chin with the crowbar, deflecting the attack, and the woman severed the hand at the wrist, whoever it belonged to screaming bloody murder in retreat. The teeth kept chomping for Scarla until—*click!*—she slapped the adult store handcuffs around the woman's wrist, hooking her arm to the twisted door frame above them. A sharp elbow to the ear knocked the bitch out cold.

And the winner, by KO . . .

She rolled the big bad wolf over and pried the manhole cover up, slipping in head-first and falling the ten feet to the sewer floor, splashing into a foot of fetid water that broke her fall some. She sat up fast, coughing liquid from her lungs, saw the things tearing the truck to pieces above her.

Don't rest now. Move.

She dragged herself up, looked around. The city sewer yawned ahead, stretching as far as the eye could see, sickly yellow lights punctuating every twenty feet. The F150's steering wheel was ripped off and thrown in, just missing her head. She took off running, making a lot of noise in the knee-high water.

14

Whitey sprinted into the parking garage, immediately spotting the white Escalade parked at the far end, in a spot reserved with a metal SUCHOZA sign bolted to the concrete wall in front of its grill. Some wiseacre had drawn a cock-and-balls on it with black Sharpie, illustrating janitorial's views. He looked back and saw the station's star sportscaster a few yards behind, sucking air in a mad dash, with the winged abomination just over his shoulder and closing fast. Not everyone stayed as able as they were at eighteen, and Whitey put Such's odds of making it to the garage vs. dropping dead of a coronary at fifty/fifty. Maybe the coronary was the better option, since the dreaded third possibility looked most promising of all. The mosquito was a grotesque vision, with a once-pretty brunette's leering face set atop a glistening insect thorax. Digesting blood was visible inside her transparent abdomen, yet she thirsted for more. Her elongated mouth still bore the pouty red lips that made her attractive to the boys, and they desperately wanted to suck. It was the first time a man wasn't interested, but she wouldn't take no for an answer.

Whitey cringed, as the mosquito woman swooped at Such's neck.

"*Watch out, bro!!!*"

A loud chirp echoed through the garage and he jumped, hoping not to see a giant monster canary. The Escalade's taillights blinked warm yellow, its door locks popping. Such ducked the mosquito's lunge, waving his remote key, voice breaking as he screamed.

"*Front seat! Under my front seat!!!*"

Whitey nodded, running to the truck. The thing plucked Such off the ground in mid-stride, long prickly legs coiling his torso, holding him tight. He watched his phone fall from his pocket, shattering on the concrete below. She wasn't strong enough to carry him up, up, and away, so they floated a few feet above the lot, her mutated mouth stabbing at his head and neck, trying to tap a vein and get some juice. He flailed, managed to grab her snout, held her lips shut.

"What the hell *are* you?!" he rasped, not expecting an answer and not getting one.

They locked eyes. He took note of the milky pupils and vacant stare, the same as Karly's. The lights were on, but nobody was home.

Splat!

The woman's face exploded, dousing Such with gore yet again. They nosedived into the concrete, Such landing on his back with the mosquito on top, half its head gone. His skull cracked the pavement hard, scrambling his brains, the blunt force to his torso nearly popping his lungs like balloons. He stared up at the night sky, into a bright white light, certain he was dead. He thought about mouthing a prayer, but didn't know any. Then he saw Whitey's twisted face. Looming over Such, gripping a 9mm handgun from the truck, he stared in horror, afraid he'd killed them both. Such's face was a mask of blood and brains, the source unclear.

"Oh, *fuck* . . ." Whitey whispered, tears welling in his eyes.

Then Such blinked. Whitey grinned like a lunatic.

"*Yeah,* boy!"

He tucked the gun in his pants, rolled the mosquito woman off his friend, yanked him to his feet. Such stumbled and fell into Whitey, who held him up, half-laughing, half-crying.

"Don't scare me like that, you bald motherfucker," he gushed.

"Fuckin' pussy," Such mumbled, squeezing Whitey's shoulder hard as he did. "Nice shot." They exchanged a glance and a nod. Such handed the keys over.

"You drive."

"You got it, bro." He lifted the camera cables off Such's shoulder. "Where to?"

"I need a drink. Think we can make last call?"

Whitey paused. "We'll play it by ear, how 'bout that?"

"Sounds good."

Such doubled over, coughing up blood. It may or may not have been his. Whitey helped him into the Escalade's passenger seat, threw the cameras and cables in the back. As he closed the hatch, an explosion ripped through the television station, blowing the windows out of the upper floors. Whitey watched debris rain down on the lot with wide eyes, saw stars where the building used to be. A smoldering office chair hit the pavement, followed by a steady rain of flaming papers, as far as the eye could see. A man's charred body splatted flat in the garage exit lane, with more bodies pounding the concrete all around him. Whitey jumped behind the wheel and peeled out of the garage, running over the corpse on his way. Such laughed, coughed, then laughed again.

"I knew I'd live to see this shit. Fuckin' *knew* it."

15

Scarla moved carefully, working her way along the sewer wall in the glow of the nauseating yellow light, falling into darkness again every few yards. She liked the dark. Nothing could see her. She couldn't even see her. The air smelled of rust, mold, motor oil, gasoline, piss and shit. But it was relatively quiet, the crazy city above muted behind concrete and steel. May as well have been another world. She wished it was. Something splashed in the stream running alongside her. She eyed the silently flowing waste without stopping, realizing that if she let her guard down for even a moment, she could fall victim to . . . any number of possibilities. Until she found safety, the world was her enemy. The sentiment wasn't as foreign as it could've been, and she got the distinct feeling she was accustomed to being an outsider.

If the shoe fits . . .

Another sound grabbed her attention, this time stopping her in her tracks. She faded into the shadows, listening. Ticking, clicking, snapping noises seemed to surround her. She stood stock-still, unable to pinpoint them. As she peered down the length of the sewer, turning left and right, waiting to see what the lights picked up, the walls around her began to shift and slide. Leering faces, blinking eyes, clawing hands, gnashing teeth, unfurling tentacles, swishing tails, all filled the dark spaces between the light, packed into the stretches of shadow so tightly, their bodies had *become* the walls and ceiling. Scarla's eyes finally adjusted, saw the movement all around her. She stepped left, stepped right, spun around and saw the darkness teeming, countless limbs reaching for her. She recoiled, leaping the sewage stream to the other side, as the tunnel came alive around her. There was no safe place, nowhere to hide, so she ran, threading the two-foot-wide concrete path between the squirming wall and the rippling sewage, watching her step as best she could. A fin cut the putrid water, then another.

Shitsharks.

Serpent-like things slithered around the fins, sliding onto the pathway and over her feet, veiny and flesh-colored, with wide slit mouths that snapped at her ankles, revealing gleaming brown teeth and leaving greasy slicks in their wake. She raised a work boot and stomped one, crushing it with a loud splat. Blood and puss blew in every direction, half its body smashed to the concrete in the shape of her treads, the other half whipping and writhing in mute pain. She felt its warm slop oozing down her calf, kept moving. The idea of repulsion was losing its meaning, existing only by degrees in her mind now. Up ahead, a lump drifted along in the sewage. At a glance, she took it for debris, but as she passed, the thing burst from beneath the surface, grabbing for her. It was a man—or used to be—naked and covered in dark slop, toothy mouth stretched wide around a flattened snout, grotesque erection jutting from between his legs, with armor-plated skin bearing scutes like an alligator. She jumped straight up and his mouth snapped air under her feet, then landed with her legs spread wide on either side of his head. He rolled onto his back and she dropped a knee across his throat, then didn't know what to do. He was strong, almost threw her, and she had nothing to hang onto for traction, just her own weight and she was half his size. He rolled again, knocking her off balance, sending them both tumbling into the water. It was too murky to see, but she inadvertently took a deep breath, surprised that the rank water didn't affect her lungs.

You want a fight, big boy? Or something better? Bring it on.

She burst from the water, ready for anything—except what happened next. The alligator man was ready, lunging with an open mouth. She grabbed his jaw, stopped him in his tracks. As she slowly forced him back, an army came to life, rising from the water, slithering off the walls, dropping from the ceiling. She was grabbed from all sides, felt teeth and claws tearing her flesh. She opened her mouth to scream and an oily tentacle shot down her throat. She was dragged underwater, gagging and struggling, to no avail. Her hands combed the sewer bottom for anything that might be a weapon, raking through sludge, muck, feces. Worm-like creatures coiled around her fingers, cinching them tight, cutting into the skin. Her left pinky was severed clean, but she didn't register the pain. She felt something cold and hard snake up her skirt and penetrate her. She tried to close her legs, but they were forced back open. Another appendage slid up the back of her thigh, entering her from behind. She groaned, dry heaving as a tentacle forced its way deeper down her throat. A shooting pain rocked her abdomen and her body went limp, letting the damn things have their way with her. Was there even a reason to fight? How much would be enough? The thought crossed her mind that it just didn't matter at all, and it only pissed her off. She wasn't a quitter in the last life, wouldn't be a quitter in this one either.

Pressed facedown to the bottom, her body bent backward, ankles held tightly above her, she gritted her teeth and started crawling, elbow-over-elbow, as the darting worms nipped at her face, ears, hands, stinging and bloodying her with tiny bites. They swarmed her, slithering over and around, in and out, squeezing, caressing, crushing, piercing, slashing, thrusting, until her mind floated away with the feces she was submerged in. She was dead, whether she kept fighting or not, and she knew it. She was warm all over, the pain fading fast, turning into a tingling blanket of numbness. She wondered if she was even still whole, or had been torn to shreds and was floating away for real, the last flickering thoughts of a dying brain.

That wasn't so bad. At least it's over. Now turn off, dammit . . . turn off . . . lights out . . . goodnight . . . ring the bell . . . ring the bell . . . ring the bell . . .

16

"*Ring the bell!*" yelled Big H, pounding one fist on the mat and throwing the towel with the other.

It was the last thing he ever wanted to do to a fighter, but the girl just wouldn't quit. Scarla slumped in the corner, beaten to a pulp, as the ref pulled Claire Conninger off. It took a moment for the challenger to realize she'd just taken the title, but when her corner's elated shouts finally registered, she leapt clear over the ref's bald head, bounding around the ring like a loosed gorilla in blue spandex, until her cornermen caught her and hoisted her high on their shoulders, for all the world to see. Seeing the celebration unfold through her good eye, Scarla remembered the feeling. As Big H made his way across the canvas to her, Conninger's trainer cut him off to shake hands. Ever the sportsman, H paused for quick words and she was glad, as it gave her a moment to clear the cobwebs and walk on her own. It'd been a helluva ride, but it was over and she was okay with it. She'd accomplished a lot in a short period of time, and fell in love along the way. With a wedding looming and a world title not meaning as much as it once did, it was the perfect way to go out. On her feet, no less. She staggered out of the corner and into H's waiting embrace, his mouth in her ear. Dentyne, winter fresh.

"You okay, old girl?"

"Never better, you?"

"Oh, I been better. Waited long as I could, champ. Can you walk?"

"Gimme a hand on the steps, yeah?"

"Yeah. Wanna congratulate this bitch?"

Scarla looked over his shoulder at Conninger, whooping it up for the crowd, and smirked.

"Nah. She's doing it for me. Let's go home."

H nodded, guiding her past the ringside doctor who was waiting to check her out. The guy raised a finger and got H's hand in his face. They walked back to the dressing room in silence, the rest of the corner trailing behind. She was relieved, though she'd never admit it. Before they were out of sight, all she could think about was a big bowl of ice cream.

17

The Escalade barreled down the center line, passing burned-out shells of cars and crumpled, lifeless bodies—if they were lucky. The unlucky ones scrambled for cover, racing for safety though nobody knew exactly what that was, or where to find it. Such dropped his seat all the way back, but kept peeking out the passenger window, his fingers reflexively pressing the door lock even though he knew it was locked. Whitey jerked the wheel hard right to avoid an overturned shopping cart and Such's head bounced off the window. He didn't react, just kept staring, marveling at how rapidly their world was falling apart. An hour ago, he was prepping his news segment. Now, he was a killer battling killers. The thought made him smile.

"*Fuck, yeah,*" he mumbled, loud enough for Whitey to hear.

"What's that, bro?"

Such turned, confused. "Huh?"

Whitey hung a hard left, peeling tires around the corner, repeating himself once he'd straightened out. "You said somethin' over there, but I didn't hear you."

Such shook his head. "Just thinking out loud. You know where we're goin'?"

Whitey eyed him. "Where?"

Such laughed. "I'll take that as a no."

He winced, studied his blistering forearm. It looked bad. Blood still flowed freely down his pant leg. Whitey took note.

"Yo, we gotta get you to a hospital, why don't we try that?"

Such nodded, lying back. "Fo' shizzle, my nizzle," he sighed.

Whitey grimaced. "While we're there, I'll have 'em update

your white ass on street slang."

Such laughed. "Overlook ER's the place to do it, man."

Whitey grinned. "Hey, it's ghetto as hell, but it's close."

An explosion blew out a bar's front window to their left, splashing the Escalade with debris and body parts.

"Maybe we don't want close," Such offered.

Whitey didn't answer, straining to see through the spiderweb cracks in the windshield and pressing the pedal to the floor. The Escalade shot to the end of another block, clipping a fire hydrant as Whitey whipped the wheel right onto a one-way street. A white geyser erupted behind them, shooting twenty feet in the air. Such pumped his leg, realized he'd lost feeling, reached down and undid his belt. Whitey noticed.

"What're you doin'?"

Such eyed him, looping the leather around his thigh and cinching it tight.

"Playin' with myself. Can't get hard with no blood in my dick."

Whitey got the idea, leaning over toward Such to try and see through the cracks, to no avail. Such patted him on the head, tying off the belt.

"Wanna blow me, big guy?"

Whitey scoffed and leaned left, his cheek touching the window. "Don't getcha hopes up, cock ring. I can't see shit outta this window."

Such brought his good leg up, kicking out the windshield with two stomps.

"Better?"

"Better."

"Watch out for flying things, huh?"

"Oh, I will, don't worry."

"Me, worry?"

Such flinched, turning away, hand to his face. Whitey grimaced, taking his eyes off the street.

"You alright, bro?"

Such nodded, rubbing his eye. "Got somethin' in my eye."

"Fuckin' pussy," Whitey scoffed, looking up ahead, his jaw dropping. *"Fuck me."*

Such kept fingering his eye, didn't look. "Thanks for the offer, rim job, but I don't think of you that way."

Whitey didn't answer. Such looked at him with a watery left eye, noticed his friend's face was ashen, even by the dashboard lights.

"What's wrong?" He'd partly asked because he was afraid to look, but when Whitey still didn't answer, Such followed his eyes out the missing windshield, bracing for the worst.

"What the hell is this?" he wondered aloud.

A gauntlet lined the block, scores of unnamable mutations on both sides of the street, buzzing and flapping overhead, all eyes fixed on the gleaming white Escalade. They were once men, women, and children, but those lives were over and now they were something else. Whitey slammed on the brakes, laying a strip of deep black, smoke streaming from the wheel wells. The engine purred. They sat staring. Thinking. Hoping. Praying. But the dinner bell had already been rung.

"Whitey," Such whispered, keeping his eyes on the salivating army before them.

"Yeah," Whitey whispered back, feeling like crying, but not allowing it.

"We got no windshield."

"I know. You kicked it out."

"Let's back up."

As if by invocation, the Escalade's back wheels bounced under the weight of something heavy landing on top of it. The guys both turned, saw nothing, then eyed each other, livid. Whitey pulled the 9mm from his pants, pressed the barrel to the roof and started firing.

Blam! Blam! Blam!

They both winced, grimacing in pain, unable to hear anything but the high-pitched *weeeeeeeee!* ringing in their ears from the ill-advised shots in close quarters. The monstrous army started to advance. Such squirmed, drew his legs up into a crouching position on the passenger seat.

Blam!

"Those are the only bullets I have!" he shouted, way too loud.

Blam!

"How many's left?!" Whitey screamed, even louder, eyeing the smoking barrel.

Blam!

Such's eyes got wide.

"You're the gangsta, check the clip! I've never used it!"

"Gangsta, my ass! What the hell you got it for then?!"

"In case!"

"In case of what?!"

"In case of trouble!"

"In case—guess *what,* motherfucker?! We're in trouble!"

Such wiggled his fingers in his ears, pointed to the advancing horde. "Let's split, yeah?"

Whitey nodded, eyed the bullet holes above them and threw it in reverse.

"I think I got whatever it was," he said, more to reassure himself than anything.

Before either of them could register the sentiment, a hand smashed through the driver's window and grabbed Whitey's face. His foot slammed the gas and the Escalade shot backward, spinning out in a sharp donut, t-boning a parked car.

"Get it off me! Get it off!"

They both tried to pry the hand loose, but whomever it was had superhuman strength and Whitey was stuck in a clawhold from hell. Such looked around in a panic, saw a wild array of animals—freakishly large roaches, spiders, snakes, wolves, bats, mosquitoes, bees, all surrounding the truck, all with greasy human anatomy making up some part of them. It was ghoulishly fascinating enough to just stare until they overtook him, but Such wanted to live and didn't have time to ponder the unsavory possibilities. He threw the truck in drive and stepped over to mash the gas. They zoomed forward, mowing down anything in front of the grill, and Such jerked the wheel to stay on the street, crushing even more bodies under the wheels. Whitey groaned, the hand mashing his nose and white-knuckling his face.

"Bite it!" Such shouted, and Whitey opened wide, chomping down hard on the flesh between the thumb and forefinger, growling as blood spritzed his eyes. They rocketed through an intersection, just as a teenaged girl stumbled off the curb, barefoot in a blood-soaked slip dress, waving her arms and screaming for help.

"Please! Please help me!!"

Such kept the pedal to the floor and didn't swerve, hitting the girl at top speed and watching without emotion as her head slammed off the hood, leaving a blood splat on the point of impact. The Escalade bounced as it ground her under its tires and kept going. Whitey thrashed his head like a mad dog and tore the fleshy pad clean out of his assailant's hand, blood spraying around the cab like a fountain, but it didn't loosen its grip on him. Such watched the street ahead, working the wheel to thread the needle between an abandoned car and debris from an overturned pick-up truck. He glanced at Whitey and grabbed the thing's wrist again, trying in vain to pull it off.

"Talk to me, man, you okay?!"

Whitey nodded with watery eyes, his mouth full of bloody flesh.

"It won't budge!" Such yelled, dismayed.

He grabbed the gun from Whitey's hand, put the barrel to the attacker's elbow, pulled the trigger.

Blam!

With a muffled groan, the arm fell limp and withdrew. The guys winced again, their eardrums close to blown. Whitey watched Such's mouth moving, but couldn't hear a thing. He reached up, felt his nose. It was broken by the hand's powerful grip. And that was all it took. Just like his glory days on the gridiron, Whitey Collins saw red. Some things never changed, even with the world coming down around him.

"You okay?" Such asked, still driving from the passenger seat, but even he couldn't hear himself talk.

Whitey reached out the window, eyes blazing, and grabbed the body that still clung to the roof overhead. He pulled the person down by the neck and came eye-to-eye with the milky-white, hollow stare of a wiry street kid. Blood streamed from a bullet hole in the kid's cheek and another in his shoulder, both having passed straight through. He wouldn't be so lucky the third time. Such pressed the gun barrel between his glowing eyes, but before he could pull the trigger, Whitey head-butted the kid, then dragged him off the roof and let him go. The Escalade's back tire crushed the urchin's head like a melon, its deep treads sucking up his blood and brains. Such eyed Whitey, who sat shaking his head.

"How many times you think you're gonna fire that fuckin' thing in my face, bro?"

Such shrugged, tucking the 9mm between the seats. "Just trying to help."

Whitey took back the wheel, kicking Such's foot off the pedal. He was still crazy pissed, but stabilizing. "Motherfucker broke my nose. Ain't nobody ever broke my nose."

Up ahead, something caught Such's eye and he reflexively chopped Whitey's chest with an open palm. *Smack!* Whitey frowned, gritting his teeth.

"Hold up," Such projected, able to hear himself that time. "You see it?"

Whitey leaned over the wheel, straining to see though bleary eyes. A few yards out, a manhole cover was rising in the middle of the street.

"What the hell's *that?*" Such wondered aloud, but Whitey couldn't have cared less, flooring the pedal and speeding right for it. Alarmed, Such gripped the dash with both hands.

"What're you doin'?"

No reply.

"Whitey."

The truck hit sixty . . . sixty-five . . . seventy . . .

"Watch my truck, man!"

Whitey scoffed, waved him off.

"Look around, Such! Your shit's *totaled,* bro!"

He was right. Such held on, watching the steel lid rise higher and tip back to face them. A naked arm reached out from behind it, gripping the concrete. The Escalade hit seventy-five.

Ka-clang!

They blasted right through, slamming the cover shut on the pavement—and on the arm—and it bounced back up to hit the Escalade's underside hard. They both turned to see what it was, but couldn't get a good look at eighty mph. Whitey dug his phone out of his pocket, eyed the screen, frowned. "Ain't got no recep—"

SMASH!

The impact snapped both their heads around, the street a blur of spinning colors, the Escalade twirling three full rotations in the air, like a pricy, mangled, metal boomerang. Time seemed to stand still, as Such studied the glistening shards of the passenger window that floated past his face in slow motion, everything weightless for what seemed an eternity. He saw the runaway city bus that had hit them streaking by, the overly-suntanned cast of the latest bad reality TV show grinning bleach-toothed smiles from its digitally-printed side. They looked obscene to him, like a soon-to-be-extinct species that was doing the world a favor by disappearing. In the next instant, the ride was over, the Escalade bouncing off a light post and tumbling end-over-end down a parking garage ramp, obliterating the aluminum gate leading to the first underground level and spinning out in a shower of sparks, wailing a cringe-inducing *SCREEEEE!* that echoed off the concrete and steel-enforced walls, until finally coming to a rest in a cloud of smoke that slowly crept through the empty level.

Silence.

Such and Whitey both hung upside down in their seatbelts, semi-conscious, but miraculously unhurt. Such eyed Whitey.

"You alive?"

Whitey hung with his eyes closed, pushing up with his large hands on the smashed roof.

"Think so. You?"

Such looked out at the topsy-turvy grey sprawl. "Yeah, unless heaven's a parking garage."

Whitey still wouldn't open his eyes. "Who said you were goin' to heaven?"

Such scoffed, combed his waist for the belt latch. *Click!* He dropped on his knees, head smacking the glove compartment, and stayed put, breathing. *In . . . out.* Collecting his senses, he reached up to unclip Whitey's belt. The big man lowered himself with his hands, struggling to roll over in the small space. Such crawled out the front window, elbow-over-elbow, passing tiny bits of the cameras on the way, then their mangled shells, then the master tape spools, blowing through the garage in the wind. *There goes the evidence,* he thought, laughing to himself. When he was clear of the wreckage, he rolled over to lie flat on the concrete, blinking into the overhead fluorescents. Whitey squeezed out of the cab and crawled after Such, spotting the 9mm on the concrete and slipping it back in his pants, before slumping facedown next to his friend.

"Where are we?"

Such lifted his head and looked around, recognizing the place instantly. He laughed, coughed, laughed again.

"*Perfect,*" he spat, shaking his head.

Whitey looked up. "I'm seein' double, bro, where the fuck are we?"

Such sat up, wincing. "I take it back, maybe we *are* dead. Where else would two mofos like us end up?"

Whitey rubbed his eyes, thought about it. "Hell?"

Such pulled himself to his feet, extended a hand to his friend. "The Badgers might agree with you after last season. We're in fuckin' *Wire Media Arena,* champ."

Whitey looked up, accepted the hand, stood and surveyed the area. "Oh, yeah." Pause. "Think the concession stands are open? I could eat."

18

Scarla dragged her limp body out of the manhole, hand-over-hand, fingers clawing the concrete, untold things still clinging to her legs, not wanting to come into the light, trying to drag her to hell. Her right elbow was bruised and swelling from the weight of the lid being slammed on it, and she'd lost sensation in her forearm and hand. She lifted one leg out, the knee scraped bloody to the bone, then the other. She was barefoot, slimy tentacles coiled tightly around both ankles with no intention of letting go. It didn't stop her from pushing forward, crawling on her hands and knees, using every ounce of strength she had left. Every foot she gained was soon lost, as the tentacles pulled taut and slowly dragged her back to the sewer, strips of skin and blood streaking the pavement. It might've seemed a backhanded consolation, but she took some comfort in the fact that her body was so ravaged, she'd gone numb, watching as little pieces of her were torn away, as though it were happening to someone else. The separation freed her up to kill the next unlucky sonofabitch dumb enough to get close. And, lo and behold, a batter stepped up to the plate.

He scrambled out of the sewer hole, naked and wet, sharp teeth chomping in a frenzied mouth, cone-like snout twitching and sniffing for his prey, back arched like a rat, spine elongated into a soft cartilage tail. Earlier in the day, he was working as a junior partner at a law firm around the corner, which was arguably not much of a switch. He scurried onto Scarla's back with unnatural speed, sinking his teeth into her shoulder. Blood sprayed, but she didn't bother screaming—she had no pain, fear, or rage left. She acted without contemplation, sure, strong, and steady, which was no small feat given her situation. She hooked the rat man's legs with her arms, rolling onto her back and pinning him under her, his fangs still buried in her flesh. The tentacles wrapped her ankles tighter, trapping her legs together. All things considered, she was ok with that. She'd deal with them soon enough. She reached back with one hand, sinking two fingers into the bastard's eye sockets, wincing at the shrill scream he let rip in her ear.

"You scream like a girl," she rasped, pushing deeper and hitting skull.

He thrashed, clawing at her face with wild hands, and she pushed harder still, breaking through bone and piercing the brain. It was squishy and hot, like a microwaved melon, and the rat was dead before she withdrew her hand. She sat up fast, saw two more rat people emerge from the sewer, a man and a woman. Both were naked, him wiry and her voluptuous, and they lunged at Scarla with teeth bared. She dropped back, using their own momentum to slam their heads together, then grabbed a handful of the woman's hair and face-planted her on the concrete. The man kept coming, playing right into the trap, and she easily caught his head in both hands and violently twisted, breaking his neck in one sharp move and ripping his lower jaw clean off. He dropped, dead on impact, and she rolled him off just in time to catch the woman's second lunge. Scarla hooked her hair again, forcing her head back and tearing her throat out in one smooth motion. The woman fell, still biting air, twitching as she bled out.

Four more long, black tentacles reached out of the manhole, combing the concrete for Scarla. What they were attached to, she didn't know, only that it had followed her through the muck below and had no intention of letting her go. She dropped flat and rolled. The arms slapped the pavement and swooped over her, barely missing. She knew it was only a matter of time before she'd be roped by too many to fight off. She had to break free, and fast. No weapons, no leverage, no help. The godforsaken things didn't even have bones to break. That left only one way to kill it. Probably the last thing the beast expected, and definitely the last thing she wanted to do. She tucked and rolled back to the manhole, tentacles swarming her body as she dropped into the darkness.

* * *

The thing was an abomination even by Scarla's standards, a cross-species mish-mash of invertebrate and human, as if so flush with transformative power that it forgot what it intended to do in the first place. The tentacles slowed her fall before she hit the thing's fleshy underbelly, eight insect legs slapping their sticky hooks into her from head-to-toe, one nearly gouging out her eye. She had enough presence of mind to know that if she wasted too much time, she'd be dead—or worse—in seconds.

Do what you have to do. Make it count.

She could barely make out the guy's face in the shadows, hollow-eyed and sunken, with sallow cheekbones so sharp they were jagged, like his skull was pushing to bust out of his face. His mouth was open wide, tiny brown razor teeth bared, long thin tongue lashing back and forth like one of the crushing tentacles that seized her. She eyed the thing's exposed belly, snaked an arm free and pounded it with a hard punch. Pain exploded in her hand, shooting through her arm into her neck, making her ear ring. She winced and saw that what looked like fleshy pads were actually two hardened plates protecting the thing's vital organs. She didn't hesitate, grabbing the edge of one and ripping it off with one hard tug. A nauseating Velcro-like sound echoed off the concrete and she caught a warm, dark spray in the face. The monster's legs went wild, a tentacle wrapping her neck and squeezing tight. Her air was gone in an instant and she felt herself rising as it lifted her away from doing more damage. Around her, shapes scurried up and down the walls, whizzed by her face, slammed into her from all sides, some clinging fast to suck her blood. She was weakening, knew it wouldn't be long.

Goddamn, just finish it already, one way or the other.

She squeezed her fingers between the tentacle and her throat, managed a quick breath and was able to slip the appendage over her chin, just close enough to her mouth to—*bite!* She clamped down hard and chewed right through it, severing it clean as the beast went berserk, slamming her into the walls over and over, the impact buffered every time by the bodies that surrounded them. She wondered if she'd turn, then wondered why she hadn't. But there was no time for ifs and whys.

Get it done and get the fuck out.

Another sentiment that sounded all-too-familiar. In the split-second that she was close enough to get another shot at its exposed belly, she tensed her hand into a claw and swung with all her might. The momentum she had sailing through the air multiplied the force of her strike, and her hand plunged right into its chest cavity, like punching a fresh-baked cherry pie. She couldn't do that type of thing to a regular person—as far as she knew—so maybe the multi-legged abomination was just in a vulnerable state. Exactly *how* vulnerable, she was about to find out. With her hand buried past the wrist in the thrashing thing's torso, Scarla closed her fingers around the first thing she felt and yanked, tearing out its still-beating, enlarged, blackened heart. All of its tentacles and legs fell limp in an instant, dropping her. She landed right on top of it, straddling it with her hands and feet in the muck. Flying things and swiping hands struck and slashed her faster than she could react, and as she swung to backhand some fluttering menace, the heart slipped from her fingers and splatted against the sewer wall. It fell with a wet thud and was promptly pounced upon by a half-dozen ravenous creatures, big and small. But it was what happened next, she wasn't prepared for.

She heard them before she felt them—a strange sound she couldn't place, emanating from inside her victim's torn-open chest, not unlike the *Snap! Crackle! Pop!* of the popular breakfast cereal. It spread fast, enveloping her senses, surrounding her. Then she felt them. Swarming up her arms, over her shoulders, around her head, into her clothes, into her wounds, into her mouth. The bugs weren't cockroaches, but they were close. Shiny, bullet-bodied, hybrid babies, with more lightning-fast legs than the eye could count, all of them tri-jointed like spiders. They streamed out of the dead thing's chest cavity, thousands of them, with no end in sight. Scarla sprang up, slapping them from her hair, swiping them off her arms and legs, spitting them out. The sewer tunnel exploded in chaos, bodies pinging off the walls in all directions. She looked up, scraping a bug from her eye, and leapt back onto the metal ladder leading to the street above. Her hands and feet were slippery on the cold rungs and she struggled to hang on, bugs still swarming her.

Climb . . . climb . . .

She felt them on her face, gritted her teeth tight. Two rungs . . . three rungs . . . four . . . She felt them squeezing into the orifices under her checkered skirt, slipped and caught herself, winced and kept going.

Climb . . .

19

Such and Whitey staggered up the garage stairs to the first landing, both looking the worse for wear.

"Think anyone's here?"

Such thought about it. "I swung by this afternoon to talk to my boy, the Satanic Hispanic Sam Rodriguez, but I wasn't being chased by bugs. Pro wrestling was tonight, maybe we'll luck out with a couple dozen juice monkeys ready to lay the smack down."

Whitey chuckled, enjoying the brief respite. "Fake fighters vs. real monsters. Who wins?"

Such didn't think about it that time. "With any luck, we can get lost while they kill each other."

Whitey smirked and moved for the door, but Such grabbed his arm. "Let's go up to the colonnade, we'll be able to see everything from up there. We can head down to the floor if it's safe."

Whitey didn't argue. "Good call."

He took off, sprinting up the stairs four at a time, disappearing from view. Such leaned on the concrete wall, catching his breath, looked up and saw glimpses of Whitey growing smaller and smaller.

"Wait for me!" he called.

But Whitey Collins wasn't waiting for anything. Such took a deep breath and started climbing.

* * *

Two minutes later, he yanked the door open and stepped out into an empty upper deck hallway. It was still and quiet. He looked right and left, saw an unmanned concession stand a few yards down, still stocked with pretzels, popcorn, hot dogs, cold drinks. No sign of Whitey. Such braced himself, moved toward a curtained entranceway, C23 painted in bold black font above it. He stepped gingerly, making no sound, held his breath as he slowly reached for the red curtain. Just as he grabbed it, Whitey burst through. They both jumped out of their skin at the same time, Whitey's scream echoing off the walls.

"*Fuck,* man! You wanna give me a heart attack?" Such hissed, doubling over, hands on his knees.

"Give *you* a heart attack? Motherfucker, stop creepin' around!"

Such groaned, composed himself. "How's it look?"

Whitey smirked, held the curtain open. "See for yourself."

Such eyed him suspiciously, stepped through.

* * *

Wire Media Arena yawned before them, a sea of 17,642 empty orange seats, spiraling down two more sections to the concrete floor below, where the behemoth structure stood, still illuminated by the ceiling lights from the night's show. The 20-foot high, reinforced chain link steel cage was sealed on all four sides, including the top, completely enclosing the wrestling ring and ringside area, accessible only by a door that stood open in the cage's lower center, heavy padlock and chain hanging from it. *Rage In A Cage!*© was printed on all four sides of the three-foot ring apron, lending the ominous structure a cartoonish flavor. It was pro wrestling's most brutal match, a two-men-enter/one-man-leaves contest, made palatable to the industry's legion of young fans through suspension of disbelief and the acknowledged fact that wrestling was pre-determined entertainment. Both Such and Whitey grinned. If they were overrun, that fake gladiator set could possibly save their lives.

"That could come in handy," Such remarked. "Anyone else here?"

Whitey shook his head. "I called out, nobody answered."

Such nodded, looked around. "I'd stay quiet too, if a six-foot-five black guy busted in and started hollerin'. Stay on your toes."

Such headed down to the floor. Whitey stayed put, watching him go. "Yo, I'm gonna hit this concession stand real quick. You want anything?"

Such kept walking. "Two pretzels," he called, over his shoulder.

Whitey turned to go, when Such finally stopped and looked back.

"*Whitey.*"

Whitey paused. Such held up two fingers.

"Gimme *two*."

Whitey shook his head and ducked back through the curtain. Such continued down the stairs, having never seen the arena so silent. His footsteps echoed loud and it felt like he was descending forever. He came off the last step to floor level, moved past rows and rows of folding chairs bolted together, reached the ringside barrier and leaned on it. The action stung his burnt arm and he recoiled, shaking it off, which only made it hurt worse. He eyed it, grimacing.

"*Mother of fuck,*" he mumbled, unsure exactly what that meant.

Thinking there might be a first aid kit at ringside, he swung his legs over the barrier and hopped down behind the announce table, rooting around for anything that might help. A crude pencil sketch of a nude, busty woman sat on the desk beside two blue screen TV monitors and a closed laptop computer. He eyed it, wondering for the first time if he'd ever see a woman in the flesh again, so to speak. He bent down, looked under the desk. Cables, power boxes, a pair of men's alligator dress shoes . . . and a half-full bottle of Crown Royal. Such plopped down in a comfortable leather chair, popped the top, took a long pull and exhaled fiery dragon breath. *Down enough of this and you won't feel shit,* he thought, studying the monolithic cage that towered over the announce table. He took another swig and spotted two cameras sitting on the concrete to his right, still powered-up. Looked like the crew left in a hurry—if they were, in fact, gone. He slugged from the bottle again, eyed his belted-off leg. It had stopped bleeding, but the skin behind his pant leg was fish belly white. He sighed, took another hit, started singing.

"*Show me the way to go home . . . I'm tired and I wanna go to bed . . .*" He eyed the bottle, continued. "*I had a little drink about an hour ago, and it got right to my head . . .*"

Whitey descended the stairs, arms full with hot dogs, popcorn, pretzels, sodas.

"I found *hot dogs*, dog!"

Such spun in his chair, raised the Crown. "And I found my third wind."

Whitey made a face. "It's all you, I don't drink," he replied, his mouth full.

"*Great*," Such mumbled, spinning back to face the cage. "Still gonna need a couple more of these."

Whitey strode to the barrier, stepped over it without touching, dropped two pretzels on the desk, set down two bucket-sized sodas, scarfed half a dog in one bite and ogled the cage.

"What the hell do they do in this thing?"

Such tore into one of the knots, chasing it down with whiskey. "Clotheslines, Whitey. *Mad* clotheslines."

Whitey shook his head, chomped another dog. "In my neighborhood, your mama *hung* shit on clotheslines. You had a beef with someone, you knocked their goddamn teeth down their throat." He snapped his fingers. "*Pow!*"

Such thought about it, chewing. "And at the end of the day, all you had to show for it was bloody knuckles and a dented grill, but these motherfuckers just banked five figures with sparkly underwear and *clotheslines*."

Whitey also thought about it, chewing. "Good point. Think they're still here?"

Such was nearly done with his bottle. "Might be hiding in the dressing rooms, you wanna check it out?"

Whitey's eyes bugged. "*Hell,* no. Anything could be up in there."

"Well, what's scarier, a three-hundred pound mosquito or a three-hundred pound guy in spandex?"

"Shit, I don't like either one."

Whitey noticed the laptop and cameras, flipped the computer open. The screen sprang to life, blasting Such with light bright enough to make him wince.

"It's not the time for porn sites, man," Such cracked, but Whitey ignored him, focused.

"Bro, we can get help with this. Let people know we're in here."

His long fingers plucked the keys fast.

"What, you gonna *tweet* about it? I *hate* that shit," Such grumbled, chugging from the bottle. He eyed the screen, saw Channel 4's website, watched as Whitey punched in the passcode newzleader4, bringing up a black screen with mumbo jumbo at the bottom. It was all Greek to Such, who knew how to check email, but that was about it. He didn't need to know anything else, so he didn't. Throwing the pigskin had always carried more weight in his world than translating code, not that he'd ever get to practice either again, for all he knew. Whitey grabbed one of the cameras, set it next to the laptop, pulled a slim cable from its side panel, plugged it into the computer. Such stared like he was witnessing a magic trick. Whitey's fingers raced along buttons and past screen prompts, until he stood up straight, smiling wide.

"What?" Such inquired, genuinely curious.

"We're *live*, bro. Webcastin'. Anyone out there's still online, they can see what we're doin' here."

Such slid the computer toward him, saw the camera's static view filling its 17" screen.

He lowered the bottle, and his voice. "You mean, people can see this *right now?*"

"Well, they gotta be logged in, but yeah. We're the number one news station in town, bro. *Thousands* might be loggin' in to find out what the hell's goin' on out there, know what I'm sayin'? Somebody's *bound* to come get us out."

Such nodded, still staring at the screen, letting the information sink in. Whitey circled the desk and knelt in front of the camera, waving. Such watched the action onscreen.

"*Yo,* everyone. Me an' Josh Suchoza are here in Wire Media Arena and we'd sure like somebody to come get us the *fuck* up out here, y'know what I'm sayin'? Josh is hurt, but he's gonna be okay. We could really use some assistance though, so . . . if any help's watchin' this, we'd love to think you're on the way. *Thanks.*"

He popped a peace sign with his fingers and stood up, then quickly ducked back into frame.

"*Oh,* uh. My name's DeWade Collins—" Then, smiling, "—yeah, *that* DeWade Collins—an' I work for Channel 4, ain't that some shit?"

He stood up, took a deep breath, saw the Crown disappearing fast and held out his hand.

"Lemme hit that, bro."

Such eyed him. "Thought you didn't drink."

"Yeah well, you're killin' it too fast for me to change my mind later. Hand it over."

Such gave up without argument, turned his attention to the pretzels.

"Don't underestimate the liquid courage, kid. This could be a whole new beginning for you."

Whitey took a hit off the bottle and pulled back to eye it, hissing like a rattlesnake.

"Shit *burns!*" he growled, wiping his mouth with the back of his hand, dumping the remainder in his soda cup and hurling the bottle like a molotov cocktail into the upper deck, where it exploded like a gunshot, raining glass on section F.

Such laughed, spraying pretzel dough on the pencil nude. "Fuckin' *light*weight!"

His words were prophetic, but he didn't realize it. Whitey froze, staring at the top of the entrance ramp. Such took note and followed his gaze, swiveling the chair. Scarla stood onstage, bruised and bloodied and looking like she'd been to hell and back, which wasn't far from the truth. Looming above her was a jumbo digital screen displaying the graphic of a fiery explosion behind blackened chain link, with the company's industrial *Rage In A Cage* 3D logo bursting out of it. She scanned the empty arena, her déjà vu so intense the hairs stood on the back of her neck and gooseflesh rose around her myriad of wounds. Such stood up, squinting to see who—or *what*—she was. She focused on the men and took a deep breath, her body language calm and assured, moving down the ramp with steady footsteps. Such and Whitey eyed each other, concerned. Such stepped forward, hand raised.

"*Stop right there*. Don't come any closer," he called, not expecting her to comply.

She stopped in her tracks, bare feet gripping the steel grate ramp, and watched them closely. The guys exchanged another look, unsure.

"We need a weapon," Such whispered.

"Got one," Whitey answered, not taking his eyes off the strange, blood-splattered, scantily-clad woman.

He slapped the laptop screen shut and pulled the 9mm from his pants, letting it hang at his side. Such breathed a sigh of relief.

"You think she's one o' those things?" Whitey asked.

"*Look at her*," Such scoffed. "What do *you* think?"

They both reflexively checked her out, like lecherous construction workers. Whitey seemed oddly nervous.

"I never shot anyone before, bro."

Such arched a brow, glaring. "You've been blowing shit away all night."

Whitey waffled. "You know what I mean. *People*."

Such shrugged, studying Scarla. "I'd say it's a fine line here, man."

Whitey wasn't about to fire from where they were, not before seeing if the woman was a threat. Before seeing her up close. Besides, he wasn't that good a shot. He'd gotten lucky earlier, when his wild aim killed the mosquito carrying Such, though he'd never admit it. Given the night they were having, Such didn't need to know.

"What happened to you?" Whitey called to Scarla.

She thought about it. What *hadn't* happened? Maybe the truth wasn't her best option, but if she lied, would they know? She sized them up, letting seconds tick by while they waited for a reply. The black guy was a hulk, but he was a wide-eyed, baby-faced hulk, and he was young. The white guy was older and less physically imposing, but something about him seemed meaner... and familiar, but she wasn't able to place him from a few yards away. The air was tense. She needed to give an answer, and fast.

Fuck it. Bullshit 'em. Give the bullet points, leave out the ugly parts.

She wondered if there were anything *but* ugly parts.

"Had some problems out there," she replied, deliberately vague.

"I bet. Where'd you come from?" Whitey shot back.

She paused. "Lake house. Few miles away."

Such eyed Whitey, who licked his lips, thinking.

"You got *wheels?*" Such interjected.

Scarla shook her head. "Hitched a ride."

Such's eyes narrowed. "Where'd your ride go?"

She paused again. "Dead."

Whitey flexed his fingers around the gun handle, readying to kill her if need be.

"Where's the vehicle?" Such followed-up.

She shook her head again. "Wrecked. I got away."

"She got away," Such mumbled, wringing his hands. "How do you think she did that?"

"How'd you get here?" called Whitey, suspicious.

She took a step, advancing slowly. "I hid in the sewer. Came up outside."

Such spun around, turned his back to her. *"Kill her,"* he spat.

Whitey eyed him. "What the hell for?"

"Remember that manhole out there? I'm tellin' you, the bitch ain't right. *Shoot her.*"

Whitey pondered it and raised the 9mm, but held his fire. Scarla stopped, stared. The gun didn't scare her, but being revealed did. She'd have to play by their rules, make them think she was just a damsel in distress, if she wanted to make some allies.

"What's your name?" Whitey asked, sweat dotting his brow.

Such's eyes widened. *"Fuckin' dating game?"* he hissed. *"What're you doing?"*

"Scarla," she offered, matter-of-fact.

Such frowned, paused, then turned to face her, squinting at the battered figure on the ramp.

"Don't shoot," he instructed Whitey, who eyed him, incredulous, "unless she makes a move."

Such hopped the barrier, threading the floor seating to the ramp, keeping his eyes on Scarla the whole way.

"Sure thing," Whitey mumbled, confused. "Yo, what's goin' on, Such?" he called, getting no reply. *"Shit,"* he whispered, to himself.

Such reached the foot of the ramp and stopped, only twenty feet separating them. His face brightened in recognition.

"Scarla Fragran?"

She cocked her head, surprised.

Well, well. Your reputation precedes you, girl.

She remained on guard, breathing a sigh of relief inside, and offered a quick nod.

"Jesus fuckin' *Christ*, you okay?"

"Been better," she shrugged.

Such waved to Whitey, who lowered the gun, stepped over the barrier, joined them on the ramp.

"What's up?" he asked, to whichever of them wanted to answer.

"It's *Scarla Fragran*, man." Such commented, still taken back.

Whitey didn't react, having no idea who she was, so Such clarified. "The youngest women's kickboxing champ, fuckin' royalty. She was on my old show twice."

She took note of the remark, but didn't remember.

Whitey nodded, unimpressed. "Oh. She alone?"

They both stared, awaiting her reply. She nodded.

"Not *anymore,* you're not. You're with *us* now."

Such motioned her forward and she obliged, following him back to ringside. Whitey trailed behind, wrinkling his nose at her rancid stink, his eyes scavenging her body as they walked, noting her schoolgirl mini-skirt and her shapely, gore-streaked legs. He held the 9mm at his side, but was ready to use it if he had to. He ogled the patch on her back, frowning hard. The Northern Nazis, a white supremacist motorcycle club. He'd had an altercation with a member once, years prior, back when his gridiron injury was still fresh and he was pissed at the world, looking for any excuse to lash out, any scapegoat to vent his frustrations on. He'd found it one afternoon, at a liquor store in the suburbs, when a lone Nazi rolled in on a solo beer run. The scraggly punk bitch made the mistake of holding eye contact a bit too long, and that was all the excuse Whitey needed to *pow!* Lights out. Unfortunately for Whitey, the MC had deep hooks in said liquor store and tracked him through his credit card receipt. Three days after he blew off some steam on one of their boys, nine more scraggly punk bitches with SS skulls on their backs blew the steam back and made sure Whitey would never so much as entertain the idea of getting back on a field, lest his screws shake loose and he fall apart like Humpty Dumpty. Game over. He hadn't seen or thought of the club since . . . until seeing Scarla's cut. The rage boiled inside him, but he kept it in check. He'd play it by ear, making no promises to himself. Moments before, he doubted his ability to pull the trigger on another human being. Now, he was contemplating breaking the white cunt's neck with his bare hands. One wrong move was all the excuse he'd need.

20

They sat at the announce table in silence, Such swilling his soda and gobbling fistfuls of popcorn, Scarla picking at a pile on the desk so as not to reach into the bag, keeping one hand in her lap to hide her missing finger, Whitey nursing his spiked cola, which did nothing to sooth his ill temper. She sat at one end of the table, they sat at the other, her stench too powerful to get any closer. The faint sounds of chaos could be heard from outside: screams, sirens, gunshots, honking horns, car crashes, intermittent explosions. They didn't react to any of it, just sat eating, drinking, staring absently at the cage. It was Such who finally spoke.

"What've you been doing with yourself all this time, Scarla?"

Whitey watched intently, his face twisted into an intoxicated scowl. She chewed and swallowed, racking her brain for a good answer, coming up blank.

"I've changed a lot," she deadpanned, reaching for more popcorn.

"I see that," Such chuckled. "You still around it?"

She stared. "Still around what?"

"The *ring*," he shot back, somewhat annoyed.

She nodded to the ring inside the cage. "I am now."

He smirked. "Funny. You should pull a Mike Tyson, do some stand-up. I'd love to have you on my Channel 4 segment sometime, by the way. Like a 'where are they now' kinda thing . . ." He thought about what he was saying and paused, adding, ". . . if I still *have* a segment."

Whitey sat stone-faced. Such laughed, took a slow sip of soda, keeping his eyes on Scarla the whole time. He looked around the arena, partly making sure no one else was lurking.

"Bet *this* joint brings back some memories, huh?"

She glanced up at the empty seats, but was distracted by the intense vibes she was getting from Whitey, who glowered at her from the end of the table, gripping his cup so hard it bowed.

"I've never seen it this empty," she remarked.

Such grinned. "I'll *bet!* You were *electric* in your day. Y'know, you were the *last* marquee name that sold this place out?"

Scarla locked eyes with Whitey, answering in a quiet, measured tone.

"I didn't know that. I haven't paid much attention . . ." She paused. ". . . since I've been gone."

"Well, if you don't *knowww,*" Such sing-songed. "Now you *knowww.*"

He turned to Whitey, still grinning, but the big man was unamused. Such cleared his throat, eyed Whitey's cup.

"I can't believe you jacked the last of that bottle, man. Did they have any beer?"

Silence.

The table grew uncomfortable fast. Whitey finally broke eye contact with Scarla, looking at Such with a glare that bordered on murderous.

"Wasn't lookin' for beer."

Such's smile faded. He turned to Scarla. She looked away, reaching for more popcorn.

"*Right.* Well, I'm gonna go take a peek. We could be here all fuckin' night, and I can't do this shit sober." He stood up, eyed them both. "Anybody need anything?"

Silence.

He turned to Whitey. "Gimme my gun, I'm not takin'any chances."

Whitey didn't budge, looked up slowly. "What about me?"

Such motioned to the giant cage. "Jump in, if you have to. I'll only be a few minutes, I gotta hit the head while I'm up there."

Whitey sipped his drink, set it down, handed over the 9mm.

Such was quietly relieved, decided not to give it back if the topic was broached. In his experience, surly drunks with sidearms never helped a situation. He nodded and walked away, his numb leg almost buckling. Whitey stared hard at Scarla. She studied the cage, chewing popcorn. She felt his gaze, but this time chose not to return it. Something about him wasn't right, and was going more wrong by the second. She knew it would come to a head, it was only a matter of when, and until then, she resolved not to push his buttons in any way. Whether or not he'd push them himself, she couldn't control.

"That was some bullshit you laid down with Such," he finally grumbled.

She turned to him, staying cool. "What do you mean?"

He sipped from his cup. "'Whatcha been doin'?' 'Oh, I changed a lot.'" He scoffed. "You think I don't know what that means?"

She watched him, genuinely unsure of what he was getting at. "I don't know what you're saying," she replied, calmly.

"*No?*"

She shook her head. "No."

"Alright. We can play that game. But don't think I don't know 'bout that racist *shit* you're wearin'."

She looked down, finally understanding. *Oh.* The Northern Nazis cut. She noticed, for the first time, a slim patch on the bottom right side that read, WHITE MIGHT. She'd just been happy the damn thing fit, but it was sending a message alright. The thought crossed her mind that racial tensions should probably be a thing of the past, considering what was happening outside. But alas, some things would never change. She looked up, locked eyes with a fuming Whitey.

"It's not mine."

He laughed. "*Riiight,* it's not yours! You can just pick those up at Walmart. At least stand up for what you *believe,* bitch. You'd be a *lot* more respectable, trust me."

She saw her chance to clear up the misunderstanding, seized

it. "I'm telling you the truth. They showed up at a rest stop outside the city. They tried to keep me with them . . . I got away."

Whitey took a sip, not buying it. "Sounds to me like you're just an old lady who got lost."

Scarla didn't know the term, got offended. She was pretty beat-up, but she wasn't *old*.

"Look, I didn't have anything to wear."

"*Uh-huh*. You were hangin' around naked at a rest stop and some strange biker just offered you a cut, is that it? I told you, I ain't stupid. You gotta *patch into* that shit."

She paused, careful with her wording. "He was dead when I found him."

Whitey stared a hole through her, serious as a heart attack. "How'd he die?"

"I don't know."

He stood up, towering over the table, teeth clenched, balled fists as big as hams. *"Don't lie to me."*

She sat still, realizing nothing she said would calm him until he chose to let it go. She reached for more popcorn, but he overturned the desk. Everything went flying, laptop, camera, monitors, popcorn, but the table was gimmicked for the wrestling show and only the breakaway surface flew against the cage. They both eyed it. Whitey continued.

"Answer the question, white girl."

"I don't know what you want me to say," she replied.

He stalked around the aluminum table frame to loom over her, invading her personal space. She tilted her head back, eyeline level with his crotch, and looked way up at him, the butterflies raging in her stomach. She suddenly had the intense urge to pee, unconsciously drawing her knees together and biting her lip. She wanted him. *It* wanted him.

Control it . . . control it . . . the other guy's coming back with a gun any minute . . .

She wasn't sure if *anything* would kill her, but didn't want to be shot again to find out, and her apparent fame only complicated things. If there was still a crime-and-punishment structure in place when all was said and done, the common knowledge that Scarla Fragran was some kind of monster would definitely not bode well for her freedom and survival.

Break his fucking neck if you have to, but don't turn . . . Do not turn . . .

"Take it off," he ordered.

She hesitated, slowly unzipping the vest.

21

Such pissed like a racehorse, one hand on the white tile wall above a row of gleaming urinals, 9mm resting on the porcelain in front of him. He watched the room's reflection in the urinal pipe, but peered over his shoulder every few seconds regardless, making sure he was alone. He finished, zipped, grabbed the gun, moved to the sink, and eyed himself in the mirror.

"Fuckin' hammered shit," he mumbled, snatching a paper towel and using it to twist the faucet.

He let the towel fall, bowed his head to splash water on his face, savored the feeling. When he opened his eyes, a cockroach was scurrying along the sinktop.

"Gaaah!"

He stumbled back. His leg gave out and he fell on his ass. He sat on the floor, catching his breath, feeling stupid.

"Jesus fuckin' Mary," he whispered, not sure what that meant either.

* * *

Such walked through the concourse level, gun in hand. The place was completely empty, eerily quiet. He eyed a row of exit doors to his right, noted chains with padlocks wound around the handles of each. Without hesitating, he ran over and started unwrapping the chains as fast as he could, then rewrapping and locking each set of doors, all the way down the line. When he reached the last pair, he steeled himself and carefully pushed one open. He heard distant cries, fires crackling, random gunfire, and carefully peeked out. The air smelled of burning rubber and death. The skyline glowed orange, several buildings that used to define it, gone. A woman lay dead just a few feet from the door, wearing nothing but a blood-splattered tee shirt, her body mauled to the bones. A faint roar grew steadily louder, then deafening, causing Such to instinctively duck. Four F-18 fighter jets streaked overhead in diamond formation, flying low over the city. The lead fired two Sidewinder missiles, obliterating a high-rise apartment building a few blocks away. Such gasped, slipped back inside, chained the door tight.

* * *

Buppy's Sports Bar was deserted, only a slew of half-finished drinks, toppled bar stools, and the interminable wail of the emergency broadcast system alert on the color-barred TV screens stood as evidence that people had recently been there. Golden beer flowed from a tap marked Oktoberfest, filling Such's mug, then filling another, as he switched hands. He downed the first one quickly, burped loudly, then savored the second, breathing deep to try and calm his nerves. He eyed a telephone beside the register, lifted the receiver, machine gun tapped the button, listened. Dead. An explosion hit too close for comfort outside and he spilled some, sweeping it off the sprawling bartop with his hand. He felt his heart and studied his burned arm, saw bright red creeping through the blackened, bubbling flesh.

"Not good," he sighed. "*Not* good."

He chugged the second mug, grabbed another bottle of Crown Royal from the wall, and exited.

* * *

The door was marked FIRST AID, so Such tried the knob. Unlocked. He flung it open, gun in one hand, whiskey in the other. Empty. He shook his head, couldn't believe his luck. The room was stocked like a doctor's office. He stepped in, closed and locked the door behind him, put down the gun and bottle, untied the belt from his thigh and dropped his pants, revealing boxer shorts covered with tiny footballs. He opened a cabinet, rummaged around. Pills, ointments, antiseptic sprays, band aids, gauze, syringes. He sprayed his arm heavily, letting the Lidocaine sink in. He eyed his leg, grimaced. It needed stitches. Nothing he could do about that, he wasn't Rambo. He kept looking.

"C'mon, where's the good stuff?" he wondered aloud, as a bottle of injectable B12 shattered on the floor.

He dug deeper, tossing things over his shoulder and making a mess, until finally pausing, brow arched.

"Hello, beautiful," he asked a bottle labeled Tramadol. *"Come to daddy."*

22

Scarla stood inside the cage, arms crossed over her chest, topless. The door was chained and padlocked. Whitey sat in a chair just outside, his goliath cup almost empty. Neither of them spoke. The Nazi cut lay on the floor, near what was left of the announce table. She eyed it, remembered the handcuffs and cellphone hidden in a pocket. She had no idea who she'd call, but knew she could cuff Whitey's wrist to something if she got close enough, and once that was done, kicking Josh Suchoza's ass would be a foregone conclusion.

But you're locked in a fucking cage. Like an animal. Which is exactly what you are.

She sighed, hopping up to sit on the ring apron, regretting her choice to play along and not shred the drunken bastard where he stood, once he'd decided to throw his weight around. It was going to come back to haunt her, and there was nothing she could do about it behind 20' x 20' of sealed chainlink. She made up her mind not to let a chance pass if it presented itself again. Suddenly, the house lights cut out, the cage glowing like a beacon in the overhead lights.

Walk the walk, punk!

The snarly voice blasted over the arena speakers, startling both Scarla and Whitey. A crunching guitar riff erupted, roving spotlights swirled around the arena, and Such appeared at the top of the entrance ramp, clad in a sparkling red robe with his arms raised high, bottle of Crown still in one fist. They didn't react as he showboated down to ringside, flexing and pointing at imaginary members of the crowd. He bounded up to Whitey, jabbed a finger into the big man's chest.

"*Ohhhhh, yeah! You're goin' down, jabroni!*"

Whitey eyed the finger, stone-faced, then stood and scooped Such off his feet without warning, holding him over one shoulder.

"*Whoa, whoa, whoa! Okay, put me down!*" Such yelled, dropping the act fast.

Whitey sneered, helicopter-spinning him faster and faster, until Such's face dropped and he went green. Both men were feeling the effects of their drinking and wrestling was a bad choice of activities, as they would soon find out. Spinning like a top, Whitey lost his balance and staggered, sending Such headfirst into the side of the cage in a blur of red sequins, before face-planting on the concrete. Scarla looked on, impassively. The theme music and light show stopped. The house lights slowly rose. Both men were wiped-out and groaning. Such dragged himself up the cage, holding his head, still loopy from shooting the Tramadol. He came eye-to-eye with Scarla, noting her nudity.

"Uh . . . did I interrupt?"

She didn't answer. Whitey did, still splayed on his back, eyes closed.

"She ain't right, bro. I don't trust her."

Such composed himself, felt his head and eyed his hand, checking for blood. "Were you playing strip charades, or—"

His face dropped and he turned away fast, projectile vomiting on the floor. Whitey sat up, getting his bearings, trying to slow the spinning arena.

"Bitch is *racist*, I don't care how you know her. Read that leather. She ain't wearing it around me."

Such moved to the Nazi cut, stared down at the lightning bolt skull, nodded.

"White power, eh?" He eyed her. Still no reply. "Well, it's a moot point now," he shrugged. "I took a look outside." He paused for effect. "You *don't* wanna know."

Whitey got up and grabbed his cup, let Such continue.

"I locked up all the concourse doors. Like it or not, I

think we're gonna be here a while."

He studied Scarla, thinking. The slop on her body was dried and crusting.

"Scarla, why don't you hit the showers?"

Whitey glared. "I think she should stay right where she is."

Such raised his hands. "Hey, y'know what? I dunno about you, but it kinda stinks in here and it's not doin' anything for my stomach, I'll tell you *that*. This joint still has power and water, though maybe not for much longer, so I say we should take advantage of it while we can." He turned back to Scarla. "No offense, sweetheart. You're still a knockout, but you reek like death in an outhouse and I'd love it if you rinsed off, know what I mean?"

Such and Whitey locked eyes, neither blinking. Whitey finally nodded consent, finished his cup, threw it aside. Such moved to the cage door, eyed the padlock.

"Where's the key?" he asked, rattling the chain.

"What key?" asked Whitey, indifferent.

Such looked at Scarla, sighed. "I saw bolt cutters in a utility closet. Be right back."

He walked away. Whitey followed. Such paused, eyed him.

"What's up?"

Whitey shook his head. "From now on, I go where that nine goes."

23

Scarla stood under the hot spray, running her hands through her hair and instinctively probing for a bullet hole. There wasn't one. She felt her teeth, too. All there. The shower room was cavernous, with five nozzles lining one wall and another five opposite them. She only ran hot water, filling the room with dense steam, which was what she wanted, since Such and Whitey were lingering just outside the door, able to get a good look anytime they felt like it. Thus far, she'd managed to drop no hints that she might transform into a random beast at any time and snap their heads off like lollipops, and she wanted to keep it that way. *So far, so good.* The shower was making things difficult, though, forcing her to try and disassociate, to think other thoughts. The hot spray on her body, the probing eyes that stole looks around the door jamb at intervals, her exposed flesh, all conspired to swell that tingle in her belly. It was barely detectable at first, brewing just under the surface until she slid her hands down her sides, over her hips. Her knees grew weak, hands trembling, heart skipping in her chest, breath catching in her throat. Gooseflesh rose on her body as her senses sharpened, every sound, every smell, every touch, suddenly magnified by a thousand. And though the shower spray hid it well, she was dripping wet between her legs.

No, no, no . . . concentrate . . . control it . . . they'll kill you, and this time they won't stop until you're really dead . . .

She turned her back to the doorway, one hand sliding helplessly down her navel, slipping between her thighs, fingers caressing her lips, massaging her clit. *Pop, pop, POP!* She saw stars, like the flashbulbs that drove her crazy back in the day, and closed her eyes tight. When she opened them, her pupils blazed white. Her jaw shuddered and her lips rippled, resisting the urge to sprout into something else. Her fingers twitched and her triceps jumped, fighting the call to transform. An old guy-joke sprang to mind, splitting her focus. *Just think about baseball.* Maybe there was something to it. She didn't really know baseball, had only seen a few games in passing, but gave it the old college try. A strapping batter in tight pants materialized in her imagination, wagging his smooth, bulbous club in preparation for the pitch. *Who the fuck thought* this *was a good idea?* Or maybe guy jokes were guy jokes for a reason. She sank to her knees, gripping the floor with both hands. Such peeked in, still wearing the red robe, and spotted her pose. At first, he thought she was about to do some pushups, then he realized something was wrong.

"Hey, you *okay?*" he called.

No answer.

"Scarla?"

Still nothing. Whitey appeared over Such's shoulder, his face a mask.

"*Hey!*" he shouted, his deep voice booming around the shower walls.

She flinched at the noise and sat up, her back to them. Such ogled her muscular shoulders, his eyes floating down to the firm ass resting on her feet. He and Whitey exchanged a look. Without a word, Whitey strode in and reached down, hooking Scarla's arm to pull her up. With her limp hand just inches away, she cupped his crotch and gently squeezed. Whitey's eyes widened, but he didn't object.

"Go on back down, bro. Make sure the place is still ours," he called over his shoulder. "I'll handle this."

Such waffled, unable to see what was going on from his vantage point. "I locked up the ground level, man, we're good. Besides, you wanna stick with the gun, remember?"

Whitey raised his voice, testy. "I *said* I *got* this. Go hang tight. I'll make sure she gets dressed."

Such hesitated. *"Alright there,* Marvin Gaye," he mumbled, before exiting. "Clothes are on the chair here."

24

Scarla's vision was in sharp focus—so sharp she could see the contours of each individual spray of water from the shower nozzle. Everything slowed down, like she was watching a movie in sixty frames-per-second, as opposed to the normal twenty-four. Water beads snaked up her forearm like living things, twisting and contorting until they dropped off her elbow, sailing through the air like sparkling, animated blobs and plopping on the tiled floor, where they exploded in streaming, white eruptions of liquid. It was a viewpoint few would know, and fewer still would live to describe. She kept her eyes cast down, knowing if she looked up at him, he'd see those otherworldly eyes and she'd be found out. *Why are you hiding? Why do you care?* She had no answers.

She heard the clink of Whitey's belt being undone, followed by the growl of his zipper dropping. Her heart pounded in her chest, her breath quickening to a pant. His large palm cupped the back of her head, drawing her closer. She closed her eyes, lips parting in expectation. She heard the rustling of cotton, the snapping of elastic, smelled the sweet and slightly musty aroma that was unmistakably human flesh.

"You want some o' this, don't you, white girl?" he purred, his voice all rumbling bass and intent.

Yes. Yes, I do. Yes, it does.

25

Such stood at ringside, eyeing the cameras that sat on the floor, thinking. A chill crept up his spine and he shuddered, glancing around the arena. The sea of orange seats stared back at him. He got another chill, looked straight up. All clear. He chuckled, shook his head, grabbed the jettisoned camera off the floor and studied it. He had an idea.

26

On the concourse level, a distant rumble could be heard outside the chained and padlocked doors. The noise grew steadily louder, until it seemed to surround the arena. It sounded like motorcycles. A set of doors rattled, held firm by their chains. Then, the next set did the same. So on and so forth, down the line. After all the doors had been tried, there was a pause. The sound of another chain unspooling, then clinking against metal. An engine revved, then revved harder, and a middle pair of doors were blown clear off their hinges, flying out into the night. They were dragged across the concrete, away from the arena at forty miles-per-hour, kicking up a shower of sparks for yards. Choppers began to stream into the concourse, one after another, roaring like fearsome iron dragons from a damned and extinct planet. It was the Northern Nazis—or what was left of them. Their ranks decimated by misadventures on the road, there were only a handful of riders left, but it was still enough to lay siege and raise hell. Which was exactly what they intended to do in Wire Media Arena. Most of their faces were covered. All their old ladies were gone. The masked lead rider threw his kickstand down and stood up tall, over seven feet.

"Jasper, Garth," he called, to the two closest men. They turned to him. "Sweep this place. Anyone's here, flush 'em out. Shoot first, bullshit later. I don't want any surprises."

They nodded, spun their bikes around, tore back through the concourse.

He pointed to a third man. "Snax, block that door. Nothing in or out. I want it airtight."

The guy complied, running off. The lead looked around and spotted Buppy's Sports Bar, glowing like a beacon at the end of the hall. He yanked the bandana off his face, flashing a gold-toothed smile.

"*Last call!*"

It was Tully.

27

Such stood in the middle of the ring, camera mounted on his shoulder, fiddling with the hardware's focus and functions. The laptop sat open at his feet, its screen playing his shots in real time. The noise upstairs alerted him and he looked up, staring in horror as the motorcycle club rolled through the concourse, streaking past the upper entranceways, on their way to the bar. Were they looking for Scarla? Was she a racist biker mama after all?

"*Shit,*" he muttered under his breath, collecting his toys and jumping out of the ring before anyone saw him.

He pulled the cage door shut, but didn't lock it. Crouching next to the ringpost, sweat bubbling on his brow, he eyed the *Rage In A Cage* vinyl ring apron, pulled it up, and slithered under the ring, taking the camera and laptop with him.

28

Scarla clung to the shower wall, legs spread wide. Whitey was wrecking her from behind, his pants around his ankles, hands so big around her small waist that his fingers nearly touched. He was getting soaked, but it felt so good and he was so drunk, he didn't care. He hammered with abandon, his muscular ass cheeks flexing with each powerful thrust, the smack of skin-on-skin echoing loudly off the shower walls. He studied her profile, her eyes still closed, her mouth agape in ecstasy. His face darkened, twisting into a snarl.

"You like that black dick, don'tcha?"

She didn't answer, so he pounded her until she whimpered.

"You listenin', bitch? What color's that dick?"

Still no reply, so he grabbed her wet hair and threw her to the floor. She landed on her stomach with a splat, found herself turned-on against all reason, body rippling and coiling like a cobra. She focused, controlled her breathing, let herself go limp, watched the water swirling like gleaming crystals down the drain in front of her. She lowered her head and put her ear close, listening to the sounds in the hollow pipe. Gallons of water rushing down, down, down to nowhere, and underneath it all, the hissing, screaming, laughing of a thousand morphing savages, all waiting to be loosed. Always waiting, just beneath the surface. Whitey kicked off his pants, stepped over her and planted a boot in the small of her back.

"I don't think you're hearin' me," he spat. "How 'bout we test your ears?"

He shifted his weight and she groaned under his boot heel.

"Black dick's the *best* dick," he instructed.

She said nothing, so he pressed harder.

"Black dick's the best dick," she repeated softly, unable to breathe.

Whitey sneered, succumbing to his worst impulses in the heat of the moment. He wasn't a bad guy, but he had certain detonators and Scarla Fragran mixed with hard liquor had managed to trigger them all. He fell on top of her, his hands smacking the wet floor on either side of her head. She watched the sparkling water drops fall in slow motion around her, felt his still-hard cock slide between her ass cheeks, his hot breath in her ear.

"That's right, it *is*, white girl. They never told you *that* in your little motorcycle gang, did they? All those scared white motherfuckers."

She watched the far wall, letting him do as he pleased. Through the haze of steam, she watched a lone spider spinning its web in the upper corner, slowly, methodically, making it just right. A failproof trap. At least until the next time janitorial made rounds. Whitey took Scarla by the chin, raising her head in his hand.

"Look at me," he commanded.

She paused, reluctant to show her eyes, but knew he was going to force the issue. Baseball apparently didn't work for the ladies, so she chose the sport she knew best, recalling an involved combination she'd developed in the gym. It came to her in detail, out of the blue, with timing that couldn't have been more perfect. With her mind distracted from the runaway freight train that was her libido, she took a deep breath and exhaled, slowly turning to look Whitey in the eye. He didn't react.

It worked. You controlled it. You can *control it.*

Before the thought went any further, Whitey spat in her face. She flinched, closing her eyes, but he squeezed her chin hard, not letting her turn away.

"I don't like the look on your face, don't look at me like that. *Smile* when you look at me, y'hear?"

She nodded. He slipped two fingers into her mouth, hooking her cheek.

"I think you need more training, what do you think?"

She wasn't at liberty to answer, nor did he wait for her to.

"I think those Nazi motherfuckers been brainwashin' your ass, keepin' you from what you really want, what do you think?"

Again, he didn't want a reply. He reached down with his free hand, grabbed her ass, smacked it, grabbed again.

"What say I give you what you been denyin' yourself? What you been wantin' and needin' all that time you was spreadin' your legs for those little white dicks, hmm?"

He grabbed his shaft and slid into her from behind. She gasped as he filled her, thrusting with long, deep strokes, pumping like an oil drill, hammering with bad intentions.

"You want a little nigger baby, don'tcha? Don't be shy, you can ask me for it," he cooed, working faster. "I wanna hear you *say it,*" he growled in her ear. "Say, *'Mr. Collins, may I please have your nigger baby?'* Say it. I know that's what you're thinkin', right? *Say it.*"

He pushed up off her, taking a fistful of hair in one hand, pressing the other one into the small of her back, pounding her without mercy.

"*Say it!*" he roared, causing her to flinch and buck under him.

"Mr. Collins, may I . . ." she began, then trailed-off, inaudible over the hissing shower.

Whitey let it go, head back, mouth slack, racing toward climax. "*Uhhhh* yeah, girl. *Fuck!* I want you to have this baby in your little white clubhouse, wherever the fuck y'all play. You have your nigger baby in front of 'em. Hold it up an' show it off, y'hear me?"

She gripped the floor, waiting for him to finish, and as she did, she came hard. He felt it and smiled, then erupted inside her before she was done.

"*HAAAAARRRGGHH!!!*"

Whitey's war cry orgasm drowned out the sound of the

motorcycle engines that were, by that point, close enough upstairs to be heard in the locker room showers. Riding the wave of her climax down, Scarla's eyes blazed white once more. Her jaw popped and cracked, breaking itself to elongate into a wolf-like snout, her teeth sprouting into razor-sharp fangs, bloody drool mixing with the hot water still spiraling down the drain beneath her. Her spinal vertebrae rippled and expanded, arching her back into a skulking predator posture. Whitey wasn't paying attention, his eyes on the ceiling, frowning at the roar of the bikes.

"The fuck's that?" he mumbled, jumping up and grabbing his sopping wet pants.

Scarla—or what *was* Scarla, seconds before—spun to attack, eyes blazing like LEDs, toothy maw opened wide, body chiseled with lupine muscle, fingers and toes curled into flesh-rending claws.

The room was empty, Whitey gone.

29

Tully Jr. and Jag were bellied-up to the bar, both fisting beers, both staring at the color bars and listening to the droning emergency broadcast system alert on the overhead screens.

"This is my favorite fuckin' show," Jag cracked, stone-faced.

Tully Jr. nodded, took a big swig. He was frazzled and road-weary, looked five years older than he did at the rest stop, like a man in the throes of his ugliest tour of duty. Which is what he was.

"The music really makes it," he replied, flashing a tired smile.

The reprieve of the arena was tenuous at best, but more helpful than any of the surviving Nazis would ever say out loud. A third man grabbed the telephone, listened for a dial tone, let it drop when he heard nothing and snatched a bottle of Cuervo off the wall. Tully stepped up, laying a hand on Junior's back, causing the kid to jump out of his skin.

"Relax, Joon," Tully whispered, easing onto the bar stool and flexing his hands, cramped from riding too hard and too long. "We'll hole-up here for the night, see what things look like after sun up. Don't waste it, get some rest."

Junior eyed him, wanly. Easier said than done.

* * *

Jasper made his way down the stairs of Section 8, police-issue pistol in hand, combing each row of seats for anything that moved. Directly across the arena from him, Garth worked through Section 26, sawed-off shotgun raised cavalierly, in one hand. They looked like twins, and maybe they were. Viking raiders in leather and denim, unholy horsemen on steeds of steel. They reached the floor at the same time, turning to scan the upper decks once more. Jasper eyed the cage, grinning wide. Garth eyed the entrance ramp, wondered about the dressing rooms and loading docks.

"Yo," Jasper called, getting his partner's attention. "I wonder if they're back there." Garth grimaced, not sure who 'they' were. "The *wrestlers*," Jasper continued. "Y'know . . . Batneck Bob, Sgt. Spitz . . ." Then, grinning even wider. ". . . *Missy Cummings*."

Garth shook his head, unfamiliar and unamused. It didn't stop Jasper, who jumped the ringside barrier and shook the cage's chainlink, like a kid in a candy store. In the shadows under the mat, Such froze, sweat streaming down his face.

"This cage is *way* bigger in person," Jasper marveled, studying it up close. "Whattaya think the dimensions are?"

Garth started up the ramp, shotgun ready. "Looks like gaytimes-gay to me, get yer head outta yer ass and c'mon," he called, over his shoulder.

Jasper snapped out of it, returning to earth and running to catch up. If he'd turned the other way, he'd have seen the Northern Nazis cut lying on the floor. But he didn't. He joined Garth about halfway up the ramp, when a towering figure stepped through the curtain onto center stage, under the jumbo screen. Both Nazis raised their weapons. Whitey recognized them and glared, eyes full of hate, fists balled. Garth noted his soaked clothes, stifling a laugh. He'd been in the club posse that took revenge on the kid years ago. They stood in a tense standoff, only Jasper unaware of the past history between Collins and the club.

"Whatcha doin' in here, boy?" Garth called, accusatory.

Silence.

Whitey didn't flinch, or back down. "Fuckin' your *white bitch* is what I'm doin', hillbilly."

Garth's face went cold. Jasper knew what the look meant and tried to assert himself in the situation.

"Yo, shut your fuckin' mouth, nigger!" he yelled, because he just couldn't bring himself to pull the trigger on a stranger.

Whitey went for it, pounding his chest, throwing out his

arms. "Or *what,* motherfucker?! You can't step to this! Tell ya what, you bitches can name my baby *Whitey.* W-H-I-T-E-Y, if y'all hillbilly dumbasses don't know how to spell it. He'll fit right in, only he'll be all smooth an' brown an' beautiful an' shit. Give my baby mama a kiss for me, peckerwoods, an' have her repeat what I taught her."

Jasper's brow furrowed. "What'd you teach her?"

Pause.

Garth eyed Jasper, annoyed. Whitey laughed.

"I didn't hear anything funny, coonskin," Garth snapped, through gritted teeth.

Whitey raised two middle fingers and spat in their direction, fiery eyes searing holes through both men. Garth pulled the shotgun's trigger, blasting Whitey off his feet. The big man landed on his back, arms and legs splayed, eyes wide open, torso shredded by buckshot. Jasper stood frozen, as Garth slowly walked up the ramp to see the damage. He stopped and stared. Whitey's finger twitched. Garth leaned closer, saw his lips move.

"Fuckin' cockroach," he frowned. "He ain't dead yet!" he called over his shoulder.

Jasper cringed and steeled himself, knew he had something to prove to the club. He did his best impression of Garth's stone face, stalked up the ramp, leveled his barrel between Whitey's eyes, and said a silent prayer that was mostly made-up. Whitey raised a shaky middle finger with his right hand, struggling to hold it.

Bang!

DeWade "Whitey" Collins, 25, once-famous wide receiver, succumbed to a fucked-up world in no uncertain terms.

* * *

Such held perfectly still beneath the ring, listening closely. *Did they just shoot Whitey?* He held his breath, trying to hear something, anything. Silence. *Fuckin' hell, the bastards* shot *Whitey.* It wasn't a friendly visit, and it sure as hell wasn't the cavalry. He clenched his fists, racking his brain for an escape plan, then remembered the 9mm. He didn't know how many were out there, versus how many rounds remained, but figured from the sound of things that it was going to get ugly. Or *uglier*. Scarla would surely tell her gang there was another guy running around somewhere, and not just *another guy* either. Sportscaster Josh Suchoza, in the flesh. And they'd surely come looking. He drew the gun, steeling himself for a fight.

30

Scarla moved along the hallway wall, past a dressing room where gear bags still littered the floor, following white papers taped to the walls every few yards, with the words *Gorilla Position* underlined with an arrow that pointed the way, written in bold black marker. The Gorilla Position was pro wrestling lingo for the waiting nook just behind the curtain at the top of the ramp, so named after the legendary wrestler/announcer, Gorilla Monsoon. It was also a particularly acrobatic sexual position, detailed in the Kama Sutra. But she didn't know any of that. All she knew was that those arrows were pointing somewhere for a reason and it might be an exit or a place to hole up, so it was worth a shot. Still wet from the shower, she wore a t-shirt from the merch stands that depicted the raging maniac of a man known to fans as Batneck Bob, all flowing hair, synthetically-altered muscles, and intimidating tattoos. Her shorts were lightweight polyester-drawstring waist-four-way crotch cut-knee-length MMA style, with the *Rage In A Cage* logo emblazoned down both legs. She was a walking advertisement for the show, and the show meant less than nothing. She rounded a corner, the last arrow pointing her to a short steel-girder staircase leading up to a shadowy landing that was shrouded in black commando cloth curtains. She quietly scaled the steps, the cold steel stinging her bare feet, and pulled aside a flap of the velvety cloth. It was a makeshift tent, six monitors stacked three and three on a folding table, headset and clipboard lying in their white static glow, wooden stool sitting empty beside another paper taped to the wall, showing a list of paired names, half of them x'ed off. She cautiously stepped in, letting the flap close behind her, and saw light leaking in from the other side. She crept to it, leaning close to the part in the curtains, and peeked out. She saw Whitey lying dead a few feet away, his face a bloody swamp, one glistening eyeball jutting straight up to catch the overhead spotlights. She studied him, with a fleeting smile.

Got what you deserved, motherfucker. And it was quicker than it would've been with me. I'd have made you suffer.

She saw the arena looming beyond him and started to back away, when Garth suddenly burst through the curtain and grabbed her.

"*What do we got here?!*" he bellowed, bulldozing her into the monitors and pinning her to the table by her throat. He studied her face by the light of the screens, sneering slowly. "*Well, well.* Long time no see, chickadee. Someone'll be *real* interested to see ya again."

She recognized him, too. He was wearing the same expression the last time they met, in the dirt behind the rest stop. Jasper hovered over Garth's shoulder, rattled by the Whitey incident, but trying to play it off. Behind him, the gang could be seen streaming down the arena stairs, alerted by the shots, knives and guns drawn. Scarla rolled her eyes, not interested in a repeat of last time. She grabbed Garth's forearm, using it as an anchor to swing her legs up and scissor his head. She took him down before he knew what hit him, broke his elbow, then broke it again, broke his wrist, then broke it again. He screamed in pain and she smashed his teeth out with her heel before he'd finished. Jasper drew his gun, but did so with the sludgy reflexes of a guy in shock. She front-kicked it out of his hand, caught his wrist, broke it, pulled him into a single arm takedown, broke his elbow with a fast strike, then knocked him out cold with one punch. *Small price to pay, guys.* She darted back through the curtain, leapt the steel stairs, raced down the hallway and rounded the corner.

* * *

Tully bounded up the ramp, followed by Jag and Junior, pausing to grimace at what was left of Whitey's head. Jag spotted Jasper's feet sticking out from under the curtain and grabbed Tully's arm, pointing with his gun barrel. All three raised their weapons. Tully raised a hand, signaling them to hold fire. He reached up, yanked the curtain open. Garth and Jasper, laid out. He scowled.

"Find whoever did this. Shoot first and skin 'em alive if they don't die. I want their heads."

Jag nodded. He and Junior stormed through the Gorilla Position, out the other side, down the stairs. Tully turned to watch his remaining men approach the steel cage. All five of them.

"Heads up! We got company!" he called, keeping them on their toes.

They nodded, one of them jumping the barrier at ringside. He looked down and his bearded face went livid, then he looked up at Tully, then back to the floor. Tully knew something was wrong.

"Whattaya got, Balls?" he called.

Balls reached down and lifted Scarla's discarded Northern Nazis cut, holding it up for all to see. Tully's face dropped.

"Joon!" he shouted, charging through the Gorilla Position to catch his only son, before she did.

31

Scarla ran down a long empty hallway, the arrows still pointing back the way she came, and rounded the corner into another yawning hall. A few yards down, she saw a door on the right. She ran to it, tried the knob. Locked. A few yards further, she saw a door on the left. She ran to it. Also locked. She kept going, rounding the next corner.

* * *

"What the fuck's a Gorilla Position?" Junior asked, passing one of the arrow signs, gun raised.

Jag ignored the question, partly because he didn't know, and kept moving down the hall. They reached a door and braced themselves. Jag ducked to the side, tried the knob. Locked. He stepped back, took aim, shot the lock, kicked it in. He was ready to kill. Janitorial closet. They both breathed a sigh of relief, continued on.

* * *

Tully heard the gunshot and clenched his teeth, hoping they'd put one in her head. Silence. Maybe it was that easy. Maybe it was over. Deep down inside, he knew better, but it reassured him somewhat to think that there were two of them, both great shots, and one of her—as far as he knew—unarmed. Maybe that was it. They'd put the bitch down for him.

* * *

She turned another corner in the sprawling, windowless, underground labyrinth of Wire Media Arena, and couldn't help but smile. There was a door at the end of the hall and above it, a glowing green EXIT sign. Looking back the way she came, she could hear their footsteps getting closer. Maybe two turns away. The door was about twenty yards straight ahead, no doorways, no surprises. She bolted for it.

* * *

"There gotta be *at least* three of these motherfuckers, and that's if they're *big*. No *one man's* gonna drop Garth, not to mention Garth with backup," Junior whispered, as they made their way down the hall, nearing a turn.

Jag studied the floor, his brow furrowing.

"But they got no *guns,* else they'da blown our boys away. When we find these sonsabitches—"

Jag cut him off with a hand, pointed down. Junior's eyes followed his finger. A trail of barely noticeable water drops sprinkled the concrete floor, stretching up ahead and rounding the corner they were about to turn. Junior's eyes widened. He and Jag exchanged a look. Jag nodded. They crept toward the corner, guns aimed.

* * *

Tully jogged down another long stretch of hallway, his various metal accessories jingling as he went. He was beginning to tire, not used to running. He'd taken some wrong turns, hit some dead ends, had to double back twice, and didn't want to call out in case it alerted foes instead of friends. With his sense of direction mixed up, all he could do was roll the dice and hope to find his men intact. And Scarla Fragran—if that's who was lurking—in pieces.

* * *

Scarla hit the exit door at full speed—and bounced off. Locked. *No! Goddammit, no!* She tried it again, then stepped back and thrust-kicked it with all her might. The metal door dented, but didn't budge. Her heart sank. She spun around, stared down the hall. Going back would deliver her right to them. Capture was not an option.

* * *

Jag and Junior slunk down another hallway, as quietly as possible, keeping track of the drops. The trail was barely noticeable, but still there. As they neared another turn, Junior took the lead. Jag frowned, but let him have it. If the kid wanted to earn his stripes with the whole world falling apart, why not? Open air riders and flying predators were a match made in hell, and they'd all be there by next week, at the rate they were going. Junior eased against the wall, sidestepping to the corner. It was so quiet, they could hear a pin drop.

He paused, gun pointed at the floor, then turned to Jag, silently mouthing an unnecessary, *"Three . . . two . . . one,"* before spinning around the corner, gun raised.

Crack!

Scarla's bare foot hit Junior square on the chin, dropping him like a clipped marionette. The impact rang through the halls like a gunshot. Jag froze, barrels aimed at nothing he could see. He eyed the pool of blood spreading from under Junior's head, licked his lips and sneered.

"I'll be damned. Wolf Girl. You're one tough bitch, ain'tcha?" he called, awaiting a reply that didn't come.

He stayed put, weighing his next move, addressing the painted-white cinder block wall again.

"Now, listen. I got a gun, you don't."

He scanned the floor, looking for Junior's weapon, but didn't see it. Sweat bubbled on his brow. He flexed his fingers around the shotgun barrel and continued.

"Who got the advantage here?"

The question stuck in his throat. Still no answer. He inched forward, looking for a Mexican standoff. He'd been in those situations a few times in his life, and whenever the bullets flew, he was the last man standing. This time would be no different, he told himself. Then he told himself again. He was so focused, he didn't hear the footsteps approaching from behind him. But she did. Tully's voice broke the silence, shaking Jag's concentration.

"*Joon!*" he called, eyeing Junior in despair.

Jag glanced back, out of reflex, and that split-second was all Scarla needed. She ducked out from behind the corner, gun aimed, and fired once. Jag crumbled straight down like a demolition job, shotgun spinning across the floor, eyes wide, bullet hole in his forehead.

How do you like it, asshole?

Tully stared at his men, rage muting sorrow, and dropped his gun. Silence.

"You know those bullets ain't gonna do shit to either one of us, girl," he called, ringed fists balling tight.

She stepped around the corner, gun still raised, and they locked eyes.

"You sure about that?" she hissed, trigger finger itching.

His hands relaxed. His jaw clenched. "I ain't sure o' nothin' anymore."

He eyed Junior. "You kill my boy?"

She shook her head, not taking her eyes off him. "I wouldn't do that. But he was gonna kill me, so I had to put him to sleep for a while."

Tully cocked his head, studying Junior, seeing his chest rise and fall. He was unconscious.

"The blood . . ." he began, then let it hang for her to finish.

"Hit his head. It's as gentle as it's gonna get."

He smiled. "You're a real piece o' work, you know that?"

"I'm starting to figure that out."

His Cyclops gaze fell down her body, studying her gear. "Liked you better in our cut."

"Why don't you go get it?" she shrugged.

He shook his head. "Can't do that."

"Why not?"

"Cos we just found each other again."

"There's no *we*."

"I remember different," he purred.

Pause. She leveled the gun on his face. "If you don't walk away, I'm going to unload this into your head."

His eyes widened, but he didn't budge. "That so?"

"Yeah."

They stared into each other's eyes, neither backing down.

"*Well*, then," Tully remarked, slowly undoing his belt.

Her eyes floated down. The butterflies raged. *Don't give in . . . focus . . . you control it, it does not control you . . .* He lowered his zipper, half-erect cock dropping out of his jeans.

"Why don't you take those silly clothes off?" he cooed, stepping toward her.

She stood firm. *"Walk away."*

He smiled, kept advancing. "I told you before. We belong together."

She thought about it, felt control slipping away. In that moment, she hated herself, hated the *disease*. Or whatever the hell it was.

"We belong dead," she whispered.

He moved right up to her, leaned down, pressed his forehead to the barrel.

"Maybe we do, Scarla." He slid a hand around her waist, squeezed her ass. "But until we are . . ."

She hesitated, every cell in her body screaming to have him inside her. Screaming to turn. Her eyes fluttered. He smacked the gun aside, blasting her on the jaw with his other fist. She went down.

Blackout.

* * *

Tully stood over Scarla, staring impassively, cold-blooded revenge in his good eye. ". . . let's have some *fun*."

32

She woke to blinding white light. Her first reaction was to head the other way, but she couldn't move. She blinked, then squinted, realized she was staring into the ceiling lights of the arena. *Weeeeeeeee!* Her ears were ringing and she tasted blood. As her eyes focused, the chainlink ceiling came into view. She groaned, pulled herself up on her elbows, looked around. She was lying naked in the center of the ring. The Nazis—minus Jag—surrounded ringside, just outside the cage. Junior sat near the ring bell, slack-jawed in a daze, Garth and Jasper slumped in floor seats behind him, both nursing rag doll arms. Tully stood at the door, his face a grim mask. She didn't know what lay in store, but it didn't look good.

"Rise an' shine, sweetheart," Tully's voice boomed.

She locked eyes with him, noticed her legs were spread in his direction, drew her knees together. He smirked, continuing.

"Glad to see you didn't up an' die on us. Woulda been a real shame." He began doing standing pushups on the doorway's top bar. "Seein' as how you're such a feisty little bitch, with such an accomplished competitive background, I thought we'd try a little workout, whattaya think? You look rested."

The Nazis around the cage snickered. Tully didn't. He motioned to the nearest man.

"Snax, you feel like sparrin' a couple rounds with this broad?"

Snax sneered, pulling a butterfly knife and spinning it until the blade locked. Tully's eye narrowed. He stepped aside.

"Sounds like *yes* to me." Then, over his shoulder. *"Bell!"*

Junior lifted a small hammer and struck the round brass bell.

Clang!

Snax strutted into the cage, sleazy smirk plastered across his face. Tully slammed the door behind him, tying it shut with the bolt-clipped chain from earlier.

"Go get her, Snax! Teach her, son!"

Tully cheered loudly, imitating a rabid fan, clapping his huge hands hard. The others followed his lead, whistling and shouting. Scarla rolled over, keeping her eyes on the portly biker storming her way. She pulled herself off the mat, set her stance. Snax rumbled up the ring steps, raising his blade high.

Thwuck!

He stabbed the turnbuckle, pulled the knife out, grinned maniacally. The Nazis roared. Scarla didn't react. As Snax bent down to step through the ropes, she sprang, scissor-kicking him square in the chops.

Crack!

His front teeth sailed through the chainlink and sprinkled ringside, the pink tip of his tongue plopping onto the floor. Snax face-planted on the apron, out cold. Silence. She grabbed the top rope, kicked his bulk off. He hit the floor with a thud. Such peeked out at the downed biker and his severed tongue, snickering with wide eyes. The nearest Nazis saw him and froze, drawing their guns. He looked up, found himself staring down two barrels, gulped. Tully stepped into view, fixing a cold eye on the unexpected visitor, and Such raised his hands in surrender.

"Hi. You probably know who I am."

He waited for a response. The Nazis stood, stone-faced. He cleared his throat, continued.

"Josh Suchoza, Channel 4 Sports."

Silence. Scarla eyed the door, but there was no point in going for it, since they could shoot her well before she could untie the chain. She took the opportunity to scan the cage for any weaknesses. It looked rock solid. *Shit.* She saw her Nazi cut hanging on one of the ringposts, wondered why it was there. Tully nodded, and the Nazis dragged Such out from under the ring. Two of them held his arms, two more trained barrels on his face. Tully approached and Such looked up, thinking fast.

"You're that motherfucker from the news," Tully growled.

Such nodded. "Josh Suchoza. How ya doin'?"

"How long you been under there, Josh Suchoza?"

"Well, I heard the commotion and didn't know, y'know, what it was, so . . ."

Pause.

"So, you hid."

Such nodded again. "*Yeah.* Spur of the moment thing, y'know."

Tully pointed up the ramp. "You with that nigger we put down?"

Such turned his head, saw Whitey's body for the first time, lying at the top of the ramp. He played it cool, glanced over his shoulder, saw Scarla standing naked in the ring, arched a brow. He shook his head.

"Met him when I got here. Think he was a janitor, or something."

Tully smiled, his gold tooth gleaming in the ring lights. "A janitor." He eyed his men, amused. "Who the fuck's gonna clean this place up, if you boys go shootin' all the goddamn janitors?"

Laughter. Such joined in, and Tully's face dropped. Everyone fell silent.

"What do you suppose we do with *you,* Josh Suchoza?"

Such pondered the question. "Hopefully, not what you did with *that* asshole," he quipped, jabbing a thumb toward his friend.

Silence.

A slow smile crept across Tully's face. "Let him go," he ordered.

After a beat, the men released Such. He rubbed his arms, regaining circulation.

"You're funny, I like that," Tully said, hiking up the ring apron and kneeling down to eye the camera and laptop. "What do we have here?"

Such took a step back, bumping into Balls, who stood right behind him. He waffled, choosing the truth . . . sort of.

"I, uh, hooked that camera up to the laptop and logged into the news station's live webstream. Thought maybe I could get help."

Tully eyed him. There was an uncomfortable silence.

"But *you guys* showed up. Maybe I can ride with you," Such suggested, voice trailing off before he was done. Everyone stared. "Or *not*, y'know . . ."

Tully pulled the camera and computer out. "Show me."

Such took the equipment, turned to use the announce table, but it was dismantled. He sat down, opening the computer in his lap. Tully circled behind him, watching the screen. Such mounted the camera on his shoulder, focusing on Scarla. Her blurry image became crystal clear onscreen.

"Smokin'," Such mumbled, under his breath.

Tully laid a hand on his shoulder. "Can people see this right now, Josh Suchoza?"

Pause.

Such tensed. *Can people see this right now, he wants to know. What's the play here, Suchster?* All eyes were on him. "Right now? Well, not right *now*, y'know. I need to, uh . . . switch over."

Tully watched the screen. "Switch over to what?"

Pause.

"To . . . the live feed?" Such answered.

"You askin' me or tellin' me?"

"I'm *telling* you, to the live feed," Such shot back, irritated.

"What's the matter, newsboy? You upset?"

"*No.* Why would I be upset?"

"Cos your ass is on the line."

Such lowered his finger over a keyboard button, hovering.

"You *wanna* go live? Right now, on *her?* We're the *number one* news station in the city, four million viewers-a-*night*. Communication's *down* out there, but the web doesn't die, baby. Could be thousands, *millions*, logged-on right now. Say the word, I'll broadcast this *fight* live."

He was bluffing, had no idea what the button would do, if anything. Truth was, the camera had been streaming the entire time. Whitey set it up, Such never turned it off. Wouldn't know how to if he tried. He scanned the faces of the four bikers looming over him. Two held guns, two were empty-handed. He ogled Scarla, still on display in the ring.

What a goddamn motherfuckin' piece of Grade A ass she was.

It was undoubtedly one of the most depraved scenes he'd ever been witness to, and surely about to get worse, but all he could think was what a waste of good pussy it was gonna be.

Tully eyed Scarla too, weighing the consequences. "*Do it,*" he spat.

Such took a deep breath and tapped the key, then nonchalantly reached down and drew the 9mm from his sock.

Blam!

He shot Balls in the gut. The biker fell. The other gun-wielding Nazi raised his weapon. Such shot him in the chest, before the others dove in and subdued him, taking the gun away. He struggled, to no avail. The laptop and camera hit the floor. Tully snagged the camera cord and slung it under Such's chin, pulling it tight.

"*Fuck yourself!*" Such rasped, before his airway was cut-off.

"No, *fuck you,* newsboy," Tully said, keeping cool as he drew the garrote taut, with all his might. Such watched Scarla, his face turning shades, eyes bulging and flushing red as his blood vessels exploded, foamy spit blowing from the corners of his slack mouth. They locked eyes and he managed a pained smile, hoping she understood. *Two less to fight off, sweet lady. Two less.* The remaining Nazis gathered around their felled brothers, at a loss. Balls writhed in agony, legs kicking in a spreading pool of his own blood, while the other one was shot through the heart, dead before he hit the floor. Such laughed at them, but couldn't draw a breath to make a sound. Tully reared back on the cord, knuckles white, fists quaking, until Such stopped squirming.

"It's gonna be okay, Balls! Relax, man!" Junior pleaded,

knowing it would be a slow and painful death, if they didn't get medical assistance fast. "Look at me, *look at me!* You gotta calm down, man, you're losin' too much blood!"

Tully finally released the cord and upended the chair, leaving Such flat on his back, legs in the air.

Josh Suchoza, Channel 4 Sports, died laughing.

33

Tully walked away from his men, approaching the cage and gripping the chainlink, staring hard at Scarla. She stood without emotion, holding his gaze.

"Put it back on, you can come outta there," he called, nodding to the cut on the ringpost.

She eyed it. He shrugged.

"Or don't, you won't. Doesn't get any easier than that."

Junior looked up at him, eyes pleading. "Dad, we gotta get *help!* He ain't gonna *make* it!"

Tully glanced down, casually. "We knew how this was gonna go down when we kept riding, son. Ain't no turnin' back now."

He rejoined them, stood over Balls, who eyed him, teeth clenched, shaking uncontrollably. "What do ya need, Ballsy?" Tully asked, matter-of-fact.

"*M-M-Maker's Mark,*" came the reply, with a scared smile.

"*Done.* Somebody go grab a fifth of Maker's. We'll ride this out."

The Nazis eyed him, demoralized. Jasper hung his head and went for the stairs, arm flopping uselessly at his side. Tully lifted the camera, held it out to Garth.

"You got one good arm, you're on camera."

Garth took it, clueless. Tully strolled away, circling the cage, his voice booming through the arena. *"Who's next?! I want an able man in there! The Northern Nazis are gonna teach this bitch a lesson!"* Nobody moved. *"C'mon, ain't got all fuckin' night! If she ain't wearin' our cut, I want new bike seats! Made from her fuckin' skin!"* He pounded the cage with his fist, his large rings creating a steel-on-steel echo. The two remaining uninjured men stepped up, steely resolve in their eyes.

"Two-on-one or nothin', Tull," one of them offered.

Tully shrugged. *"Two-on-one, it is! Garth, you okay over there?"*

Garth attempted a thumbs-up, but his arm didn't work. He winced, nodding instead, camera mounted on his good shoulder. "Got it, Tully," he called.

"Alright! Let's get it on!!!" Tully undid the chain, opened the door. "Blades, no guns. I want hand-to-hand."

The two Nazis entered, circling the ring like jackals, in opposite directions. Scarla stood in the middle, watching them. With one in her sights, the other jumped onto the apron. She spun around. He jumped down, the other jumped up. She spun again, heard a click. The guy on the floor brandished a switchblade.

"Shame, what this'll do to those nice titties," he snarled.

The other guy drew a buck knife from his boot, stuck a leg through the ropes. She lunged at him. He slipped back to the floor, criss-crossing with his partner.

"All you gotta do is wear the cut, Scarla. Put it on, zip it up. Think about it, sweetheart. Is it *really* so bad?" Tully called.

She thought it over. It didn't make any sense. Was she expected to don the cut, then join in a group hug? They'd surely gut her like a pig. But Tully was another story. She knew what he was, wasn't sure the others fully understood it. One thing was abundantly clear: every last Northern Nazi had to die, before she'd make a decision like the one he was demanding. And maybe he had to die, too. Maybe most of all, because a snake with no head wouldn't be much of a threat. She watched them circle her naked flesh, around and around, drawing out the inevitable. She knew the game they were playing, knew they were trying to get inside her head. She caught movement in her periphery, spun to see Jasper descending the arena steps with a bottle of Maker's Mark. Switchblade climbed onto the apron, slowly. Behind her, Buck Knife did the same. She set herself, looking back and forth, as they lingered. Switchblade swung a leg through the ropes. Buck Knife followed suit. She steeled herself for whichever bastard had the guts to charge first, and then . . .

Shink!

Snax's butterfly knife burst up through the mat, inches from her foot, then withdrew. The sonofabitch was under the ring. Tully banged on the door, drawing her attention.

"Looks like it's *three*-on-one! It's not too late, baby!"

The blade sprang up again, inches from her other foot, then disappeared. Switchblade and Buck Knife laughed, climbing through the ropes in unison. She rotated her stance, kept lifting and planting her feet. She eyed Tully. He pointed to the cut. She tried to listen for any movement under the mat, but couldn't hear past Balls' agonized ringside groaning. Suddenly, Switchblade charged. She dropped and spun, sweeping his legs. He hit the mat, but didn't lose his blade. She looked up in time to catch Buck Knife swinging wildly, dropped and rolled to the ropes.

Shink!

The butterfly blade punched through the mat, missing her head by an inch. She cleared the ring and stumbled, bouncing off the cage and regrouping. Buck Knife and Switchblade jumped out to the floor on either side, cutting off the ringside and slowly advancing, leaving her no choice but to roll back in. Tully appeared behind her, grabbing her hair through the cage, mouth close to her ear.

"Take the cut, Scarla," he commanded. "And I'll call 'em off. It's your only chance."

She yanked herself away, losing some hair in the process, and slid back under the bottom rope. She moved to center ring, setting and re-setting her feet. The Nazis climbed back onto the aprons, faces leering, knives waving. They had her and they knew it. It was only a matter of time.

Just take the fucking cut and see what happens. What is there to lose?

She had no answer, eyed the cut, decided to go for it.

Thuck!

The butterfly blade stabbed up again, severing the middle toe of her right foot. She winced, stumbled, and they came through the ropes for her. She wheeled around, took two long strides to the corner, leapt up on the second rope and snatched the cut off the post, losing her balance and slipping off the top, dropping the ten feet to the floor and landing hard. Switchblade and Buck Knife closed-in fast.

"*Hold!*" Tully yelled, stopping them in their tracks.

They eyed him. Outside the cage, Junior stood up, his face white as a sheet. Tully saw him, waited for the news.

"He's *dead*. Balls is dead . . ."

Silence.

Snax crawled out from under the ring, blood streaking his chin, tears streaking his cheeks. He moved to the cage near Balls' lifeless body, sobbing. They'd been friends, brothers. Tully stood quietly, watching his men. The mighty Northern Nazis. Broken, battered, nearly extinct. He realized the riders in the room with him were all that was left. Sure, there were other charters out there . . . somewhere . . . maybe. But this club was the flagship. The ones who started it all. And there was a distinct possibility none of them would leave Wire Media Arena alive. Tully hadn't cried in over twenty years. Law of averages said that was a very long time. He turned away, scanning the empty seats, thinking. Behind him, Scarla pulled herself up the ringpost. She was wearing the cut. When Tully turned back around, he wore a different expression.

"We're done here," he called, voice flat and cold. He leveled his good eye on Scarla. "Kill the bitch and let's ride."

34

She didn't wait to see who'd come first, turned and jumped onto the cage, started climbing. She moved fast, her foot on fire as her remaining toes hooked the chainlink. Outside, Garth lowered the camera, watching. Tully took exception.

"*Hey,*" he spat. Garth turned. "That battery dead?"

Garth shook his head.

"I didn't tell you to stop."

Garth got the message, hoisted the camera back onto his shoulder, found Scarla in the eyepiece. He tried zooming in on a beaver shot, but yelped when his broken wrist disagreed. Switchblade and Buck Knife started climbing after her, their motorcycle boots giving them a tougher time on the chainlink than her bare feet. Snax followed her with murderous eyes, from the floor. What goes up, must come down . . . She reached the top and looked back. They were still climbing, frenzied and relentless, Buck Knife gripping his blade in his teeth. She sidestepped left, onto the other wall, working around the perimeter. When a wild-eyed Switchblade was almost within arm's reach, she reached up and hooked the cage ceiling, kicking away from the wall and moving hand over hand, out into the center, twenty feet above the ring. All eyes followed her, dangling naked, wearing nothing but a Nazis cut, her coiled and sweat-soaked body a thing of glistening desire. Tully shook his head, turning away before he changed his mind again. He could feel it coming on, and knew damn well that the *urge* superseded his club orders. None of the boys had seen him change, and he planned to keep it that way. The last thing he needed to add to his list of problems was the risk of being fragged by one of his own frightened men. He was good at keeping himself in check when needed, though. He'd been doing it for months. One of the added benefits of deep prison meditation he'd honed long ago.

Scarla hung from the ceiling, her hand throbbing wildly, missing digit trickling fresh blood up her arm. She watched Switchblade grab onto the ceiling links and swing out after her. His sweaty hands immediately lost their grip and he fell, dropping straight back, twenty feet down to the ring. She locked eyes with him, the moment seeming to play out in slow motion. His body landed square atop the steel ringpost and he snapped backward with force, breaking his back instantly, the deep crack of shattering vertebrae resounding throughout the arena. A collective groan rose from the Nazis. Switchblade flopped facedown onto the floor with a sickly thud, eyes blinking, fingers twitching, legs as still as the dead pegs they'd become. Snax knelt over him, his rage multiplying, but it would do no good. Scarla eyed Buck Knife, still clinging to the cage wall. He pulled a pistol and took aim. She kicked her legs, swinging side-to-side. His first shot missed. Outside the cage, Tully drew his gun. The others followed suit, except for Garth, who got no signal from Tully, so kept recording.

"Fire!" he shouted, and the Northern Nazis unloaded everything they had into the half-naked woman swinging from the top of the wrestling cage.

She bucked and spun as wildly as she could, but there was no way to avert all their bullets. Hot lead ripped through her torso, hips, and thighs, shredding flesh and muscle, blasting her to the bone. Her raised arms and shoulders did a good fighter's job of protecting the head, but with slugs pounding every bit of exposed flesh, she just couldn't hang on, and her fingers let go. She sailed through the air, twisting like a macabre ballerina, landing flat on her back and bouncing up in a spray of blood, finally splatting in the center of the ring, still and lifeless, eyes staring up into the ceiling lights for the last time. The Nazis lowered their guns and their heads, eyes far away, no satisfied faces among them.

They'd lost too much, and were beginning to realize they'd just keep losing. An enemy down only meant there were countless more at the gate, clamoring for another pound of flesh. And they'd get it. Tully understood more than most. He holstered his gun, took a long deep breath.

"*Glückwünsche!*"

The Nazis turned, guns aimed at the upper deck. A tall, middleaged man in an expensive Brioni suit stood at the main entrance of Section C117, clapping his hands slowly. His skin was pale to the point of translucence, his bone structure sharp and angular, as if he were cut from granite, his eyes deepset and piercing, their striking whites visible from the floor. He didn't react to the weapons trained on him.

"Ein Job gut gemacht, in der Tat," he continued. "Wenn Sie nicht wissen, was du tust, das ist."

The Nazis exchanged looks. They recognized the language of the fatherland, but none of them were fluent. Tully stepped front and center, sizing up the peculiar interloper.

"We speak *English* here, Adolf," he called. "How 'bout you take it from the top? And start with your fuckin' name."

The man smiled, offering a polite bow, never taking his eyes off Tully. "*Of course*. It wasn't my intention to be rude," he replied, in perfect English. "My name is Keeper Reinstein. If, perchance, I've intruded . . . please accept my sincerest apologies."

He eyed a gold Rolex around his wrist and started down the concrete stairs, alligator shoe heels clicking loudly. Tully aimed and fired, without hesitation. The slug hit a seatback, a few feet to Reinstein's left. He stopped in his tracks. From where the Nazis stood, it looked like he was smiling. But it could've been a nervous reaction. Probably was a nervous reaction. Tully kept his gun raised.

"I didn't hear anyone invite your ass down, Kraut," he called, message clear. "What're you doin' here?"

Reinstein did smile that time, raising skinny hands, with long, white, spidery fingers stretching from wide, fleshy, almost glowing palms. It looked like he was offering two jellyfish. "Ich bin gekommen, um meine Tochter zu holen," he replied, catching himself and shaking his head, before translating. "I've come to fetch my daughter."

The Nazis stared, in silence. Tully looked at Scarla's body, sprawled in a puddle of blood, in the middle of the ring.

"'Fraid you just missed her," he called, drawing a laugh from Buck Knife, who hopped down off the cage wall. "Anything else we can help you with?"

Reinstein studied Scarla from where he stood, cocking his head from side-to-side. "Yes," he calmly offered. "You and your men can lay down your weapons and leave in peace . . . or not."

The Nazis exchanged smirks. Tully wasn't laughing. Buck Knife exited the cage, sidling up to him.

"Want me to gut his ass?" he asked, under his breath.

Tully shook his head, watching Reinstein. "Funny you say that, we were just about to leave. Where you *from*, Schnauzer?" he shouted, louder than previously.

The suited oddity paused. "I'm *from* the Center for Disease Control," he answered, matter-of-factly, before striking a more ominous tone. "Though you may wish to be more concerned with where I'm *going*."

With that, his lanky frame vanished in the blink of an eye. The suit collapsed in a heap, its operator gone. Four thousand dollars-worth of pashmina piled on alligator shoes, with a gold watch ticking nearby. The Nazis watched what looked like a puddle of black tar oozing down the stairs, moving faster and faster, heading their way. Without prompting, they unloaded their weapons into it, to no avail. The tar reached the floor and rolled toward them, streaking around chair legs, blacking-out the aisle like a great yawning mouth. Garth lowered the camera, to see it with his own two eyes.

"*What the fuck is that?*" he grumbled, dropping the camera and drawing his knife.

The Nazis hurried to reload. Junior slammed a clip into his

Glock with shaking hands and aimed, looking for the mysterious liquid in the aisle. Nothing. Scanning the rows, he didn't notice it ooze off the ringside barrier to puddle around his feet.

"Where'd it *go?!*" he yelled, to no one in particular.

Everyone was armed and ready, but all eyes were looking in the wrong place.

HISSSSSSSSSS!

The steadily rising sound got their attention. It seemed to be all around them, but no one could pinpoint it. Suddenly, the black ringside barrier exploded to life, hundreds of cobras springing up in all directions, their hoods spread wide, snapping at any Nazi within striking distance. Tully recoiled fast, pulling Junior by the collar. A pair of venomous fangs sunk into Jasper's eyeball, dropping him instantly. He thrashed, screaming. Buck Knife was bit on his tattooed hand, pulled back, smacked the snake away. Another one bit his arm. He hacked off its head with his blade. Still another bit his chest, then his neck. He went down, slashing wildly, chopping two of the beasts in half. Garth swung like a maniac, lopping off snake heads left and right, until a cobra stretched out of the barrier right in front of him, sinking its teeth into his crotch.

"Aiiiiieeeeeeee!!!"

He dropped and rolled around ringside, like a man on fire. The thing followed him, picking its spots, biting at will, and his energy began to fade. Garth dropped his blade and Buck Knife picked it up, hacking and slashing with two weapons. It was proving fruitless. The more snakes they killed, the more sprang from the barrier—or rather, from the black ooze that coated the barrier. A wide-eyed Snax refused to exit the cage, retreating to the far top turnbuckle, where he perched precariously, sweating bullets and hyperventilating, as his brothers were steadily felled around him. He watched as snakes slithered through the chainlink and swarmed Switchblade, whose mouth gaped in mute agony as they attacked his paralyzed body. A cobra lashed out and bit his tongue, while others took his cheeks, ears, eyes, and throat.

Bloody foam streamed from the corners of his mouth, as he lay convulsing, praying for merciful death. As it was, it proved too much to ask. Snax looked around, distraught, and spotted Tully and Junior hightailing it upstairs, to the concourse.

"*Heyyyy! Don't leave meeee!*" he screamed, nearly falling over the top rope. "*Tullyyyy!*"

Junior stopped and turned, speechless, his face a mask of regret. He turned back, kept running. Ever the fearless and iron-fisted leader of the Northern Nazis, Tully never slowed down, never looked back. On the floor, Buck Knife and Garth slumped next to the cage, both struggling for breath, the highly toxic snake venom rendering them lethargic. Cobras surrounded them on all sides, hissing and growling, lashing out to sink their teeth into random body parts. The guys groaned, trying to fight, but growing slower and less-coordinated by the second. Snax whimpered, watching as snakes began coiling around the ringpost below him, slowly working their way up.

"No, no, no, no, *no!*"

He panicked, leaping into the ring and stumbling, nearly paralyzed with fear. Everywhere he turned, snakes slithered over the apron, closing in.

"*Get away from me!*" he shrieked, kicking at them as he backpeddled.

He took one too many steps and tripped over Scarla's outstretched legs, landing flat on his back, momentarily stunned. A knife hole in the mat - one of the souvenirs of his earlier cat-and-mouse - caught Snax's eye as it ruffled, inches from his face. He turned his head, frowning into the dark eyehole slit, saw something gleam. His eyes widened. A small snakehead crept out, tongue flicking at him. He gritted his teeth and pounded it with a hammer fist, pinning it to the mat.

HEEEEEEEEEEEEE!

The sound froze Snax. Whatever it was, it was close. Right behind him, from the sound of it. He gulped and slowly turned, coming eye-to-eye with the biggest King Cobra he'd ever seen.

The thing was twenty feet long, head to tail, its hood as wide as his shoulders. The pitch of its hiss was deeper and weirder than any snake he'd ever heard, almost human. Clear venom dripped from its bared fangs, forked tongue wagging in his face, as if to taunt him. He stared into its marble eyes, hypnotized for a moment, then opened his mouth to scream, but his breath was gone. The beast was . . . majestic. It opened wide, then wider, and swallowed his head whole. In less than two hours, it would digest all of his two-hundred-forty pounds. Snax, indeed.

In the concourse, Junior knocked down the MacGyvered doors Snax had put up earlier, as Tully mounted his bike, covered his face, and donned his helmet. He revved the engine hard, waiting for Junior to mount up, then nodded to other last living original Northern Nazi, before they tore out into the ravaged night of the new Amerika.

35

4:13 a.m. The city was quiet, a shell of what once was. Scattered fires nobody bothered to put out, raging fires nobody could. The streets were full, gridlocked for miles, but there were only shiny metal boxes with no drivers. Storefronts were looted, but the looters didn't seem to bother taking their booty home, leaving pillaged goods to litter the sidewalks and streets in every direction. Bodies dotted a stretch of sidewalk under the windows of a cheap six-story motel, some clothed, some nude, their skulls burst like water balloons on the concrete. A police helicopter whirred into view, combing the rooftops with its spotlight. It roused an army of bats that poured from an array of chimneys to swarm the chopper, breaching the cabin. The pilot flailed, struggling to maintain control as he was attacked, but it was a losing battle. The copter went into a tailspin, clipping an office building on the way down and bursting into flames, raining burning debris down the street. One of the blades slammed down on the roof of an abandoned Volkswagen, like a guillotine, chopping it clean in half. On its hood lay the partially nude, ravaged corpse of a busty young blonde, milky white eyes staring lifelessly, hands and forearms twisted into hard crustacean pincers. A pack of a dozen blackback jackals roamed freely, darting in and out of open doors and broken windows, weaving through the automotive graveyard the boulevard had become. One mounted the Volkswagen, sniffing the dead blonde before tearing off a chunk of flesh and chewing greedily, as the others circled. It reared back its head, sounding its distinctive high-pitched call, somewhere between a coyote's howl and a horse's whinny. The call was returned from blocks away, echoing off the buildings and down the avenues. The pack followed it, disappearing around a corner under a flickering, greenish streetlight. Soon, their numbers would multiply. And they'd become something else entirely.

36

The snakes had gathered around Scarla before they dissolved, leaving her in a pool of bloody black slime, the gigantic King Cobra coiled at her feet, patiently awaiting her return. Nazi corpses littered ringside, rigor mortis already setting in under the hot lights. The cobra began to sway, slowly rising to loom over her body. A bulge in its belly showed that Snax had yet to fully digest, but it was likely the bones that were taking so long. The thing lowered its head, long tongue flicking Scarla's face, moving down her leather-clad chest to settle between her legs. Her skin was cold. It slid its forked tongue inside her, working in deep. She didn't stir. The snake kept at it, slowly liquifying until it spilled over the sides of the ring. Out of the black muck that soaked her, Keeper Reinstein lifted his head, sliding his translucent hands around her thighs.

"*Komm zurück zu mir, Liebling,*" he whispered, dipping to kiss the lips of her vagina.

His tongue swirled around her clit, unnaturally long, still more snake than man.

"*Lassen Sie mich sehen Sie bei all Ihren Pracht,*" he hissed, licking two fingers and easing them in deep.

Still nothing. For all intents and purposes, Scarla Fragran was dead . . . again. Reinstein sat up, dripping black slop, naked and erect. He unzipped her cut and hiked her leg, entered her slowly and started thrusting.

"*Sie sind exquisite, mein Lieber,*" he complimented, his breath quickening.

He drew her foot to his mouth, sucking her severed tow

stump, and laid a hand on her belly. His brow furrowed and he quickly pulled back, studying her.

"*Oh, my.* You've been busy, haven't you?" he asked, switching languages without thinking.

The revelation didn't take him from his task, however. He relished having his way with her limp body, penetrating her relentlessly, watching her face all the while. He came in silence and withdrew, sitting perfectly still, cross-legged at her feet, hands on his knees. Waiting... After five minutes, Scarla's foot twitched. Reinstein's eyes were far away, detached on the upper deck, but the movement promptly caught his attention. Her leg jumped. He smiled. Small seizures rippled through her body, growing in intensity, until her chest heaved with another first breath. Her head thrashed side-to-side and her eyes sprang open, pupils pinning in the bright lights. Her mouth gasped for air, filling her lungs with the stench of blood and death. She lurched upright, legs splayed, hands in her lap, and stared at Reinstein, utterly confused.

"Willkommen zurück, mein süßer," he said, softly. "Mein Name ist Keeper Reinstein."

She stared, eyes falling down his slime-streaked torso to his still-hard cock.

He shrugged. "Notwendiges Übel, ich fürchte."

She looked up, eyes blazing. "Hast du Spaß haben?" She paused, surprising herself. *Where the hell did that come from?*

Reinstein blinked, taken aback. "Es ist alles für Sie, mein Lieber."

She scoffed, drawing her legs together. "Tot umfallen."

He smiled, somewhat sadly. "Das ist, warum ich hier bin."

Without warning, Scarla got to her feet. Reinstein sat still, gazing up at her nude body. She resisted the urge to kick his head off his shoulders, dropped the Nazi cut on the mat instead. *Good riddance.* She looked across the ring and saw a mangled, steaming pile of bones in the corner, skull sitting on top, web-thin strips of flesh still clinging to the cheeks.

She nodded to it. "Friend of yours?"

Reinstein eyed the bones. "Dinner date," he replied, without a hint of irony.

She circled the ring, eyeing the corpses scattered around the floor. She paused on Switchblade's swollen and disfigured body, remembered his back-breaking fall, turned back to Reinstein.

"*You* did all this?" she asked, suspicious.

He nodded. Her eyes narrowed.

"*Why?*"

He stood up, his erection wilted. "I told you. I did it for you," he affirmed, unblinking.

She laughed. "Where the hell were you when I *needed* you, asshole?"

He cocked his head. "You never needed me. You merely needed to understand what you are," he replied, cryptically. It pissed her off.

"And what the fuck am I?"

Pause.

"You, Scarla Fragran, are the embodiment of natural selection. The harbinger of the new heritable advantage. The first genotype of your kind . . . and a mother . . . *proud,* I would hope."

She stood silent, a chill creeping up her spine, as Reinstein continued.

"You're part of the first wave. A shining example, really, of the evolutionary synthesis. To my knowledge, there hasn't been an instance of successful fertilization in a hybrid host—" He smiled. "—until now."

Without thinking, she touched her stomach with her bloody hand. "How do you . . ."

He stepped toward her. She reflexively stepped back. He stopped.

"All will become clear in time. No secrets remain buried forever."

He paused, knowing she had so much more to ask. Alas, he wasn't there to play teacher or guide, and the motorcycle club had only gotten in the way of things. He was there to serve one purpose.

"If you *must* have answers, know that the origins of your, shall we say, *condition* . . . stretch back to a very specialized series of antibiotic resistance and gene fusion testing, carried out under the Führer's direction in wartime Germany, in the summer of 1942. Quite a while before you were born. You've probably heard campfire stories, parlor jokes, about all that the Reich was devising in secret. Well, I can assure you, the truth is stranger than any fiction. The doors those tests opened, and the speciation secrets they laid bare, were *very* close to being honed and used to bring about the extinction of the human race, back in World War II. Alas, the war ended as it did. But those secrets moved across the sea, along with most of our finest scientists. Esteemed guests of your government, of course. The United States of America was not about to damn minds like theirs to trivial comeuppance. They continued their work for generations, with blessings and funding from your own heroic leaders, patiently awaiting the rise of your great empire's fear culture. There was *never* any doubt, you see, that it would flourish and eat you from within. The very scientists who engineered the biological fusions in '42 rose to positions of power in your government. All while your babies *ssslept.*"

He hissed the last word, glancing at her hand on her belly, frowning at her missing finger.

"And while your society cowers in terror, watching your planes fly into your buildings, counting down to your next seasonal doomsday, the *true* seeds of your destruction have taken root right under your noses. It was introduced months ago, through your water supply. With the number of pollutant factories lining your riverbanks from state-to-state, it was hardly difficult. Men and women have been bred to fill the required positions for decades, heroes and heroines, dedicating their lives to drudgery and banality, merely awaiting their orders. They performed spectacularly. Next, we focused on the airborne, with aerosols being an even easier and more varied means of delivery."

He started moving closer again.

"And the next step, of course, was *direct* implantation."

He slowly extended a spidery hand, ran his fingers along her belly, slid them between her legs.

"More difficult for us to control, but at this point, we don't have to. After *seven decades,* gestation has come to fruition."

He worked a finger inside her, eyes narrowing to slits. She was wet.

"Oh, darling. You've only *begun* to realize what you're capable of."

She felt the butterflies swirling and closed her eyes, the tingle growing stronger. The creepy fucker knew how to push her buttons. Her lips parted, head tipping back. He kissed her deeply, their tongues swirling in a death match. She stroked his cock with one hand, feeling it stiffen. She grabbed his wrist with the other and kicked his knee out, in one smooth motion. Reinstein crumbled. She grabbed him in an armbar before he knew what hit him.

"If I say *uncle*—" he chuckled.

With a sharp yank, she dislocated his shoulder, then elbowed him in the face, opening a deep gash above his eye. His blood ran black. He kept smiling.

"*I'll break your fuckin' neck!*" she growled.

"Yes. I *heard* you were forceful," he laughed.

She jumped up and stepped on his throat, leaning close, murder in her eyes. "*How did you find me?*"

He choked, unable to answer. She eased off and watched him, waiting.

He coughed, cleared his throat. "Ich liebe eine starke Frau."

She shattered his cheekbone with her heel. He rolled over, moaning, down for the count. She mounted him from behind, applied a rear naked choke, blood splashing her forearms as she tightened her grip.

"I'm gonna ask you one more time. How did you find me?"

He struggled for air, not laughing anymore. "*The stream,*" he groaned. "*The webstream . . .*"

Of course, it was the webstream. She drove his head into the mat and stood up, her feet planted on either side of him. Her nerves were rattled. Why did he think she was pregnant?

Games. It's all bullshit.

Reinstein rolled over, his face a bloody mask, and smiled up at her.

"You're not fin-ished yet," he laughed, in a creepy sing-song voice.

She frowned, looked down, saw that he was hard.

Run. Get the fuck out of—

He sprang up at her, all gaping maw and drooling razor teeth, but she was able to catch the sides of his head and pivot, using his momentum to hip-toss him back to the mat. His eyes were rolled-back white, his head cone-shaped and all teeth, gnashing relentlessly. Like a shark. He hooked her legs and brought her down with him, again lunging for her head. She ducked, his teeth slashing her shoulder deep. She groaned, scrambling for the ropes, and he shot across the bloody mat after her, on his hands and knees. She dropped out to the floor, landing on Switchblade's corpse and pulling it on top of her, just as Reinstein's jaws came crashing down. His teeth sunk into Switchblade's shank, jaw locking on like an iron vice, head thrashing from side-to-side. Scarla slipped out from underneath, charging for the door. He noticed, cast the mauled body aside, bolted after her. She dove out of the cage head-first, hitting the concrete and kicking the door shut, holding it closed with her bare feet. The Reinstein shark barreled full force, hit the door . . . and exploded into a hundred piranhas. They flew through the chainlink, raining down on Scarla in a myriad of vicious bites. She thrashed on the concrete, helpless against the tiny razor-sharp teeth shredding her flesh. Blood splattered. She was losing a lot of it. The fish kept attacking, insatiable. She threw her head back, screamed. A few feet away, the camera lay on its side, staring at her. Its lens danced on auto focus, still recording, still streaming. Scarla slipped in-and-out of focus on the laptop screen, until a pirahna flopped wildly across the keypad, ending the live stream. The screen went dark, but for a bright blue 4 in the lower left corner. The fish kept biting and biting, as she rolled over and crawled, arm over arm, losing steam, trying in vain to reach the ramp.

Let go . . . stop fighting . . . the pain won't last long . . . give in . . .

"Ring the bell!" Big H shouted, white towel in his fist.

No . . . no fucking way . . . not this time . . .

She raised an arm, not realizing it had become a bloody wing, then raised the other. She was changing. She lifted off, pirahnas still clinging to her body, and circled over the cage, like a hawk hunting prey. The tables had turned. The fish jumped and flopped at ringside, defenseless as she swooped again and again, picking them off. She chewed them to pieces and spit them out, until only one remained. She scooped it off the floor with her teeth and flew to the top of the cage, slumping on the chainlink roof, bloodied and exhausted. Her wings slowly morphed back into arms, slashed and punctured, from wrists-to-shoulders. She held the ten-inch wriggling fish in her hand, studying it with tired eyes. Its strong jaw kept biting air, its cold blank eye staring into hers. She knew it was the last of Keeper Reinstein, whoever he was, but never did find out why he'd come for her. She thought about letting the fish go, about throwing it into the stands as far as she could, about leaving it/him to fate. But that wasn't how things worked in Scarla Fragran's world. There was no mercy. There were no second chances. Fate was what you allowed to happen. And she was hungry, but what she wanted wouldn't be found at the concession stand. She'd never leave a loose end again, not as long as she was still breathing. She brought the piranha up to her face, staring at it, eye-to-eye.

What the hell did you want with me?

To her surprise—or maybe not at all—it pursed its lips to speak.

"Ich wollte, dass du deine Stärke zu sehen. Sie sind alles, was Sie sein wollen. Ist es nicht schön?"

She paused, still amazed she could understand every word. It *was* beautiful. Yes, it was. She bit into the fish's underbelly, tearing out a mouthful and chewing slowly. It thrashed in her hands, its jaw chomping furiously. She swallowed and took another bite, watching it die . . . watching the strange man who called himself Keeper Reinstein die . . . and his secrets along with him. But there'd be others. There'd always be others.

37

The custom chopper tore through the countryside, not slowing or stopping for anyone, or anything. The night was beyond black, the thick smoke from burning buildings and burning bodies enough to hide all the stars in the sky. By the time she reached the lake house, the morning sun was peeking over the horizon. It, too, was affected by the new world, its vibrant orange dulled to a muted and burnt brown, maybe forever. She cut the engine, dropped the kickstand, and stretched her legs. The back of her white jumpsuit read *Mighty Missy Cummings,* in cursive red. The merch stand said it was a small, but Scarla was swimming in it. Her wounds were nearly all closed, but her shoulders ached from gripping the ape hangers on the long, non-stop ride. She rolled them and shook her arms, eyeing the house. It looked the same as she had left it. She moved to the patio door, pondering a shower, then stopped. She turned and slumped into a deck chair, watching the sunrise over the lake. It was peaceful. It was exactly where she wanted to be. She stood and unzipped the jumpsuit, letting it fall, walking down to the water in the nude. Her feet padded along the wooden dock and stopped at the edge, planting nine toes over the line. She studied her reflection in the water. The fish slowly gathered near the surface, watching. They numbered more than before. Soon, there'd be one more of her, too. They seemed to know. Just like they knew she'd return. She knew it too, even if she never admitted it to herself. She took a step and dropped off the dock, smiling as she sank.